T0148466

Lucid Dreams

L. V. Tamez

iUniverse, Inc.
Bloomington

Lucid Dreams

iUniverse books may be ordered through booksellers or by contacting:

iUniverse
1663 Liberty Drive
Bloomington, IN 47403
www.iuniverse.com
1-800-Authors (1-800-288-4677)

ISBN: 978-1-4759-2656-9 (sc)
ISBN: 978-1-4759-2655-2 (hc)
ISBN: 978-1-4759-2654-5 (e)

Library of Congress Control Number: 2012909138

Printed in the United States of America

iUniverse rev. date: 5/29/2012

For: My Lui

Darcy sat up in a pool of her own sweat. Feeling gross and a little hazy she got out of bed and made her way unsteadily to her restroom. As she shuffled across the hall, the sound of her footsteps brought the memories of her dreams back. She ran back to her bed, reached over the half empty bottles of water on her nightstand and just behind it. She hoped it would still be there, and then she pulled out the dusty black journal. She knocked over her alarm clock; “shit 3:34 am,” she thought, completely aware she probably would not get back to sleep. She opened it and wrote the date and time in the corner and began scribbling everything that would come to mind. For as long as she could remember, she’d been dreaming lucidly, ferociously and quite vividly. Like most people’s they were full of mysteriously unfamiliar people and places.

As she continued on with an alacrity she’d managed to conjure up, oddly enough she was reminded of an argument she had had when she was ten with her neighbor Ricky Furbes over her dreams. She had fatuously revealed to him this ability to dream floridly. His grandmother said that normal people dreamed with purpose or not at all, and colored dreams denoted something unnatural and evil. Darcy knew she wasn’t evil and as far as she could tell at 17 there was absolutely nothing unnatural about her at all. He never played with her after that afternoon, but she was quick to get passed it. She was quick to get passed most things in life. Darcy had a hard time connecting and made it a point never to do so. “Le sang des mes veines coule de mon coeur et le votre a partir de votre cerveau,” her mother often made it a point to tell her, but Darcy never learned her mother’s native french, so she never cared what it meant. Besides she’d always dreamed in color and this particular night, one color stood out above all others.

As the pencil beneath her fingers grazed over the pages effortlessly, she began describing the faces in her dream and that’s when she had a revelation of sorts. It was those striking blue eyes that she’d seen before. It was one of her most reoccurring dreams, the all too familiar house, the white pillars, the crack in the door, it was weird but as soon as she would see the crack, it’s almost as if she knew exactly what would happen next. She’d walk through the door, passing in still motion as if she were being filmed by an old, still framed studio camera. The only thing different this time was that through the familiarity of the unfamiliar faces and voices, he was there again.

DARCY (FROM THE BEGINNING)

Darcy had never really been interested in her dreams until she was twelve; up to then she thought it was all relatively normal. Ashamed to admit it even to and especially to her self, he was the one that ignited her interest turn peculiar obsession with them. She often had reoccurring dreams where the events of almost the entire thing were predictable, everything but the boy; which made her even more curious. His appearances were very random in the different dreams and she had never remembered seeing anyone like him in her everyday existence, he was just another figment. She'd first begun to take notice of him when she was twelve or so. At first he seemed to fill a space in the void of strangers and then as time went on, he became more profound. In the dreams, he never spoke to her, but she noted that he would stare at her with a gaze of intrigue. He seemed to be about her age twelve or so, he had dark hair and seemed ordinary enough, except for his strikingly bright blue eyes. They were royal blue and she had never seen anyone with eyes like his. Beautifully piercing.

During those first couple of years, Darcy continued to pass her dreams off as a normal reoccurrence. He would appear once in a while, but they never exchanged more than glances. She would simply see herself pass him over, or see him staring at her from a distance. Back then she was dreaming as an audience member might be viewing a play. Watching the sequence of events unfold before her and even if she was in it, she could only observe herself from a distance.

The year she turned fifteen, she noticed something so significant, it triggered her desire to start her dream journal. The boy with the blue eyes returned again that year except he was not really a boy anymore. He was changing, his physique, his face, he was older. The first time she noticed the difference in his appearance, she woke up in a cold sweat. As far as she understood, the people in her dreams were a fictitious product of her over active imagination; could it be possible that her brain was complex enough to create a character that could age. That night she began the journal.

As time went on, she noticed that she started seeing him less and less. That year something else changed as well, although she could always tell when she was dreaming, she could only witness them inactively, but then one night, she found her self walking up a familiar path, she was a little confused at first, but as the crack on the door came into focus, she realized she was dreaming.

This time though she was seeing everything through a new set of eyes, her own. Everything continued to happen exactly as it always had and she even reacted the same way she had before; it was all very mechanical. When she awoke that morning, she felt no different then she had any other morning, and as she recorded the event of the night she wondered if her dreams would continue on that way. They did.

By the time Darcy turned sixteen, the boy had disappeared all together and she had abandoned her journal. That year she had too much going on in her actual life to continue with her asinine infatuation. She'd outgrown it.

DARCY: UPBRINGING

Darcy lived in a less than suburban neighborhood. Her father was a financial advisor to the elite and her mother had once had a very lucrative, but short lived modeling career. In fact, although Darcy did not acquire any of her mother's vanity, she had her beauty and then some and the best part of her was that she was genuinely unaware of it. She grew up in the best of everything and she had everything life had to offer. Like every normal teenage girl, she enjoyed movies, music and socializing, and although she always had a desire to swim out to the deeper end of the social pool, in her neck of the Hollywood hills she was forced to wade in the shallow waters.

Darcy went about her senior year of high school with anticipation and eagerness for what was to come. She was filling out college applications and longing for the year to pass with haste. Much to own surprise she had even been eyeing a boy in her advanced history class. Attracting the opposite sex had never been difficult for Darcy; she found she had a harder time returning their affections. Harley seemed a bit different though. They actually had conversations about things other than what he drove, who he knew, where he liked to party, or how much money his family had. He also seemed to be genuinely interested in her as well. When she found out her parents were throwing her a surprise 17th birthday party that year, she made sure her friends saw to it that he would be there. He was.

It was a typical party as far as high school shindigs went. There was a lot of music, gossip and skin. She knew about half of the people there and she didn't mind too much because she had Harley's attention all night. That's the night he first kissed her and made their situation more serious. When she fell asleep that night she was in a state of bliss, and that's the night he returned as well.

When she woke up at 9:30 that morning, the first thing she did was reach over to grab the journal. He hadn't returned to the second dream of the evening, but she remembered he had been in the first. She pulled back on the satin marker and began to read.

Friday October 11 (17 birthday) 3:34 Am

It started out in a shopping center, it's large and open, and I've seen it before. I walk over to a bench and drop myself onto it. I just sit there superciliously and watch the people walk by. All of a sudden I am talking to my Aunt Emily about some horse or something I'm not too sure. I must have remembered my birthday because mom comes over with a cupcake and as I am about to blowout the candle the scenery changes.

Now I am walking through the playground of my old elementary school and I find myself on a rusty swing looking up at the stars. Then I see someone and I feel butterflies in my stomach. At first I'm not sure, but then as I look at his eyes, I can see it's him. A pain rises up in my throat as if it hurts to breathe, but I can tell it resonates in my chest. He's gotten so much taller, and broader.

He was standing on a small hill in the distance and as I looked up our eyes met. I stared at him for a while and he looked at me this time with a strange look of confusion and disbelief. I remembered I was dreaming and I was actually able to take a little bit of control. I stood up and took a step in his direction and his eyes widened. Then, as I get to the steps of the house as usual the pillars and crack are exactly the same. I walk in and as I go down the hall through all the people I can see him walking away and he stops and turns back to me and suddenly everything seems to be animated in movement and black and white like an old movie. Everything looks like different shades of grey except his beautiful blue eyes. He still looks shocked that I'm staring at him. I must have woken up, because that is all I can remember.

She lay back on her bed and closed her eyes tight. With everything she could muster up, she tried to remember him. He was tall, about 6'1" and she could see his face in bits, but couldn't fully bring it into focus in her mind. She remembered his black hair was not long, but a bit over grown and tapered to his head on the sides and it went up in all directions on top, it suited him. He had a very distinct jaw line and his bottom lip was plump and seductively ripe. His eyebrows perfectly framed his striking eyes. He had dreamy eyes, they didn't open very wide, and they made him look sad, but the color made her feel warm. He was perfect. Everyone in LA had aspirations of being famous, so she had encountered various handsome faces on a daily basis. She wondered if her brain hadn't put together all the best features and created this painfully perfect face. If only he were real.

She sat up in her bed and had flash backs of her party from the night before. Realizing she was a year older, she ran to the mirror to see if there weren't any major physical changes she should be made aware of. She pulled the dark, wavy, unruly locks of hair back out of her face and up into a messy knot atop her head. She looked up into her own eyes, which she seldom did without flinching at the reflection that stare back at her. She was not too keen on eye contact, not even with herself, especially not with herself. She studied the different bits of color that made up the aquamarine pigment of her iris and then she thought of the cerulean eyes in her dreams and as she was about to once again drift into the face of the dream boy, she quickly thought of Harley. She smiled at the notion of the kiss that had been exchanged. Harley's eyes were dark and on the very opposite end of the chromatic spectrum, but she found them mysterious and equally as enticing. It was still very hard for her to believe that she'd found someone she actually liked and that was a huge relief, because she was beginning to feel like the odd man out in the typical high school relationship scene.

That Saturday evening she had made plans to meet up her girl friends for dinner. She usually declined, and had aptly earned the nickname Buzz Kill. It wasn't so much because she didn't enjoy the company, because truthfully when her friends were out of the watchful eyes of the high school body, they were fun to be around. Mostly it was because Darcy enjoyed staying home and embracing the sweet escape a good book offered her. She never really had experienced any kind of tragedy in her own life and it made her feel inadequate and undeserving.

That night, she felt like letting loose a little though, so she threw on some jeans and a black t-shirt, pulled up her hair and set out. She walked over her driveway passing her mother's Porche and her father's slue of impractical and unnecessarily pretentious cars. When she turned sixteen, she knew her father was going to get her a car and ostentation was not a quality she could tolerate; she asked for a "regular, normal" car. Hoping to receive a car that would better suit her reticence, instead her father surprised her with a black Chevy Camaro. According to her father the initial idea of her driving a Chevy made him grimace, but he was actually quite fond of this particular model. She hated to admit it, but so was she and she couldn't very well argue with the alternative fuel tank, it would have been ecologically irresponsible. She walked over to her guilty pleasure and hopped in.

When Darcy arrived at the trendy, over priced pizza parlor, her friends were already inside. She walked in and sat down. The smell of the baking cheese was over whelming; her friends were indulging in salads but she couldn't possibly pass over pizza. She ordered a cheese pizza and smiled smugly at her friends.

"Sorry guys, I'm not a Rabbit," she giggled.

"Well, Darcy don't start to complain when you have an ass the size of a Beluga Whale," her friend Amanda countered. "Now Darcy, you know what we're all thinking."

A bright red flush ran across her face. "Yeah Darcy, Harley Reede?! What in the world?" Stacy never let Amanda make her point without interrupting.

"What, he's really nice." Darcy said through her breath.

"Yeah, but he's really weird and kinda scary." Stacy always whispered, like it was making everything she said justifiable.

"Well, I mean he is pretty hot Darce, especially for someone named Harley. I mean he has that dark Johnny Depp thing, but like seriously, I've heard stories you know about his many female encounters? I was surprised he showed up, I mean he doesn't really strike me as the party type. Or any type really. Does he have any friends who aren't lovesick girls? But anyway how come we didn't even know about this? Is it serious; I mean is it a fling or do you like, like him?" Amanda's whole life revolved around the social scene and what was going on in everyone else's life.

"Well he does play soccer and I've seen him with those guys. And I mean come on Mandy, they were like a few moves short of making babies." Stacy joked. "I'm kidding Darcy; we all know you're still well let's say virtuous. But I mean seriously he looked pretty willing, do you think you might be ready?"

"Change of subject please." Darcy never talked much about her personal life and she wasn't about to open that can of worms, but Stacy had brought up a good point.

On the drive home, Darcy thought about it more and more. The sad reality about her generation was that there weren't very many girls left unconquered. Also, it wasn't so much of a question of virtue or morality for Darcy it was more the lack of opportunity. She had never even had a real relationship before, usually it fizzled out before it got to that point. She tried to concentrate on the road ahead, but she thought instead about her mother, how easy it all came to her, the flirting, and the teasing; in fact sometimes she felt embarrassed by the fact that it came too easy. Where Jeannette, her mother, was concerned, no man was out of bounds and so many of her teachers, coaches, friend's fathers, had fallen victim to her mother's seduction. She figured that in denying herself in that respect, she was somewhat making up for all of her mother's immoral transgressions. She decided she still had plenty of time before that opportunity would present itself again, so she turned up the radio and sped off in to the night.

Sunday morning, Darcy woke up disappointed. She thought she would see him again, but his return wasn't permanent. Her dream was strange enough to tempt her to record, but she decided not to raise old habits. That night Harley invited her out for coffee, but she wasn't in the mood for scrutiny, so she offered instead a movie at her house.

Darcy:
Hopeful Expectations

When Harley arrived she smirked at the mere sight of him, in jeans and a grey t-shirt, he really wasn't much of a Harley. He wasn't too tall, but he was fit and his hair always seemed to frame his face perfectly. His high cheek bones helped make his crooked smile irresistible, and his dark, almond shaped eyes could easily draw in anyone. He had a couple of movies in tow and she led him in.

"Come on we'll go watch em in my room." She took his hand and led him down the long corridor; Harley eyed the house in amazement. It wasn't its immaculate size or the gaudy overpriced furniture that bombarded the space; it was the pictures on the wall that caught his attention.

Most homes had walls adorned with family portraits. Tacky overdone poses, forced smiles on forced vacations, the products of photographers paid thousands to capture the family's best pretended demeanors in a bogus natural element. Instead, there were pictures of Darcy's dad Mr. Whitten with all sorts of musicians and actors. There were also plenty of photographs of the infamous Jeanette Sergey. He noticed the framed magazine feature covers and couldn't help but smirk a little as he passed some of the more daring and revealing photographs. He couldn't imagine friends walking into his house and seeing such compromising pictures of his mother hanging around. Then again his mom didn't look anything like she did. It didn't escape his attention though that there were not very many of Darcy; in fact, he was sure he'd seen just two. As he furtively eyed a topless picture of Mrs. Sergey-Whitten on a beach with her arms folded over her bare breasts, he couldn't help but think how much prettier Darcy was than her mother. With his devious thoughts suppressed he smiled and followed her into the bedroom.

"Do you think your parents will mind?" he asked in a somewhat hopeful undertone.

"Mind what? That we're watching movies?" Darcy asked somewhat sarcastically.

"No, my being in here, you know, parents?"

"I seriously doubt they'd even notice. If I truly had to rely on my parents for sustenance, I'd of died by now." Darcy caught herself mid-thought and quickly stopped talking before she could divulge too much.

She smiled and pulled him over to a small chaise lounger she had positioned in front of her bed. He was surprised by the state of her bedroom.

It was really nice, but somehow it didn't seem to coincide with the rest of the décor in the house. The chaise he sat in was soft lavender and white striped silk, framed by white wood, the shape was curvy and delicate, it reminded him of Darcy. The small bed had a white, wood headboard with two small lavender pansies carved in. All her bedding was white and plush; it reminded him of an Easter dress a baby girl might wear. The matching nightstand held a stack of black leather journals. The only thing that gave her room, a hint of modernization was the laptop sitting open on her desk and the plasma TV hidden behind the mirrored double doors of a beautiful Armoire. Everything was so clean and pure, just like Darcy and at that thought he pulled her close against his chest.

Harley had had his fair share of girls. It was easy for him. He was captain of a state champion soccer team, he knew he had charisma, and he had a way of luring the girls he wanted. In fact, Harley had always gotten what he wanted; life in general came easy to him. When he met Darcy two years prior she was too much work for him, but he knew eventually and at some point he'd want her. She was different than most girls he'd come across, and when they first got to talking he was actually blown away by how smart she really was. Not just book smart, but aware and mature. With her choice in music and movies, she by far was one of the coolest girls he'd ever met.

She must have felt his stare burning into her because at that moment she turned her head and as he looked into her eyes, something inside him ached and he had never wanted anyone more. He placed his hand under her chin, lifting her face slightly and kissed her softly. Beneath his chest he felt her body tighten, and he realized the rumors were true; unbelievably she was still inexperienced. Afraid of pushing her too soon and scaring her off, he pulled away. He knew it was probably in his ability to have his way with her that night, but he actually kind of liked her and felt like it might be nice to keep her around a little longer.

Darcy was nervous and she could tell it was obvious. When Harley stopped kissing her, she was afraid she'd somehow done something wrong, but then when he spoke his tone was soft and reassuring. He was just being considerate and she liked that. The rest of the night went on with not too much more than occasional caresses and deep but subdued kisses. Darcy couldn't have imagined a better end to her birthday weekend. That night when she lay in bed, she thought about Harley, how tender he'd been with her and easy it would be for her to lose all her inhibitions around him. It was quite a scary thought for her, not knowing if she was willing to let go and give up control of her body to someone else. She knew Harley would take things as slow as she needed, or at least hoped he would. She still couldn't shake what Mandy had said, because for the most part it was true. She had heard about the trail of hearts Harley was dragging, how he'd slept with several girls, none of which he ever dated before or after, but maybe this time it was different, maybe she was different. She knew she wasn't dumb enough to be a one night stand, and as this had actually been their second date so it seemed she was off to a good start.

That night he was there again also. When she opened her eyes at 4:38am she reached over and methodically began writing. She rolled over and slipped away again. A couple hours later she sat up in her bed. Realizing she had an hour to get ready for school she quickly made her way to the restroom and jumped into the shower. Her showers usually lasted at least 30 minutes, but when the water streamed down her face, she remembered the dream and in record time, finished in just under 10 minutes. She rushed out dripping wet and in nothing more than a towel threw her self on the bed.

Sunday October 13 4:48am

I'm in some kind of court yard and I see Harley sitting ever so coolly beneath a huge tree. It looks like an Oak tree. I walk over and sit by him and he pulls me to his chest. I lean in and I can hear his heart beating steadily. He whispers something in my ear, but I can't make it out clearly. It's weird because although he's stroking my hair I can't really feel it. All of a sudden I'm watching from a distance again and I can see Harley stand up and ask me for my hand. He's wearing a black t-shirt and he looks very tempting. I take his hand looking a little more hesitant than I would expect and stand up then he pulls me towards him and I think we're dancing, but there's no music. I can see myself just staring at him in awe. Then across the way I spot him staring down at Harley and I as well. I get a strange feeling as I watch him watching Harley and I dance. I can see the creases in his forehead and his mouth is turned down. He looks almost pained or disappointed. I wonder if he knows I'm watching him from afar, he doesn't seem to. I have never seen anyone so beautiful. It's very hard to pull my attention away from the eyes I'd been missing, but then I notice his expression get more intense. That's when I turn my attention back at

Harley and I, I see Harley caressing the side of my face. At first I thought I might be fantasizing, but then Harley takes my face into his hands and starts to kiss me, at first I am excited but then kisses become rough and forceful. I can see myself tensing up and even though I want him, I looked frightened and I push him away. I pull free and start to walk away from him. Harley just disappears, then I look back to make sure he hasn't left also, but he's still staring down at me. I notice that as I continue to walk further away from where Harley and I had been sitting, he's staring at me with a strange expression, he takes his hand brushes his face and lets his fingers sit over his mouth, then he smirks with satisfaction and walks away as well. He doesn't seem to notice me staring this time, maybe because I'm not in my own body. I can't remember anymore, except that before I woke up when I looked back at the tree, it seemed darker and it looked more like a willow. I wonder what that means. LOOK IT UP.

Darcy never really put too much faith in dream interpretations, besides her dreams were so over loaded and she usually had more than one a night. With many details she might never finish analyzing one. However, when something stood out to her, she found it amusing to just check it out. She pulled put dream dictionary and flipped it open she decided to look up the oak tree she stood under with Harley first. TREE: To see a tree in your dream, symbolizes new hopes, growth, desires, knowledge, and life; as well it implies strength, protection and stability. Confused and still intrigued she kept going to the next thing she could recall. WHISPER: To hear someone speak in a whisper suggests the need to pay closer attention to something vital about said person, and represents anxieties that currently exist. She thought about Harley at that very moment. It was ridiculous to even think she hadn't paid enough attention to him, because all she had been doing for the past couple of weeks was hanging on to his every word and over analyzing every remark and reaction he made towards her. She thought about how stupid the whole thing was and just as she was about to close the book, she decided it couldn't hurt to look up one last thing. WILLOW: To see a willow tree in your dream, symbolizes mourning and sadness or may denote a loss of someone or something. It gave her the creeps. She shut the book and threw it under her bed. Then she realized how late it was. She finished dressing as fast as she could and made her way to school.

Jackson

Jackson knew what he was doing was not only wrong, but dangerous. He had crossed a line, and although his head urged him to go back, something inside him drove him further. He'd stumbled across her accidently and from the first moment he'd seen her, he remembered being drawn to her for some reason. When they were kids, it was mere curiosity, but now it was so much more. It was easy at first, to stay away. He had other things, important things that seemed to occupy his time then. Even though he'd convinced himself that it would be just another passing glance, just to check and make sure she was doing well, he had his doubts and rightfully so, because although he couldn't be sure, he swore she'd noticed him. That should have been reason enough to stay away, but Jackson had always been stubborn, and now at eighteen, he had learned that rules were not as binding as they seemed.

She looked beautiful that night. He knew it was her birthday because he saw her blowing out her candles. He noticed that she held her eyes closed more than most people when she blinked as if she were taking in the moments. It had been a little over a year since he'd seen her, but so much had changed. He'd always felt a fondness for her, some kind of protective feeling, but now there was something else, desire. It took him a while to realize he was holding his breath and when he quickly let the air escape his lips, he must have let his guard down as well, because at that moment, her eyes met his. It had happened before, but her gaze would usually run past him. This time when she saw him she smiled and his throat tightened. He knew what was coming, and as badly as he wanted it, with every conviction he had, he turned and walked away.

He let another day go by and felt the grating urge to go back and see her. Just to be sure, just once more. This time he'd be more careful. He was one of the best at what he did; he knew he could do it. It was a tiny slip and no one knew anything anyways. Besides what could possibly go wrong, if anything ever happened, what could she say or do? When he arrived and saw her though, she wasn't alone. A new emotion invaded him now. The more the stranger touched her the more it ached, he saw how she looked at him and felt an aggravating longing. Jackson had no idea who he was, but hated the way he gazed at her with coveting eyes. Harley, she called him by name and the distaste grew more potent. But then he noticed something; she seemed apprehensive about him. When Harley finally left, he felt relieved, but still cautious. He always knew she could never really belong to him, but yet somehow, she did.

DARCY: ALL GOOD THINGS

Darcy got to school late and as usual unprepared. She ran into her Art class and interrupted the exam that was already in progress. That set the pace for the rest of her day. She just couldn't seem to get it together, until she saw Harley. She had no idea how she was suppose to act around him now. When she first walked in and saw him sitting across the room, she felt the sudden urge to hold him, but then without fail her more sensible side held her back. She knew Harley's reputation and unforgivable past and although she never really cared what anyone thought of her, she wondered at this point. Would they take her for just another one of Harley's indiscretions, and what if he didn't want to be seen with her? As ridiculous as that sounded, she couldn't help but remember the year before when Annabelle Lackey boasted about her passionate weekend with him during gym class, and then the awful look she had on her face the rest of the day when he blew her off. Maybe Harley wasn't such a prize after all. She'd asked him about all the rumors and the girls, but he said most of what they said wasn't true. He did admit to a few, but he laughed and told her when it came to keeping score, now a days, the girls seemed to be worse than the guys. It made some kind of sense or maybe she chose to believe it did. She decided to play it cool.

She walked over and sat down next to him. He sat with his elbows on the table and his chin resting on his crossed fingers.

"What no hello?" He half smiled and sat up.

She returned the smile. "Hi."

He couldn't help himself; he grabbed her face like he'd done the night before and kissed her gently. It felt good, but she was not one for public affections and she could feel the sting of the burning stares of everyone in the room.

Harley had never been one for PDA either, but Darcy was literally irresistible. He had seen guys walk around with girls on their arms, cheap trophies, but thought it was an insane notion. He knew most of the time it wasn't love; it was the effort of trying to get where they wanted to with that girl, or her reward for letting them. Harley never really had to try that hard and he never felt the need to continue on with a girl, once he had gotten his fix on her, all it did was give them hope. Besides, tying him self to one girl closed the opportunity of endless possibilities, but Darcy Whitten, she was definitely a different kind of girl. Everyone knew she was all but unattainable and now he finally had her on his arm. As an added bonus she was insanely beautiful and no one deserved to be there more than she did.

Harley almost as equally impressed Darcy, and the more time they spend together, the more she learned about him. Everyone was well aware that he was a star soccer player and assumed his grades were a product of school politics, but Darcy knew he really was that smart. He had read all kinds of books, and had flawless taste in underground rock music. She liked that he wasn't keen on all the bullshit of high school or at least didn't seem to be. He never desired the popularity that naturally came to him, although he embraced it, he never sought it out. They spent a lot of time together away from the crowd and on occasion would make it to a get together or a party, but it wasn't her scene. He didn't mind too much because he also preferred to have her to himself as often as he could. As the weeks progressed, naturally so did the intensity of their relationship. Although Harley never pressured Darcy, she knew it was only a matter of time before he made his intentions known.

It was a couple of days before Halloween and Darcy felt apprehensive as she and Harley walked hand in hand. Looking around at the decorations she got a complacent feeling. Everything was just as it should be. It was her favorite time of year, seeing the children dress up at Halloween always made her feel nostalgia and made the artificial Hollywood lifestyle seem just a little more normal. As they walked out of the drugstore she rummaged through the bag for her candy bar.

"You know, I love that you're the only girl that would be caught dead eating that giant chocolate bar out here." He squeezed her shoulders and kissed her lightly on the cheek. She blushed, not sure whether it was caused by the comment or the kiss.

"Well, its Halloween; I'm just getting in the spirit you know." Darcy spoke through chattering teeth as a chill drew up her spine.

"Yeah, like in three days," he replied sarcastically.

"I celebrate early? Besides maybe that's what all these bitchy snobs need, some sugar in their body. Chocolate makes everyone happy," Darcy countered with a smile.

"Yeah, happy and obese." She shot him an annoyed glare. "I'm just joking; I like to make you mad, it's sexy. Besides you eat chocolate like everyday and you're just fine." He hugged her tightly from behind and playfully ran his hand under her shirt over her stomach. The feeling of his hand on her skin was both exciting and uneasy. He pushed her hair back and kissed her neck lightly. She knew it was going to come sooner than she'd hoped.

That night as she lay in bed, she thought about the past couple of weeks with Harley. The way he looked at her made the blood in her veins run thicker and louder than usual. What would she do? Darcy had no intention of saving herself, so she couldn't figure out her hesitation. She thought about how he made her feel. Physically she yearned for him as any one who wasn't completely blind might. She could picture his perfect face, his sinister smile and his eyes, his dark, beautiful, enticing eyes. Strangely enough, as inviting as they were, she could see something more behind them.

Dark circles usually outlined them and highlighted the hints of grey in the dark iris of his eyes. They weren't comforting, they were luring and that scared her a bit. Then she asked herself how she really felt about him. Did she love him, could she love him so soon? Did it really matter; after all, all they needed was desire and that was not in short supply. Darcy had always had difficulty with the concepts of love. She had never seen it first hand. She knew lust; she knew attraction, obsession and convenience all too well. Those were the only feelings radiating between her parents. She then realized her biggest fear was that she might love him and in giving in to her desires he might leave and for once, she would have to feel loss.

Halloween fell on a Friday and the air was filled with talk about who was going where. Amanda was having a party, costume optional, thank God, because as festive as Darcy was, she couldn't imagine walking out of her house with all her bits and pieces on display. Harley agreed to pick her up around 7:30. She knew that night with so much flesh on display she should at least try a little, so she wore her jeans a little tighter than normal, and her black blouse dipped down ever so slightly as to expose just the contours of the tops of her breasts. She seldom let her hair down, but that night she didn't mind so much. When she saw his truck pull up her driveway, she felt the fluttering in her stomach. She remembered thinking how lucky she was that he opted for a truck over the over compensating sports cars most of the guys in LA were insistent upon. It made him so much more desirable in her eyes. When she met him at the door, he grabbed her waist, pushed him self against her and when her back hit the wall, he leaned in, she could feel the warmth of his breath against her lips and her eyes fell closed, then he softly kissed her forehead.

"Ready?" He asked as his breath traced her lips.

"Yes" she whispered her eyes still shut as she felt his arms fall free. "Hmm? Oh to leave, yeah definitely. Let's go." She jumped up to leave, a little flushed from embarrassment. He chuckled sardonically under his breath and climbed in the driver's seat.

When they arrived at the party she was so grateful she had allowed herself to be a little more daring than usual with her outfit, because most of the girls were half naked and a few were just a string away from complete nudity. Darcy was thankful that she'd never been the type to obsess about her body, but that night she was pretty surprised at the condition of most of the girls. Then again in a town chock full of aspiring models and actresses, keeping your body perfect was almost a requirement. Now that they usually spent almost every moment together at school, people were no longer in awe to see them together; in fact they were both so attractive it made sense. The party seemed like a blur to Darcy; she was uncomfortable most of the time and watching her friends get drunk and act ridiculous just embarrassed her. Finally around 10:30 Harley was ready to go. Truthfully he'd been ready to go about five minutes after they'd arrived, because although there was plenty of entertaining and appealing scenery, most of them were trying so hard to achieve what Darcy naturally possessed, and she was his. He took her hand and led her through the crowd. He left her standing at the door while he went to bring the truck around, and she over heard two half naked girls talking about them and she wasn't sure if they lacked volume control, or if it was an intentionally loud exchange.

"Look who's leaving. Mmm he's so hot. Ughh, why is he with her?" As the girl spoke, Darcy could almost hear the gum she was chewing stick to her teeth with every word.

"Who knows I mean she's pretty I guess. But I hear she's a total prude," replied the second, less intimidating of the two. "Makes sense, you know guys love the challenge."

"Well, from what I've heard, if she's anything like her mom he won't be waiting too long." This time when the girl spoke, the echoing of the gum didn't faze Darcy as much as the comment itself.

"So you don't think they've done it by now?" As the lesser of the two spoke Darcy actually wanted to know what the response would be.

"No, hello, he's still with her."

She was relieved to hear him honk and with her head down she ran into the truck.

"Hey what's wrong?" he asked.

"Nothing why?" she lied.

He grabbed her hand. "Come on, you're too pretty to look so sad." He bit down on his lower lip. "I'll get it out of you later. I have my ways." He winked at her and she smiled. He squeezed her hand and she gripped his tighter.

When they got to her house she felt a rush of anxiety. She knew they'd be alone and wasn't too sure how things would go. They walked in and walked almost simultaneously into her bedroom. Harley watched her as she walked over to her desk and flipped on the lamp switch, and then reached over to her computer. The music came on; she had purposely selected her favorite rock band as to not create too much of an ambiance. He loved watching her walk around, she moved effortlessly almost as if she were floating. He had to have her that night. Desire no longer filled his ache it was a blunt need.

With a superhuman swiftness he was standing behind her. He placed his hands on her shoulder and brushed her hair back to one side, and then as he slid one hand over her collarbone, the other one moved around beneath her shirt and sat on her stomach. His hands were cold and his breath was hot against her neck and as she felt his lips touch her skin, her body trembled at the tactile contradiction. She reached back and grabbed his hip and the hand he had on her collar bone followed his kisses up her neck to her face and when he reached her lips, it felt as if he were trying to devour her. Her breath became hollow and useless as she choked on the words that could not find release. He pulled back only long enough to lift her up effortlessly and lay her down on the bed. When he pulled off his shirt, Darcy noticed all the muscles in his stomach tighten as he breathed heavy and as he reappeared over her, she instinctively raised her hands to his chest. He smirked and grabbed both her wrists with one hand and held them down above her head. He bent down and resumed kissing her, as he did so, with his free hand he quickly undid her pants. That's when the reality of what was happening came to her and she felt doubt consume her. Once again she tried to lift her arms, but as she did his grip tightened and she could see every tendon in his forearm. As she looked up at his face, he smirked and her eyes widened, in his dark eyes, he had a look of determination. She took in as deep a breath as her body would allow.

"Hhharley wait," was all she could manage.

"Darcy don't worry, I'll go slow. Trust me." She knew she couldn't. She tried to tighten her knees together but he caught on and slid in, positioning his legs between hers, as he was still standing at the foot of her bed it was easy for him to hold them apart. As he pushed up against her, her body quivered ferociously as she tried to break free and in a sadistic way it turned Harley on. She knew no one would hear her scream and that he was well aware of this fact. She decided to try to talk him out of what he was about to do, but when she tried to speak he placed his free hand over her mouth and slipped his finger inside just to be sure. This only triggered her gag reflex and she bit down as hard as she could but she caught her lip between her teeth and his finger. She felt the skin tare and she felt his body shake as he chuckled. As she felt him position himself on her, she gathered every bit of air she could and as he thrust forward she screamed as hard as she could. This did nothing and as she was going to scream anyway Harley lifted his hand from her mouth and proceeded to run it over her body. The same touch that made her quiver in anticipation before made her shudder in disgust. She pleaded for a merciful release that he never granted her. Hot tears ran down her face and when it was over she didn't have enough energy to even move. He left what was left of her strewn out on the bed and when he finished getting dressed, he walked over and callously kissed her forehead and he was gone.

She lay still on the bed numb at first and then as time past, she began to feel the effects of the assault. It began with the metallic taste of the blood from her torn lip, then the stinging in her wrists, the stiffness of the muscles in her body, the burning in her legs, and finally a dull pain in her waist and as she sat up she let out a horrible shriek. She threw herself on the shower floor and let the scorching water run over her in hopes she could somehow burn off any trace of him.

That night when she was finally able to fall asleep, she repeated the entire evening in a sequence of dreams, she opened her eyes at dawn and remembering every detail of the prior evening, she shot up and rushed to the bathroom, where she proceeded to vomit violently. She spent the whole of that Saturday crying in bed. That night she finally mustered up the ability to walk into her restroom. She stood in front of the mirror and stared at the stranger that now occupied the other end. She felt deserving of the bluish black surrounding her lips, the purple fingers now imprinted around her wrists, the burning red hand print on her hip bone, and the countless bruises running up her inner thigh. She cried for almost a minute and that's all she allowed herself.

She climbed into bed and closed her eyes, but she could see his face within the darkness. She could taste him and in brief moments she could feel him and her body would flinch involuntarily. Then, before she knew it, she was drifting away.

DREAMING: THE ONE THAT CHANGED EVERYTHING

Darcy walked through the crowd clinging to the sleeves of her grey hooded sweat shirt. As she hid as much of herself as she could, she could still feel the burning stares of judgment. She walked on without any sense of destination. Finally she was at her own front door, sanctity. She ran in and headed straight for her bedroom; she stumbled in and closed the door behind her. Then as she stood in the middle of the room she noticed, the atmosphere had changed. She lay down on her bed and then out of no where she felt someone staring down at her. When she saw Harley standing over her she screamed, but no sound came. There was something darker and more diabolical about him. She looked up into his eyes and that's when she noticed in the midst of the rich black color, there was not a trace of white. As he grabbed her wrists, she knew what was coming, so she shut her eyes.

He stood watching from the corner of the room, his initial reaction was to go after Harley, but he knew it was an impossibility. Instead he just stood with his hands clenched into fists at his sides; it was all he could do. Then as he continued to watch the events happen just as they had before, he helplessly fell to his knees and buried his head in his hands. He tried convincing himself that it wasn't real, and although he understood all too well that it wasn't, he was also very aware that it had been. Why hadn't he come a couple of days before, maybe if she'd been anticipating it, he could have done something, somehow. When it was over she got up and walked to the mirror as she had earlier that day and examined her wounds. When he saw her as she had seen herself in the reflection, he felt agony and if it were possible, tears of anger would have been running down his face. Darcy walked over and sat on her bed; pulled her knees up to her chest and wept. He walked over to her, reached his hand over her head to caress her hair in comfort, but realized what he was about to do and pulled it back.

He couldn't bear to see her in so much pain, but could he really go against everything, fate, destiny, nature, was it worth breaking all the rules? No one would know, how could they, he knew she'd never be a receiver and she wasn't any kind of muse. Then he heard the word that changed everything.

"Please." It couldn't have sounded sweeter if it had been whispered by angels. So he dropped his guard. At first he wasn't sure what to do or say. He didn't want to scare her. Before he could do anything, she looked up and saw him standing next to her. When their eyes first met they both froze in amazement and then she stood up. As Darcy stared into the familiar blue eyes, she could see horror and pity

and she became self aware and placed her hand over her mouth to hide the busted lip. He grabbed her hand softly and pushed it down. Strangely she couldn't feel his touch but she could see the actions. He smiled at her, and she only managed a shameful half smile and hung her head down and wept. He couldn't help himself he placed one hand on the small of her back and the other cradled her head and he pressed her against his chest. At first Darcy buried her face in his chest and wept, she still couldn't feel his embrace, but she knew he was holding her and it wasn't with dark intentions, it was comforting and safe and she wrapped her arms around him. She noticed that although she couldn't feel his touch physically, somehow, she could feel him.

He had thought about this moment since practically the first day he saw her, and now that it was here, he found he couldn't concentrate on how good it felt to finally hold her. All he wanted to do was make her safe and try to ease as much of her suffering as he could.

Darcy felt insane for finding comfort in someone she knew wasn't real, but at that moment of desolation, he was hope and security and that's what she desperately needed.

"I'm Darcy." She whispered.

"I know, I'm Jack," his voice trembled as he spoke. He kissed the top of her head, and with that the daylight touched her eyes.

Darcy: Aftermath

Upon waking up her initial reaction was to reach for her journal, but instead, she just fell back on her pillow and tried to take it all in. She could still feel the physical effects of what had transpired, but somehow she felt safe again. "Jack," she tried to figure out why she would have chosen that name, but nothing came to mind.

Darcy's phone had been ringing since Saturday and finally on Sunday night her voice mail was full, before bed she decided to listen. The first couple of messages were from Amanda and Stacy, wondering where she was, making plans around her, complaining because she didn't show up, a few from her mother in Barbados and then she heard Harley's voice. At first she was afraid to listen, the abrasive sound of his gritty voice, reignited the sensation of a thousand pinheads trying to escape her skin, but then curiosity got the best of her. Apparently Harley was sorry. Trying to sound nonchalant he started out sounding concerned for the fact that she hadn't been answering anyone's phone calls; ironically, he wanted to make sure she was okay. Then he went on to ask if she was doing alright after the other night, followed by a few "I'm sorry if I was a bit rough, things kind of got out of hand, it's just because you're so beautiful, and I couldn't help it." She was waiting for him to blame her, but thankfully that never came, instead he closed his last message with instructions to call him early if she needed a ride to school. She couldn't believe his arrogance.

Sleep did not makes its way as easily as it usually did. Her mind fought it back with a determination her body was eventually able to subdue.

Dreaming: Meet Cue

Jackson stood on the hill watching Darcy as she looked around expectantly for him. He tried to understand how she did it. He knew it happened in glitches, people realizing they were dreaming when they failed to slip off into the deepest state of sleep, but somehow she always knew and even more bizarre, she had control. Maybe it was some very rare sleep depriving condition. Whatever it was, she looked beautiful and even though he knew they were most likely still there, it gave him consolation to see her without her bruises.

Darcy looked around the empty streets, but couldn't see him anywhere. She hoped he'd come back, and then she had an epiphany of sorts. If it was her dream, then she must have some control, so she sat on a desolate bus bench, closed her eyes and willed him. Jackson watched Darcy with her eyes shut tight and her lips pursed, trying to figure out why she looked like she was struggling. If it were possible he would have thought she had a headache. Just then he walked over and sat down.

"What are you doing?" His voice was soft and deep.

"Oh." Had it worked? She wondered. "Um nothing; you scared me." She couldn't help but giggle.

"Sorry." They sat side by side, neither of them brave enough to make eye contact. "So, are you better?"

"Yes, thanks." She hesitated as she continued. "No, probably not." She caught him off guard. And he looked at her pensively. "I mean I think there might be something wrong with me, like schizophrenia or some other mental illness? I'm kind of starting to freak out a little."

He tried to contain his smile. "What, why? That's ridiculous."

"Well, I can't figure it out. Why am I hallucinating then?"

"You hallucinate?" He began to worry.

"Well, how are you here? Like, I must have created you from some weird repressed mental thing."

"Oh, you created me then, is that right?"

She worried that maybe he wasn't aware that he was in her dreams, that he wasn't real and this thought just made her feel mad. "Well, yeah sort of, like," she bit down on her lip and wondered how he'd react, "you know in my dreams?"

He felt relieved when he realized what she meant, but he couldn't help but laugh. She felt stupid. "I'm not too sure, but I don't think it's considered a hallucination if you're sleeping? Maybe I'm just a dream, or maybe you just needed a friend, or maybe I'm a fantasy," he joked. Darcy blushed and couldn't help but smirk. His tone didn't have a hint of pretension so there was no doubt he wasn't being serious.

"Well, whatever you are, I'm just still glad you're here." She usually wasn't so confident and she would never dare to be this outspoken, but she felt so comfortable around him, like she'd known him almost all her life; she playfully grabbed his arm and rested her head on his shoulder. "It's weird, you know all these years I've been dreaming about you, I wondered what it'd be like to talk to you, and now I can't think of anything to say." He suddenly got a look of worry. "What?"

"All these years?" He knew she'd seen him that once, but had there been another time? It was impossible; how could she have? "What do you mean; I thought you just created me?" He said trying hard not to sound too concerned.

"I never said I had just created you, that's sounds kinda stupid, I meant like dreamt you. Oh but maybe, I guess, you don't remember or well how could you right?" She felt awkward and ridiculous. "I don't really know how this works or how you work," she felt like the more she talked the less sense she was making.

Jackson began to get nervous. "How I work?" He tried to break the uneasiness with mocking. "What like I'm a robot or something? Do I have like powers and stuff, cause that would be kinda cool." He smiled.

She rubbed her face in frustration. "No, never mind. I guess, maybe I am crazy. Jesus, what's wrong with me, even in my own dreams I act like an idiot. Forget it. You can disappear now if you want." By this time she had her face buried in her hands to hide her embarrassment.

Now he felt bad; for as long as he could remember he had wanted her and now he was just bringing out the worst in her, but watching her struggle made him smile at her beautiful imperfections. "So, you'd seen me before yesterday?"

"A couple of times, actually a lot, but when we were younger. Like twelve or something."

"Twelve? Maybe it was someone else how can you be sure? Did you ever talk to that person?"

"No, and it, I know it was you."

"Really?" he asked playfully lifting an eyebrow. "How could you tell?"

She was way too embarrassed to tell him that she knew it was him just by looking into his beautiful blue eyes, that he had a face that was burned into her memory since the first day she saw him, that whenever he was around she felt something profound and indescribable. So she settled for… "I could just tell. Can we please change the subject?"

Jackson realized everything she was saying was true. Because she was his first and he remembered being about twelve when it happened. He still couldn't understand why or how she could have noticed him. He wanted answers, but he would never dare ask the only people that could probably offer them up. He decided this would be his last time. It had to be, so he'd make the best of it. They talked a little more about Darcy, her life, her family, her interests and as the conversation continued, he kept having to remind himself not to fall for her, so that he wouldn't be tempted to come back.

Darcy had never talked about herself so much in all her life. She felt a little egocentric, but she couldn't help it. Jack had a way of asking that made it impossible to refuse an answer. She told him everything from how hollow her childhood had been, to how awkward and unreal her life was now. She told him how living a phony life in a phony town, full of phony people, it was hard to connect to anything real, because Darcy's reality was her own practicality. She didn't mind telling him the most intimate details of her life, because he wasn't judgmental, he was interested. He would stare at her when she spoke, and that's when she decided he couldn't be real, he was too beautiful. His face, his demeanor, his sincerity. Then he stood up.

"We don't have a lot of time left." He saw her expression sadden. "I have one more question though. If you'd dreamt me before, why didn't you ever say anything?"

"I guess, when I finally got around to it, you left. I mean not left, but like didn't come back or whatever. I honestly didn't think I'd ever see you again, I mean I'm not really sure how long it was, but it was a while." She hung her head down and then under her breath said "felt like forever."

She'd missed him; he shamefully felt satisfied and happy even. He knew exactly how long it had been, because it was during his more active period; and even though he was into his own thing, he'd missed her too.

"So will I see you again tomorrow or…?"

"Can you always tell when you're dreaming?"

"As long as I can remember, why?"

"No reason."

"So? Will I see you or are you gonna abandon me again."

He knew he shouldn't but he really couldn't help himself. "Well, doesn't that depend on you? I mean according to your theory? Besides, I might not always be around, but I'll always be there."

"Be where?"

He was walking away, but turned back. "Where ever you need me to be." As he spoke, Darcy stared at his perfectly shaped, full lips, and she knew he would be. "Good morning Darcy," he joked as he continued on.

"Good morning Jack," she smiled. And with that came the day.

Darcy: A Means

As Darcy's alarm rang she sat up and listened with revulsion. She wanted so desperately to fall back asleep and see Jack, but she knew it was time to face her spurious reality. She showered delicately as to not disturb her sensitive contusions. She got dressed and headed off to school. On her way, the realization that she'd have to face Harley finally hit her. She hesitated and decided she didn't want to be victimized; she didn't want the attention, the sympathy, or the pity. She would play it by ear.

When she pulled her car into the student lot, she was relieved that Harley's truck was nowhere in sight. Maybe he was afraid she might make a scene and decided to skip school all together. She wasn't so lucky, as she kept walking; she spotted it parked in front. Apparently he felt the need to get there early; she nervously gripped the sleeves of her hoodie. As she was about to walk into the building, she was rushed off to the side by Amanda and Stacy.

"Where the hell have you been?" Stacy asked noticeably loud.

"Seriously, we thought you were dead or something," Amanda spoke in a softer less assertive tone.

"Dead? A bit dramatic don't you think?" Darcy turned back and kept walking. The two girls hurried behind her trying to keep pace.

"So, where were you then? I mean it's not like you not to answer your phone. Even Harley called Stacy to see if we'd heard anything from you."

"Oh I don't doubt that," Darcy snarled.

"Really he sounded concerned, very worried," Amanda kept on, unknowingly.

"Oh my God, poor Harley, he might have died of concern, fuck him," Darcy snapped sarcastically. Her friends both looked at her in surprise. It wasn't in her character to be curt. She felt bad for taking out her anger on them. "Sorry, guys don't pay any attention to me; I'm just acting like a total bitch today."

"I'll say. Darce are you PMSing or something?"

"I'll explain later, but just please do me a favor, just …" leave me alone, she wanted to say, but she couldn't they were the only tolerable girls in the whole city and they were her friends. "I'm feeling bad and I need some," she swallowed hard, "space. Could you help me like dodge everyone?"

Amanda knew all too well that Darcy had her days, but she also knew how Darcy had been the only one there for her when her mother had succumbed to a very untimely and unpleasant stint in rehab. Darcy had also been the only one of them to confront Stacy's pig of a stepfather when he started inexcusably walking into her bedroom at night. They would do anything for her. "Yeah Darcy, whatever you need. And you know if you need to tell us anything..."

"I will, just give me some time." Darcy walked into the building with her head hanging, if she could just make it through at least the morning without seeing Harley she'd be okay.

She got her way, the morning went smoothly, even though she paid absolutely no attention in either of her classes, the fact that she was present at all made up for it. Stacy and Amanda did well in swaying conversations and exchanges made in Darcy's direction and by lunchtime she was even feeling hopeful. She decided to stop by the ladies' room and agreed to meet up with her friends at their usual lunch spot. She washed her hands compulsively whenever she felt nervous; she knew after lunch she'd have class with Harley. She debated on what she should do and decided maybe she wasn't strong enough to face Harley just yet. Darcy knew PMS was always the easiest ticket home, so she decided to skip lunch and head to the nurse's office. She tossed the wad of paper towel into the trash and headed out of the restroom unknowingly.

"Darce!" She couldn't help but jump up a little. "Ha, sorry didn't mean to scare you," he leaned in and playfully whispered into her ear. She felt all the tendons in her neck tighten, she lost her breath and small bumps plagued her entire body. "What no hello, no kiss?" He said nonchalantly. She opened her mouth but the words never found their way out. "Look I'm sorry about the other night. I might have gone a little too far, but you know how I feel about you, I just...," he hesitated, she stared at him with a look of disgust, "look, if I'm guilty of anything, it's just liking you too much," he smiled at her appeased, "you're so beautiful," he whispered maniacally. Her look of disgust morphed into a look of amazement; she could not believe those word could even be animated.

"Really, that's what you came up with? Yes, you're definitely guilty, but it's not of liking me, you twisted moron. You know what you did." As Darcy spoke, he looked annoyed and was getting angry.

"What, what exactly was it that I did? Huh?" he whispered as he took hold of her forearm forcefully. "I had sex with my girlfriend, in her house, in her room, the house she let me into, the room we've been making out in for weeks. Look, I don't exactly remember forcing my way in or throwing you down on the bed. That was all you. All I did was finish what you had initiated." Darcy's face was burning and she could feel her lip twitching.

"Harley, don't, you know what happened in that room. You knew it was wrong. You knew I said no and I fought and begged you and..."

"Cut your innocent shit Darcy, fifty fucking people saw us leave together that night, and about a hundred have seen us together. So what? Everyone knows how this works for me, all I have to do is break it off and everyone will know exactly what kind of girl you really are." She threw back her arm and tried to walk away and he grabbed her wrist that was apparently still sore. When she grimaced, he smiled deviously. "Look I really do like you, a lot, so I'm offering you a choice here, if you really want to end this you can walk away, keep your mouth shut, and play it cool or you keep throwing around your made up fantasies and I dump you and everyone thinks, well, what can I say, like mother, like daughter right?" The tears streamed down Darcy's face and she wrestled her arm free and slapped him. She didn't wait for his face to recover, instead she ran down the hall, out of the double doors.

On the drive home, she fell apart. Her throat burned with the acids from deep within her stomach, and all of the feelings from that night returned, the nausea, the helplessness, the shameful disgust. Darcy, for once, was incredibly grateful for her absentee family. There would be no one to face or answer to when she got home, but still running into her empty bedroom, she needed someone, and she knew exactly who it should be.

HARLEY'S LAMENTING

When Harley walked into class, he half expected to see Darcy sitting there; given their previous encounter he wasn't too surprised. He could feel the eyes in the room burning into his back. He could hear the questions passing through the room and it was apparent that it wouldn't be long before the obvious would be directed at him. As the teacher began another lengthy boring lecture, Harley was grateful that he had a little time to make an important decision. He thought about Darcy and how beautiful she was; usually during these lectures, he would entertain himself by staring at her and letting his dubious thoughts take flight. This time though, he no longer had to fantasize or question his motives, because he'd conquered and victory had been sweet. He thought about how she felt, how she smelled, how she tasted, and then as his mind's eye swept up over her body to her face, a look of fear and desperation recalled itself. Admittedly he knew he had gone too far, but somehow he'd convinced himself that it was what she wanted. She desired him as much as he had desired her; she had to have. His affection for her really did run deep, he felt more for her than he had for anyone. In his own dire way, he still did and he hoped she'd wanted to stay with him, at least a little longer. Why wasn't that enough for her, why couldn't she be like every other girl and just get over herself? Did he love her? Probably not. He could say that she was sick and maybe after taking his proposition into consideration she'd agree to work things out. He realized that by her reaction it wasn't likely; and it was too bad, because he wanted her still. He knew what had to be done. He genuinely felt bad for hurting Darcy but he could see no way around it.

As the night Darcy had been praying so desperately for finally approached, she readied herself. She hadn't tried to get to sleep that early in as long as she could remember. She smiled, slid back onto her pillow and closed her eyes to no avail. Within an hour, she shot up, pressed her hand to her face and had never felt so awake in the whole of her life. She got up and paced her room. Why couldn't she sleep? She was sure on a few occasions she had dozed off, but something kept springing her back. She spotted her cell phone on the desk and reached for it, 13 missed calls, all from Mandy. She probably shouldn't have left them completely clueless in the lunch room that afternoon. She figured by explaining everything, she'd make up for it the next day. She turned off her phone and went back to bed with determination and she knew exactly how to get to where she needed to be. She flipped on the television and found one of her favorite movies, knowing very well that by the time it would get to her favorite part she'd be passed out and miss it. Darcy finally slipped away to another deliciously lucid slumber.

Darcy found herself walking through a slue of strange yet familiar houses. As soon as she realized she was dreaming she couldn't help but smile. With her hands tucked into her pockets, she walked through the brownstones and as she looked around, in the sea of faces, there was no familiarity. Slightly disappointed, she walked up and sat on one of the stoops. Listening in on the conversations she noticed that although everyone was talking she couldn't make out a word they were saying. She'd had this dream before and it often bored her. She looked down at the steps and began to slip away. Reluctantly she thought about her confrontation with Harley, but before she could dissect it, she felt a warm breeze, and looked up. He was standing at the bottom of the stoop looking up at her with his head slightly tilted and his hand casually tucked into his front pockets. When she met his eyes, she smiled, but it was not returned. "Who is he?"

"Who?" She looked around in confusion.

"Him," he sounded apathetic, but she knew it was more out of anger or disapproval. "Never mind. If you don't want to tell me that's fine."

She'd immediately known to whom he was referring but for whatever reason she could think of, perhaps in sheer paralipsis, she still raised the question. Then she looked up at him, to him, "Harley."

"Harley?" He said curtly. Darcy gave a smirk and shrugged her shoulders. "Harley, figures. What did Harley do this time?"

"How'd you…"

"I could just tell. I mean did he" he hesitated enough to swallow hard and bit down on his lower lip "hurt you again?" A pained expression swept his brow; he couldn't utter the words, because the mere idea of him touching her, of his hands being anywhere near her body, gave him motive enough to carry out the hells he was capable of.

She was about to nod her head, but then a curious thought made its way to her head; could he possibly know and how? "Hurt me?" He looked at her in bewilderment. "I mean at first I thought you meant like emotionally or something, but you didn't did you?" He averted his gaze down to his feet and she blushed in embarrassment. He did know. She pulled her hands up to her face and sighed. "Shit, I feel so stupid."

"What, why?"

"I just...How did you know?"

"I saw you, him, well you know, it. Like not when it actually happened, because I would've never let him...But the other night, I guess the day after, I mean that first night before we ..." he couldn't find a way to explain himself correctly.

She remembered the dream. "I'm not like that you know. I mean I don't just, I had never, well before then..."

At first he furrowed his brow in confusion. "You didn't do anything." He walked up and sat next to her. "I saw what happened to you and it did happen to you, not because of you, do you know what I mean? Don't feel stupid. He should feel, well, there are a lot of things he should feel." He was staring down at his feet again, but she could see the tension in his temples. "So what are you gonna do now?"

"I don't know. I thought about telling someone, but it's so, dirty and shameful. I don't really like attention, and that's the worst kind you know." He watched her as she spoke in determination, in justification. "People asking questions, making their own assumptions, people can be really stupid, especially where I'm from. The best headlines are the worst stories you know? The worst part is I still have to see him."

"You saw him today." He finally began to make sense of what had happened earlier. "Did he say anything? Apologize, promise to stay away from you, give you any lame ass excuse, anything?"

"No, not exactly. I'm not even sure he knows what he really did."

"Oh no, please don't be that kind..." he shut his eyes tight as he spoke as if the words affected his vision.

"No that's not what I meant," she now spoke apologetically and it made him feel bad. "I mean he's twisted, demented. He expected me to just let it go and I don't know stay with him or something."

"If that's what he thinks, then he really must be fucking nuts." He turned and looked at her. "You're not are you?"

She rolled her eyes. "You underestimate me that much?"

He smiled. "No not at all."

He stood up and motioned for her to follow. They walked down the streets that were now empty. He wanted to press on about Harley, but when he saw her eyes fade he decided instead against it. They continued to talk about music and Darcy sans Harley. She felt at ease and enjoyed the temporary escape. As they continued on she took his hand. He smiled. "Ahh that frustrates me."

"What?" he asked.

"It feels like my hands are numb. I want to feel you. Why cant I?"

He shrugged his shoulders and as they continued on although his insides were illuminated he couldn't help but share in her saddness. He wanted her to feel him too, and he wanted nothing more than to feel her and he knew exactly why neither one of them could. They continued on for a few more moments and then Jack stopped. "Darcy," the way she looked at him made something inside him ache. "Do something for me, please." She knew she would do anything for him. "Just," he couldn't find the right words (make sure he stays the hell away from you, so I won't be tempted to kill him) seemed too brash, so he opted for "Don't let him get to you. Stay away from him. Make it clear that you want nothing from him and if need be and if you really feel it's in your best interest not to turn him in, even though I'm not too sure I agree, assure him you won't, so he'll disappear." She smiled at him and raised an eyebrow slightly. He blushed, "I'm usually not you know, demanding. Sorry if I sounded a little..." he looked embarrassed and he quickly stuck his hands in his front pockets, he was nervous, but it was endearing.

"Jack," he looked up at her his sapphire eyes piercing, "thanks." He half smiled and her heart sped up in her chest.

He was a foot taller than she was and he bent down and pressed his forehead to hers. "Good morning Darcy."

Darcy and Daniel

As the morning rays fell over Darcy's eyes, she took a deep breath and felt hopeful once again. She walked over to her mirror and stared at her reflection, most of the contusions had yellowed over and she was grateful it wouldn't take so much make-up to cover them up. While getting ready for school, she considered maybe not going, but then again, Darcy was never one to give in easily. She decided to follow Jack's advice and let Harley know that so long as he left her alone, she wouldn't stir any trouble. She had also decided that first thing, she'd find her friends and fill them in on what was really going on and as hard as it might be she'd spare no detail. She finished dressing and ran out into her kitchen; she was surprised to see her father sitting at the counter.

"Hey dad." She walked over and kissed him dryly on the cheek. "Is everything okay?"

"Morning Princess. Why do you ask?"

"Um I don't know because you're still here I guess. You usually don't stick around for breakfast or life in general."

"Oh, I know. I'm not really here for breakfast honey; I needed to talk to you about something. Your mother wanted me to wait until she came back, but apparently she's been detained by some deal and will probably be gone for another week or so."

Darcy was curious about her mother's deal; she wondered what his name might be. Then she began to panic a little. "So what's wrong?"

"No nothing's wrong princess," she grimaced, she hated being called princess, "it's just, well, I've been offered a new position. Something of, well a substantial raise."

"Wow, that's sounds really great Dad, congratulations," she tried her best to sound somewhat enthused.

"Yes, erm, thank you. Thing is, the position requires a transfer. I'll be working out of the London branch," she knew what was coming but acted coyly, "so of course we'd have to move.'

"Really? But dad you hate the city, you always said that's why you left New York."

"Yeah, I know, so I've been looking at real-estate in more rural areas of England. It's a bit of a commute, but nothing too extreme. It's nice enough; I think you'll enjoy it. Nice scenery," he paused and looked away, "the schools are excellent and I don't think with your marks anyway, that a transfer would be difficult."

"Transfer?"

"Yes, I tried to stretch it out as long as I could but as far as I could get was the end of the month." He really had tried to extend it, he felt awful that she'd have to leave everything behind so abruptly, but with her mother almost always gone, he couldn't see anyway of letting her stay in LA for the rest of the year.

"But it's my senior year! That doesn't make any sense. What good would that do me? I mean really it's so stupid. You never ever put my needs ahead of your own. That's so fucking selfish. Did you ever stop and think about the small fact that this is my last year of High school? What the hell am I suppose to do in England Dad? Seriously, sometimes, it's like I don't even exist around here." Darcy picked up her bag and stormed out of the house. Daniel Whitten sat in unease. Having Darcy mad at him always made him feel bad. She was the only person whom he could disappoint; ironically she was the only one who mattered. Everything he did in his life was for her and his transfer was not so much of an option, it was absolute.

Now in his mid forties and with all his successes, he was still the same timid guy he'd always been. Daniel was never the Hollywood type and he was always secretly happy that his daughter didn't appear to be either. Daniel had grown up in Pennsylvania in a middle class setting. His mother was a beautiful and gentle mannered nursery school teacher and his father was a prominent banker. Finance was in his blood and he excelled at it. If NYU hadn't offered him a scholarship, he would have been content to remain in his modest yet comfortable lifestyle. His parents had also been polar opposites his father came from a stiff middle class family that had not approved of his unorthodox marriage to his mother, a strong spirited Hispanic woman. He saw a lot of his mother in his daughter and this gave him solace. Daniel hated New York, the fast pace, the crowds and the social scene. Upon graduating he was offered an internship at a prominent firm and his father was so proud there was no way he could turn it down. Before too long, his talents were recognized and soon enough, he was making a six figure salary. That's when he met Jeanette. She was beautiful and unlike anyone he'd ever met before.

It didn't take much time before she too saw his potentials. She knew exactly what Daniel was capable of, what he might be worth and she knew how to get him to fall desperately in love with her. It wasn't too hard though, there hadn't been many women in his life before and certainly none like her.

Jeanette Sergey was a fresh french import at just seventeen. After a couple of deceptively vague modeling years, by the time she was twenty she learned the rules to the game of life. Everything was a derision to Jeanette and so long as she made the right move she could always count on the results. What she hadn't counted on was Darcy. When Jeanette learned of her pregnancy, her world nearly ended. At just shy of 21, her career had finally taken off and she was not ready to settle down or set roots. However, when Daniel did the noble thing and proposed, she saw a way to make the best of the situation. Over the years, she had managed to make Daniel feel so guilty about ruining her career and robbing her of her dream, he would do anything she asked of him. Thus, the move to LA. He could never feel disappointed about his marriage of convenience, because he had Darcy and she was worth every lonely night and public indiscretion.

Darcy felt bad for being such a brat. She knew it was stupid. Her father was the only person who ever even considered her opinion vital, and she knew he loved her more than life itself. Truthfully she wasn't even that disappointed. She wasn't very fond of most of the people and her current situation was reason enough to leave California in her rear view. Would she really miss it all that much? Then she thought of Stacy and Amanda and how they had been inseparable since grade school; they had plans. They were supposed to graduate together and go to prom and now what? Maybe she could stay with them at least for the couple of months that were left of school. She was sure their parents wouldn't mind. Then she felt foolish that she had acted like such an idiot when there was a perfectly simple solution.

She got to school armed with her self assurance and Jack's voice in her head. All she had to do was tell Harley that so long as he kept his distance, she'd let it go. With one last reflection check, she got out of her car. She tucked her cold hands in the pockets of her black pea coat. Something in the air felt heavy and suffocating. Darcy walked into the school and she felt the burning of a thousand eyes, but she figured it was probably because people had caught on to the fact that Harley and her were no longer together. She decided that she'd save herself the agony and torment of waiting for the right moment which most likely would never come and find Harley first thing.

Darcy headed straight for the athletics building and walked into the boys' locker-room with full force. She was usually more reserved, but she knew she had to do it before she lost her nerve. As she walked a few guys ducked behind locker doors, it was almost amusing. Then she saw him standing by his locker in nothing but his soccer shorts, laughing along with some of his teammates. He was by all definitions beautiful. She couldn't understand how beneath all that there was a monster. Funny as it was, when she saw him there with a smile on, she was reminded of better times. She'd really cared for Harley quite a bit, and he had become her best friend. Where had that person gone? She felt bad, but not bad enough.

"Harley." He turned and seemed genuinely and understandably surprised to see her standing there. Seeing her still gave him chills. She stood there with her waves of hair pulled up messily on her head, even in her jeans and coat, her shape was appealing and her face was painfully attractive. He secretly hoped for an embrace.

"Darcy!" His friends almost simultaneously smirked and he gave them an arrogant nod. "Well what can I do for you?"

"Can I talk to you for a minute?" He looked on expectantly. "Er in private?"

"Look Darcy, I don't think that's such a good idea. I mean, why are you doing this?" He whispered a little too loudly, after which a serious of low toned "Oohs" followed.

"What the hell are you talking about?" Darcy's voice trembled nervously as she spoke.

"Darcy, seriously I really like you, so as a friend, I'm asking you to stop all this embarrassing begging and move on." He slammed his locker shut and walked out.

"Harley! Harley what did you tell them? What did he tell you?" After a series of eye rolling, a couple of the guys just up and left. "He's lying; you know you're a fucking liar!" She yelled out to no one in particular. She stood there in fury and awkward silence for a couple of minutes, then looked around and saw the judgmental eyes. She hurried out of the locker room.

Back in the main building, the prying eyes continued to appear from every doorway, the snickers, whispers and smirks came from every direction. She put her head down and just kept pace, thinking she had to get out before the security guards shut the gates, but her visceral reflexes were set in motion. She quickly reached the nearest bathroom and ran in shutting the door quickly and dropping to her knees. After a serious of dry heaves, she knew the worst was over, then she heard them talking.

"Who is that?" The girl's voice was vague and unfamiliar.

"Is she okay?" Asked another phantom occupant.

"It's Darcy Whitten I think?"

"She's probably knocked up by now."

"Poor Harley." They just went on and on.

"I know I can't believe he even went out with her."

"Well, he told Rick she was such a freak, he should have seen it coming."

"Well, I mean look where she comes from. I mean seriously."

She couldn't tell who they were and she didn't care. She folded her arms over her knees and tucked her head down. She knew they were talking loud enough purposefully so she did her best to shut them out. She waited until she could only hear the faint ripples of the somewhat stagnant toilet water and just as she was about to stand up, she heard a knock.

"Darce?"

"Yeah?" She didn't want to cry, but her voice was shaking uncontrollably.

"Are you okay? Come out."

"Stacy, I'm fine. I just..." She couldn't fake it any more. Defeated, she stood up, opened the door, fell into Stacy's arms and cried.

"Oh Darcy, why didn't you tell us you'd been sleeping with Harley? You knew what he'd do when he'd gotten his fill."

"Oh my God, is that what you think? Do you honestly believe what he's saying?"

"Of course not Darcy. He's said some pretty horrible things you know. We know better than that, but we figured you had at least slept with him. I mean he described pretty much every detail of," she bit her lip and spoke through her teeth, "well, you know, your room, your underwear, your body.

I mean he does know quite a bit. At first we doubted it a bit, but the details are pretty vivid." Darcy pushed free.

"Jesus. You all don't know shit. Thanks a lot." She started towards the door.

"Well, you keep us in the dark about everything now. How do you expect us to know anything? Don't be that way Darcy. I'm here for you just tell me what's going on with you." Stacy pleaded.

"Forget it! Never mind. I should have known better. You guys really suck you know. You should know me better; you're supposed to know me better. What kind of friends are you anyway? Making assumptions." Darcy was hurt.

Stacy was offended. "Clearly not the kind someone like you deserves. Sorry we're not all fucking mind readers like you Darce. We don't all live in our heads some of us live out here in reality."

"Reality, you think you live in reality. You never know shit and you believe everything you hear. You're as phony as everyone else here." Darcy could not contain her words.

"You know what Darcy, whatever's going on with you, obviously someone as stupid as me isn't qualified enough to help you, so fuck off. Go be a slut for all I care." Stacy stormed out of the restroom.

Darcy instantaneously knew she had been wrong in everything she said. But she was feeling so many different things that she couldn't process her guilt fast enough to apologize. She got into her car and felt numb. She drove to the gate and the security guard stopped her and asked to see her release. She just looked up at him and as he saw her bloodshot eyes welting up with tears and helplessness, he just let her through.

She headed straight for her bedroom, closed the door behind her and as she stood with her back against the door, her body went limp and she slinked onto the floor. Tears fell continuously out of her eyes, but she felt nothing. As night began to fall, besides changing position from the floor to her chaise, her demeanor had not changed. With the TV running, she was still mentally shut off. Occasionally the message icon on her phone would flash, but she ignored it. Finally she heard heavy footsteps outside her bedroom. She knew it was Daniel, probably wondering if she was still angry with him.

She wanted to reassure him, but she didn't have the strength, luckily he turned and walked away. He had seen the lights off under the door, and figured she was sleeping. She got up and grabbed her phone. There were several very apologetic messages from Stacy and she knew she didn't deserve a single one. She wanted to instead offer up a few of her own, but she just couldn't that night, not in her blunt condition. She took a long shower and the water against her skin reminded her that some part of her was still alive.

She pulled on an old t-shirt and crawled into her bed. She closed her eyes and prayed for salvation or at least consolation.

Jackson: Cruel Decisions

Jackson stood at the foot of the bed, stared at his watch and he wondered if it was possible. By his calculations he knew it was unlikely. He thought about Darcy. Would she be expecting him, more importantly did she need him? The temptation was dangerously fierce. He couldn't if he wanted to, not only would he have hell to pay, but he would raise suspicions and he wasn't sure if it could affect her somehow. He had thought about if before, but now as he had actually considered it, he wondered what she'd be facing if they knew. He could only imagine the worst and it was bad enough that she'd just have to get along without him that night. He thought about his promise, but it couldn't be helped. He looked down at the page in his hand and went on to fulfill his obligation that night.

Darcy smiled. Through the flood of people in the market she could see a small girl sitting by a table covered in dolls. She loved this dream. She continued to walk towards the table, aware that the little girl polishing the dolls was her grandmother. Everything was exactly as described, the people, the stands, and the dolls. As she watched the girl, she felt warm inside and even though the girl was fairly younger than she, the sense of security still radiated from her. Then she felt the shift and she knew the dream was about to change. As the scenery began to fade around her, she desperately tried to hold on to the image of her grandmother as a child, but she couldn't, and the girl slowly faded to a faint shadow. The grass around her was over grown and she suddenly felt afraid. She looked around and could feel eyes. Watchful, judgmental eyes stalking her from within the brush. She continued to walk through toward a green field in the distance that appeared more serene, but with every couple of steps, the thick, jagged grass grew taller. Then she saw Harley standing through the course blades and she could see something dark in his demeanor; cutting through the silence and coming from all directions, she could hear the same whispers she had heard all day. The more Darcy ran the farther she'd sink and no matter in what direction she went, every step was a step closer to Harley. She began to feel suffocated. Heaviness fell on her chest and her breathing was shallow. "Jack," she pleaded in a course voice. As she repeated his name, Harley shook his head and smiled. Fear overwhelmed her. "Jack please I need you. Jack." Her voice faded until it was gone. She stopped moving in an attempt to keep the short distance that was left between her and Harley and all of a sudden he was holding her waist from behind as he had done before.

He put his mouth to her ear and whispered "Don't worry, this will only hurt." As he slid his hand below her waist line, she gasped for air to no avail. She was dying and no one was there. As she struggled to breathe, she could hear Harley's soft chuckle and she tried to hold on to Jack's voice from before but it was interrupted by a more devious one, "He's not coming, no one will come."

Darcy sat up wheezing for air. Finally, deliverance. She took in a couple more deep breaths and stood up. She made her way to the restroom, turning on every light along the way. She splashed water on her face to shake off the dream she placed her hands over her chest to try and subdue the dull pain form within. She felt as though she'd been breathing in icy cold air and her lungs ached ferociously. Then she sat and cried again, this time she sobbed, for her fears, for her desperation, for her heartache, for her abandonment, for Harley, and for Jack.

DARCY

Darcy was terrified to go back to sleep, and it was only 5:30 in the morning. She grabbed her cotton pants and pulled on her tennis shoes. As most of the other joggers ran or walked in stride with purpose and determination, Darcy walked with agony in her paces, but at least she felt insignificant enough. She got back to her house when the sun had finally taken its rightful place in the sky. She could not face anyone, so she showered and curled up in front of her television. Darcy was terrified to go back to sleep, so she went out at noon to pick up some essentials. She was sure to arm herself with plenty of entertainment, books, movies, magazines, snacks, and just to be sure on her way home coffee. She wasn't one for piping hot beverages; she never saw the point in that, so she opted for an iced caramel macchiato.

Back in her new fortress, she sat in front of her computer and Googled London. She thought how funny the idea was that within what was bound to be the worst thing that could have happened, hid her salvation. She decided she could not return to school, she would simply tell Daniel that she was sorry and ready to move. She knew he would question her motives, so she fabricated a long story that ended with Harley breaking her heart, she was sure he wouldn't pry. The mere notion that Darcy might have a private life made Daniel extremely uncomfortable.

She wouldn't be leaving anything behind, anything she'd miss anyway, except Stacy and Amanda. She picked up her phone and began to type. The few well deserved moments of discomfort would be worth the resolution. By five o clock that afternoon both girls were at her front door. They walked into her bedroom and were astonished at the change in atmosphere.

"Okay Darcy, now I'm really worried," said Stacy.

"I know are we preparing for some kind of natural disaster?" Amanda added while eyeing the junk food containers sprawled across the floor.

Darcy giggled. "I know, I haven't been feeling well, normal lately."

"And the house keeper? Jinx!" They both giggled.

"I'm kinda on a Do Not Disturb basis with everyone in my house right now. So, I know I'm usually not the best at well, sharing I guess, so I'm going to fill you in on everything. No details spared. You know how hard and uncomfortable this is for me, so just listen."

"What do you mean by…"

"Stace, don't talk just listen," Mandy reiterated.

Darcy smiled at her and proceeded. She told them every little detail about everything that been happening, as much as she could recall anyway. During the hardest parts she would pause take a breath, close her eyes and continue. When she finished with the whole Harley thing, she went on to tell them about the move, the girls in the restroom at school, and finally her nightmare. The only thing she never mentioned was Jack. Beside the fact that even in her head it sounded completely insane, she had decided to let him go. However she could, she would try not to think about him, or anticipate seeing him again. It was just another abandonment, another betrayal, another broken promise.

When she was finally done, both girls sat there in complete silence. She laughed a little, because she had never seen them so quiet. Both girls had a looks that ran from pain to pity on their faces. "Well, aside from offering opinions, advice, or sympathies, you can talk now you know."

Amanda smiled. "I just," she was careful to choose her words, "you should know us better than that Darcy. If you really don't want to move, you can stay with me until the year ends. Besides, you know I was counting on Paris after graduation, and then we could be close."

Stacy wasn't sure she could open her mouth without releasing the sob that seemed to be lodged in her throat. She was hurting for her friend and there was no denying it, but she couldn't exactly remain mute, so she offered up what she could. "Hungry?"

"Definitely," Darcy wasn't programed to pass on pizza.

Jackson: Predicaments

When Jackson got called out again he was visibly upset. He knew he had to pull it together and appear less dubious. It was just that it was such a crucial time with Darcy. What were the odds that he'd be called out twice in a row? It almost never happened and why now? There was a brief period when he had gone almost two weeks without any activity. "Fuck," he thought. He'd been away from her longer than this before, but not since he'd made that stupid promise he should have known he'd never be able to keep. He lay back against the back board with his hands tucked behind his head, and imagined her face. There had been other girls in his life, many, but none held a candle to her. She was flawless even her quirks and insecurities were attractive to him. He had been studying her demeanor, her style, her eyes, for years, trying to figure out what it was that drew him to her. He remembered trying to convince himself that although she was beautiful, she was probably stupid or shallow, and frustratingly, when he finally got to know her she was neither.

Darcy: Wishful Dreaming

Darcy found that it was easier to close her eyes and drift away now that she wasn't so eager to sleep. Then she sat up in an instant. What if she had another nightmare? With that in mind she felt sleepier than she had in a while. She tried to think of something distracting, maybe if she fell asleep thinking about something funny or pleasant, she'd project that in her dreams. She reached over and stuck her I pod into her alarm clock and turned it on. The music was a nice distraction but as one particular song played she stared at the ceiling and images of Jack flooded her mind. She thought of his face, the expressions in his mouth whenever he talked or smiled, his eyes; she wondered what it be like to run her hands through his hair, or run her fingers along the side of his cheekbones. She thought of them walking hand in hand and wished she had been able feel his hands in hers. She thought of his laughter and his soothing tone when he spoke and before too long, she was out.

Darcy walked into the building as if she was being pulled into it. She got to the door and swung it open. The room was a bright almost metallic white from floor to ceiling. In the corner was a folded over piece of paper. She walked over and picked it up, just then she heard a heavy door slam shut. She ran over and tried the handle, but it was locked. As she looked around the room, she noticed something changed, she felt more enclosed; the room seemed smaller. She looked back and the door was gone. She stood in the middle of a still, white cube. Darcy worried she might begin to panic so she walked over and stood at the back on the room, or what had originally been the back, when there was a door. She kept reminding herself it was a dream, hoping to calm the claustrophobia that seemed to be flaring up. She looked down at her hand and realized she was still holding on to the note. With shaky hands she slowly opened it. Don't look up. Tempted she averted her eyes to the floor, that's when she noticed her feet were bare and as brushed eyes over her legs and further up, she noticed her clothes were gone. She quickly sat in the corner and pulled her knees up to her chest and folded her arms over her knees. It was then she noticed, making their way to the surface of her skin as they had that night, the bruises. She sat still for a few moments, afraid that any movement might cause a change that would prove to be worse than before. Then she heard a faint tapping. She knew where it was coming from, but she was too terrified to look up. The tapping got louder and louder until finally she could no longer ignore it, so she looked up at the wall towards the ceiling.

The room seemed to have stretched, and then she saw the long rectangular window, like the observation windows used by students to witness a surgery. She could see faces in the distance and as they became clearer and forgetting she was naked, she stood up to try and make them out. Soon they were all clear enough, Harley, Stacy, Mandy, Daniel, amongst many others were just staring down at her each with a different expression. Harley wore his infamous half smile, her friends held the look of pity they had earlier in the day, the strangers seemed to be talking back and forth as if they were studying her, then she saw a horrible look of disappointment in her father. It was an expression that had never made itself known to her before. She quickly remembered she was exposed and returned to the corner. This time she buried her head in her folded over arms and prayed to wake up. Every time she'd pick her head up, the window seemed to expand and more and more people would appear. Finally she closed her eyes tight and when she opened them again she was relieved by the familiarity of her bedroom.

That morning Daniel was once again waiting for Darcy when she walked through the kitchen, with the remnants of her dreams still lurking she averted her eyes. When she saw him sitting there staring down at his cup of coffee, she couldn't help but feel guilty for being so stupid and brattish. It was then she noticed that there was something pained in his eyes. People always assumed Darcy's looks came from her mother, but just then she noticed how attractive her father really was. He was a classically handsome man, and he had the most engaging heir about him. She hated the loneliness she knew he carried. He deserved better. She would always love her mother, but she hated that she had robbed her father of any kind of life worth living. "Hi Dad."

"Oh, um morning Prin, er Darcy."

"Wow, two mornings in a row, must be a record," she tried to be humerously crass, but it just came off as catty.

"Well, I just wanted to tell you in person. I have some great news. Well, I couldn't extend the move until next year, but I convinced them to hold out until after Christmas. I figured that might give you a little more time at least with your friends. Then I figured you'd only be stuck with me for six more months, until you know, college. I'm sure under the circumstances, well you're a bright young lady, so..." The words almost choked him.

She was tempted to tell him how ready she was to leave, but she just couldn't. Instead she walked over to where he sat and wrapped her arms around his neck. She hadn't done that since she was a little girl and it felt great. Daniel was equally thrilled by the expression. "Thanks dad," she whispered and as he watched her walk away, he got a strange feeling inside, like his whole life was walking out that very door.

The drive to school seemed unusually short. When Darcy got to the front of the school, she was tempted, to drive off, but then she'd be back where she started. Besides, Darcy had never been one to shy away from anything. She pulled down the vanity mirror and took a minute to check her reflection. She couldn't recognize the insecure face staring back at her, she'd never been weak natured. Enough was enough. She quickly devised an ingenious plan and walked out of her car. She pulled out her iPod, stuck her earbuds in and turned up the volume. As she walked with slow heavy paces, at first she noticed the faces and mouthed whispers, but as she walked on, she realized that listening to her favorite music, drowned out everything else around her. She felt like she had a small sense of herself back. She passed Mandy and Stacy in the hall, and as they realized what she was doing they smiled and she returned with a wink.

The day passed by quite smoothly with her newly shielded disregard. She would only take out the buds to hear lectures. The girls didn't mind her selective hearing during lunch too much either. On her way to her last class, she hesitated. As much as she wanted to be strong enough, it was just too big of leap. Instead she walked into the library and sat at a study desk in the back. Darcy figured that so long as she was there, she might as well finish off her homework. When the day was over, she actually felt a little normal.

He ran through the trees unaware of what he was running from. He never saw anything or anyone in particular, but the whispers seemed to be growing more and more concentrated. He could hear shrieks and every time one pierced his ears his heart skipped a beat. His breathing was tight in his chest and when he became so tired he could no longer trudge on he couldn't stop. His mind was fighting his body for a merciful release. He finally came to an abrupt halt. He threw himself onto the ground covered in twigs and rocks. He felt his knees tearing beneath him. When he placed his head in his hands to regain some sense of calm, vile pictures flashed in his mind and even when he opened his eyes for surrender, they were still there. He screamed, but no sound ever came to him. He knew someone was watching him and he could hear the whispers growing louder. He still couldn't make them out, but every instinct told him he should be terrified. "Please stop," he pleaded to the sky, "somebody help me!"

After her shower, she sat on her chaise and flipped through some of the tabloids she'd picked up during her self condemned solitary confinement. As she stared at the new pictures of Hollywood's newest and hottest import, she was impressed by how good-looking he was. One movie and already he was the talk of the town, linked to just about every thriving starlet. She wished she could envy them for even just having the potential to be the possibility of someone that beautiful, but she didn't; she'd seen better. She couldn't believe how stupid she was, relating to someone who wasn't even real. "Leave it to me to get dumped by my imaginary friend," she sighed.

As she climbed into bed and rolled over to hug her pillow, Darcy feared the worst. She wasn't sure she could really survive another nightmare. It had been quite a while since she'd been scared to close her eyes and fall asleep. She knew thinking about pleasantries hadn't made a bit of difference. Instead, she flipped on the TV and decided to watch reruns of one of her favorite shows. Maybe the comic relief would make its way into her subconscious. She lay back and thought about how her life had been so different just a few weeks before, she longed for those days, and desperately wished she could somehow go back and change things. She tried to hold off her sleep for as long as she could but as her eyes grew heavier, the weight became too much and she drifted out of consciousness.

As soon as Darcy realized she was dreaming, she readied herself. As she stood there in front of the pillars, she decided that no matter what awaited her passed that cracked door, she would confront it fearlessly. Darcy walked leisurely through the halls, usually they were riddled with faces and voices, but this time, she found they were empty. As she passed the parlor and several rooms, she realized that she had never paid any mind to the fixtures and furniture in the house; everything was quite nice, and yet yellowed over with an antique finish. She wondered if she should just sit down and brace herself for whatever hells were about to commence. Just then she heard the creaking of the door, and when she turned to face her certain anguish, there he stood in the doorway. She was so hurt by his absence during the past couple of nights, which coincidently happened to be the worst she'd ever had, that she assumed by now she'd be immune to him. But as he stood there in his grey t-shirt, casually tucking his hands in his front pockets, she felt her heart race in her chest.

"Hi," he said light-heartedly through his half smile and with a strange look of contentment.

"Hmpf," Darcy rolled her eyes and headed off in the other direction.

Jack stood there confused and a little surprised. He was pretty certain she might be upset, but he didn't expect it be this bad. "Darcy, hey Darcy!" He grabbed her arm to stop her. "Hey, wait, stop a minute. Look I'm sorry, but..." he chose his words carefully, "I haven't been around."

"You think I haven't noticed?" She asked sarcastically. "In case you didn't know, it's been a little hard for me not to. Oh, that's right how could you?" She felt her lip quiver and knew what would come next. She couldn't stand to have him see her cry. She looked down at her arm which amazingly enough was still in his grasp, she didn't feel him. As the tear rolled down her cheek he felt something inside him burn. He put his hand to her cheek and pressed his forehead to hers. "Why weren't you here?" She cried.

"I'm here now. I'm here now. What happened are you okay?"

"No." She sat down on the old wooden stairs and proceeded to tell him about the past couple of days and the nightmares that'd been haunting her. The guilt he felt, though inevitable, given his current situation was still inexcusable.

"Let me make it better, please. Give me a chance. Tell me what I can do; I'll do anything. Is there anything you need?"

She knew he really did feel bad and that he was sincere in his plea, but she also knew the truth. "I needed you Jack." His glance fell and he took a step back. "I just needed you," her voice fell, "and you weren't here."

"Not because I didn't want to be." He raised his voice and she was surprised to see him so worked up. "I really couldn't. I want to explain, but I just can't. Do you really think for one second that I'd ever want you to hurt? Seriously?"

She wondered if it really was in his control to even be there at all. After all, he was her creation a sheer product of her lucidity. Maybe he really couldn't be there. How did it work? It was obvious that she couldn't will him there because if she could, he would have been there countless times before. "Jack?"

"Yeah?"

"Why couldn't you be here? Like how does this work?"

He hesitated with all his heart he really wanted to tell her the truth no matter how ugly. "I don't know."

"I mean sometimes you seem so real to me."

"Well," he bit down on his lower lip nervously; she found it endearing, "maybe in some way I am." They stared at each other in silence for a moment. She smiled and he realized that it was finite although he could never have her, he'd always be hers. "Where are we by the way? What is this place?"

"I have no idea, but I come here quite often." As she spoke her eyes moved over the house and she realized how comfortable she felt there.

"It's creepy," he spoke under his breath.

"Actually it kind of grew on me. Feels homey." They both giggled.

"Well, you can live here by yourself."

"Oh, come on it might be nice. You really wouldn't stay with me?" She stood and offered him her hand. He took her hand knowing that he would stay with her in the deepest pit of hell if he had to. And very quickly the faint idea that he just might have to entered his head. He quickly dismissed it and led her out to the court yard.

She wondered why she had never seen this before. It was old and the ground was covered in dead branches and roots that seemed to connect to nothing in particular. As they walked silently with nothing but the crunches of the ground echoing through the air, Darcy looked up at the house. From behind it looked larger and as she stood there admiring the old widow's walk that surrounded the upper portion of the house she felt Jack pull her over to a stone bench.

"Well, now I really want to live here," he said sarcastically.

"Okay, if you could live anywhere in the world where would you want to live?" After she asked the question, she felt a little stupid and wondered what he could possibly know of the rest of the world. She was too embarrassed to ask, so she nervously waited for a response.

"I don't know. I guess I'd like it to be some place calm and very basic." He thought for a moment, "I guess I'd want to live in Alaska."

"Alaska?! Who in the hell wants to live in Alaska?"

"What? You said anywhere! It seems like a peaceful, desolate place."

"Yeah, because nothing wants to live there voluntarily." She realized they were locked in a silent gaze and she spoke again to relieve the emotional build up. "I guess we could try Alaska. I mean it might be nice to see snow for a change, a white Christmas like in the movies."

"Okay how about Switzerland then?" Jack gazed off into the distance and as a look shot across his face, Darcy knew it was about that time. "Well, I guess I should wish you a Good Morning?"

"I kind of wish you wouldn't."

"Why, it bothers you when I say that?" He had a look of genuine concern.

"No," she looked at her shoes, "it's just, now I'm afraid it'll be like ten more years before I see you again." She looked up and half smiled at him. The site of her face made his jaw clench and she saw the strain it took him to hold back what was obviously a smile.

"Good morning Darcy." He smile and kissed her hand. She closed her eyes, hoping if she concentrated hard enough, she could feel the wet warmth of his breath against her hand. Instead she was pulled back to face another day.

The last of Darcy's week went on as it had since she developed her "out of sight, out of mind" plan the previous day. She went to school, clad in her hooded sweat shirt and ear phones. She got through her classes, skipping, the last one, steering clear of Harley and the gossip that she hoped was dying down by now. She spent her lunch hour sitting in her car; occasionally, her friends, whose initial intolerable sympathy was thankfully wearing off, would visit her. They invited her out for pizza, but Darcy's mother was coming back home that evening, and although she was sure, it would be a short-lived reunion, she was really looking forward to it. As much as it felt somewhat perfidious to admit it, she missed her.

The news of the move made Jeanette happy. It had been years since she'd made America her home, but it would be nice to at least live back in her home continent. Maybe being closer to France, she could visit her home more often and it might give her chance to share something of hers with Darcy. Jeanette was well aware of the distance she had placed between her daughter and herself. Undoubtedly she loved her daughter and what was often mistaken for resentment, was actually fear. Being a mother doesn't always come easy or naturally, especially for someone like herself. She had basically been on her own since she was twelve and had no experience taking care of anyone but herself. It seemed that as soon as she learned to use her talents to make herself a place in the world, she was pummeled with the news of Darcy's impending arrival. She raised Darcy as much as she could, but she found that she had such a horrible fear of ruining Darcy or leading her into a life of indecency, she found it was easier to maintain a distance. She knew her daughter was beautiful and although she secretly envied her for it, she found she envied her daughter's humility and intellect more. Her resentment towards Daniel unfortunately was genuine and seemed to be permanent.

The night was a success where Darcy was concerned. Her parents actually got through a meal without a huge blown out scene. As ridiculous as it seemed and as far and few between as it occurred, there was always something about having both her parents home that gave Darcy a false sense of security and comfort. As she lay in her bed that night, she hadn't felt so carefree in as long as she could remember, she lay back and allowed herself to get enveloped in the embrace of the down stuffed satin. She smiled as she thought of what awaited her on the other side of existence.

Darcy walked through the darkness and as she lifted her face towards the sky, she could almost smell the flowers that covered the streets. Jack stood at a distance at first confused and taken aback by the events taking place. He watched the masked people walking in a disturbingly slow pace. It seemed an unusual paradox, everywhere he looked death seemed to march along waves of beautifully colored flowers. He wondered if Darcy hadn't taken something, to induce such a trippy dream. He realized that she must be in a frightened state and quickly looked around for her. Then he knew that if it were at all possible, his heart would have stopped still in his chest. She was standing in the middle of all the commotion. She was completely at ease; her face looked even more striking amid the flickering of all the candles, the mixture of colors in her eyes popped out against her black blouse. He desperately wanted to rush over, but instead he watched as she looked through the crowd at nothing in particular. She lifted her head back as if to inhale the ghost aromas, and as she did this she picked up her waves of carbon colored hair and tied them up on top of her head. When she returned her gaze in the direction of the crowd she had the most enticing smile across her face. The relentless want inside him hurt. She looked across the sea of skulls and met his gaze. They walked over to each other.

"Darcy, what the hell?" He asked under a giggle.

She giggled as well. "What?"

"If you're gonna be dreaming weird psychotropic stuff like this, I might be tempted to stay away. What in the world is all this? Are you some kind of gothic cult girl or what?"

"No. Sorry, I can't really control the atmosphere you know. Umm well, I've actually had this one before and to be honest it's one of my favorites," she admitted through pressed lips. He shot her a puzzled look. "My grandmother on my father's side is Mexican and every year she sends me a postcard on all souls day. She's kind of traditional that way. I mean I've never actually seen the celebration, but from what she describes, this is how I picture it, I guess."

"Hmm still, creeps me out."

"I don't know, I kind of like the idea of celebrating something so morbid, it kind of makes me less afraid of what it really means you know?"

"No, not really." He really didn't understand what she meant, but he loved to listen to her speak.

"My grandmother she had this past, like real beliefs and faith and stuff. She has traditions and history. Like she descends from the Aztec, and she has pictures from when she was younger of pyramids and artifacts. She tells me these stories and…" she caught her self getting carried away amid the sound of her own voice. Jackson looked on with a genuine look of interest. "Sorry, I know I get like carried away."

"Don't be, I like hearing you talk." She blushed. "It's just…"

"What?" she asked.

"Want to walk a little? The skeleton people are really starting to freak me out a little."

She smiled. "Sure."

"So, you're close to her? Your grandmother I mean."

"As close as I can be I guess. I don't see her much, but she writes and I try and call." It made her sad, because she knew that the move would really sever what little ties she still had left. "Like my grandfather and my dad say she's insane, but

honestly she's the most genuine person I know. My dad says she's very strong and he says I remind him a lot of her. I guess I can kind of see that, except..."

"Except?"

"In what?"

"I don't know, humanity, life, death for that matter. I wish I could believe in anything that wasn't so, concrete. I'm not very, you know religious. I mean I believe in heaven and stuff, but I guess I wish I was more sure of myself or what I believe." He was still listening and she felt embarrassed by the direction the conversation had gone in.

"Heaven's a good start," he smiled.

"Yeah, I suppose so. The Aztec believed there was more than one heaven and like lots of hells. Well they weren't like what you and I think of hell, they were more like layers of existence. Like when you die you just go into one of these other worlds and some were darker. Not like evil or bad, just darker. Maybe that's why my grandma's not scared of anything, maybe she doesn't believe in evil."

"Do you.." he hesitated for a moment, "is there evil?"

She looked up at him. "It's hard not to believe otherwise."

"Well, that would explain the skull thing." Darcy smiled and shrugged her shoulders.

"Maybe they're right. I mean maybe you and I are like in another layer of existence right now."

"Maybe." Jackson shrugged. He knew her grandmother was wrong at least about a couple of things. He knew very well of the evils that existed and he knew of the kind of hell, that was not only dark but overrun by revolting malevolence.

"Okay, too deep, lets change the subject." Darcy's words came at the most opportune time. Just then the darkness seemed to lift. They spend the rest of their time just having smaller yet meaningful conversations.

Monday's lunch period seemed to be shorter than usual. Damn Einstein and his stupid relativity. The thought of facing Harley seemed to speed up time. As she walked through the hall, sans I pod, she drew up all the strength she could conjure. When she reached the doorway she felt the burn of a thousand eyes. Then she saw Harley's face; there was something different about him. His crimson coated eyes were highlighted by deep shades of mauve and his expression looked worn like something had been taking a toll on him. Instantaneously the blood seemed to drain from his face and that's when Darcy noticed, despite all her fears, she still knew the truth about him and maybe she still had the upper hand. She unintentionally looked dashing in her v-neck sweater and jeans, she walked in casually and headed straight for her old desk and took the vacant seat next to his. The sound of gasps filled the air and she couldn't help but smile, when she saw Harley's neck tendons flicker.

"Welcome back Miss Whitten, you had us worried there," her teacher murmured in false concern.

"Oh yeah I was feeling a bit off, but I'm well, over it now." She knew the very intentional pun was well received.

"Glad to hear it, lets get on then."

After class Harley leaned in and asked "Hey Darce, can I talk to you for a minute?"

She knew very well, even though he was trying his best to whisper they had an audience. So she turned and smiled. " Oh Harley, I don't really think that's such a good idea. You know its like I've been saying, maybe you need to just move on and get over it already, I have. Look I'm sure it happens to most guys," she winked. The faint sound of gasps confirmed her theory. Darcy walked headstrong and head set free to her car, she stopped and searched her satchel for her keys. Just then, she felt a solid grip around her forearm.

"What the hell are you up to Darcy?" Harley was clearly angry. Darcy felt her insides shudder, but she didn't flinch. "You really think you can hurt me?" He looked down at his hand still clenched around her dainty arm and let it loosen without completely removing it. "Sorry, I just… I haven't been sleeping and…"

"What do you want Harley?!" He gazed up at her with intensity.

"Darcy, you can't do this to me right now. I, I , just look…" she started to get into her car, "wait! Just, just look I'll… let's start over, I'll leave you alone and you, just don't do anything…"

She leaned in close to the side of his face and whispered. "Don't worry, I'll go slow I promise. TRUST ME," she reiterated as she pulled her arm free.

He quickly had his hand at the back of her neck and pulled her closer. Darcy hadn't expected it and she felt her throat tighten. "Look you little…" he paused as he breathed through pressed lips, "I won't let this happen. I know you still feel me at night because I still taste you," she knew he was trying to scare her.

She squirmed and pulled free, by now there were several spectators engaged in the scene. "Fuck off, you don't scare me Harley." She got into her car, "get a life." She drove off and left him standing in the parking lot, like a vulnerable sheep in a field of wolves. Gossip was cruel.

The next few weeks passed with ease. Harley's revocation was short lived, but enough to help Darcy move on. Realizing she was soon going to be half way around the world, Darcy began to spend more and more time with her friends. There were times she felt nervous, like she was expecting something bad to happen; things seemed too good to be true. Her parents were under one roof and already three weeks had past. She figured her mother was anticipating the trip and therefore decided to stay home and enjoy the last few weeks of the sweet dry air LA offered up. Judging by the amount of bags that made their way daily to her living room, she seemed to be taking advantage of the endless shopping districts LA offered up as well.

Her nights were even better, even though Jack wasn't always around, he was there most nights and they were unbelievable. They talked and laughed and sometimes just walked. It was so different, different from everyone, different from Harley. Mind you, Jack was the most beautiful person, she had ever seen, but for some reason, since the first day they'd met, she never felt intimidated by him. In fact, no one had ever made her feel so comfortable in her own skin. The chemistry between them was intense, but not so much sexual, it was much deeper. They could walk hand in hand without feeling the tension that usually drives two people. There were several occasions where he'd placed his hands on her shoulders, but she never felt uneasy. Perhaps it had something to do with the fact that she had still yet to feel the warmth of his skin. She continued to wonder about that, but had yet to figure it out.

Jackson: An Old Friend

The past couple of weeks had Jackson not only reeling with contentment, but riddled with exhaustion as well. He knew there was a reason, for the time between transactions. As he walked in for the next assignment in his vocation, he hoped the weariness wouldn't raise alarm. As he walked through the narrowed hall, he noticed a familiar face down at the other end. The familiar faced young man returned the recognition with a smile. Max and Jackson had been "recruited" at about the same time, and it had been a while since they had seen each other. Jackson remembered taking a liking to Max during those formative years. They were about the same age and had similar interests. He remembered looking forward to seeing him, as he was generally the only person he could relate to in all aspects of his existence. However, as the years, past and Max became more comfortable with his raison d`etre, he began to change. There was something cold behind his voice and even the somatic transformations were very apparent. Max and Jackson were about the same height, but Max's athletic build made him seem much bigger. Jackson had seen the humorous lanky kid, transform into a quiet robust mercenary. The light in Max's once emerald colored eyes had all but disappeared behind what now appeared to be a mixture of olive green and grey. His dirty blond hair was now dark brown almost black and cut short with just a few longer strands carefully gathered on top. In fact, the only real remnant of the boy Jackson was so fond of was his never changing boyish face.

As Jackson walked towards Max, he felt excited about seeing his friend and the feeling was returned. Max had similar affections towards Jackson. Max had already grown quite numb to the ideas of humanity and was becoming more and more immune to the marvels and sentiments that any kind of interaction had to offer. Few things in life and beyond offered him any solace and his friendship with Jackson was one of them.

"Coming or going?" Max playfully asked Jackson as he shook his hand and patted his back.

"Coming. You?" Jackson asked still surprised at the runion.

"Same. Summoned or routine?"

"Not quite sure yet actually. It's really great to see ya, but what brings you here?"

"Same here, well, apparently I get to study abroad this year. Uh, Cambridge presumably." Max smiled as he spoke and it just look contradictory to his frame.

"Wow, cheeky bastard how'd you swing it?"

"I have no idea, believe me it wasn't a personal transfer." They nodded in acknowledgement of the fact that it was the higher ups that had transferred Max over for some reason, they would never be made aware of.

"Well, I've still got a bit left before I'm done; couple of months," Jackson spoke eagerly and it made seem almost normal.

"Oh yeah that's right still in High school," Max teased.

"Secondary," Jackson corrected.

"Whatever, so then what?"

"Fuck if I know, probably end up frying eggs or something dodgy like that you lucky shit."

"Man, at least we can hang out now. Seriously sometimes I get so bored you know?" Max asked rhetorically.

"Yeah I know what'cha mean." Just then a light appeared through an open doorway and Jackson was summoned over and handed a small piece of paper. Routine, Jackson felt relief wash over his face and he hoped it wasn't obvious to Max. "Guess I gotta run then, but we will hang out later then yeah?" As he shook Max's hand Jackson could feel how calloused they were and it gave him chills to think of all the death they had offered up.

"Yeah most definitely. Hey by the way man, you really look like shit."

"Oh, yeah? Well, you know, exams and stuff. You don't look too good yourself, nah I'm totally lying I'd shag you."

Max chuckled, "what can I say, good looks never fade. "He smiled and went to face his destiny.

That night as Jackson lay back in his bed, his thoughts drifted towards Darcy. He wondered if she'd miss him, what crazy sort of nonsense would fill her head that night. He hated the nights he was away from her. He had never been in love before, maybe because he knew it was an impossibility, so he hadn't gotten close enough to anyone before. Jackson had girlfriends, but the attraction was mostly physical and very short lived; it was a necessary front. Lately though, his days were spent alone, and his bed had not felt the warmth of another body in a while. As he ran his hand across the empty bedside, he thought of his past improprieties, he knew Darcy couldn't even be compared. He'd never seen anyone so beautiful, and there was a deeper connection. Still, he wondered what it would be like to be able to really feel her, to touch her skin, to stroke her hair, to feel her breath on his neck. As the excitement of those very thoughts ensued, he closed his eyes and was swiftly interrupted by a vision of Max standing before Darcy, her vulnerable petite frame over shadowed by his. He sat up and tried to shake the thought, but it was no use. As he rubbed his hands over his face, flashes of the new frame Max had seemed to fill while they were apart kept popping in; he was beastly. He knew it wasn't just a possibility, if Jackson persisted in his unrealistic relationship with Darcy there'd definitely be a penance.

DARCY: MOVING

Darcy grimaced as her mother knocked on her door at 7:15am on a Saturday. Even though Jackson had already wished her a good morning and was gone, she was enjoying the extra hours of sweet, silent sleep. She left her a credit card and asked her to go out and purchase a couple of those plastic packing bins, so they could get started. Darcy reminded her very eager mother that there were still a couple of weeks left in December. But Jeanette insisted and reminded her daughter that she was planning to be in Europe before New Years Eve. Darcy finally sat up and decided to face another monotonous day. Before her nights had been so occupied, she had never noticed how little she had going on in her everyday life. She called up her friends and invited them out to lunch and for an invigorating afternoon of errands.

"So, last two weeks as an American?" Stacy asked over lunch.

"God, sometimes you're so embarrassing. She's always gonna be American; hello, she was born in America. What planet are you from?" Darcy chuckled at the ridiculous argument.

"Oh my gosh, I wasn't trying to sound all like technical or anything, I was just … shut up Mandy, like you're so perfect all the time."

"I know what you meant Stace, calm down. Yeah last two weeks. You know I didn't think I was going to miss any of this, but I don't know. Its scary you know? Not having anyone. At least here I have you guys and now I'll hardly ever see my family…" as she lost herself for a bit in thought, she reminded herself to call her grandmother.

"But it's really exciting you know, like living in a new place, a whole other country especially?" Amanda traveled every summer and spoke 5 different languages.

"I have no idea what to expect, I've never even been to England before what if I don't like it? I mean like do they have Oreos and coke and stuff?"

"Well, they have pizza and they speak English."

"Gosh shut up Stacey, really. I've been to Europe like a million times. You're gonna like it Darce. There's a lot of like history stuff and museum things that you like and the food is pretty much the same, and most of the weird music you listen to is from there anyhow. Besides, it's not like there's anywhere on the planet that doesn't get internet or some kind of phone reception. Oh and I'm forgetting about the best part, the guys."

"Oh please. I'll be ecstatic so long as they have Oreos and pizza."

"Well, in that case if you meet any send them my way."

"Seriously Darcy, maybe you'll finally meet someone that meets all your high standards and is qualified to ask you out."

Darcy rolled her eyes. She felt herself blush a little. As exciting as the very idea of Jack was, it was still a little uncomfortable. She had already accepted the fact that she might have a slight mental condition, but she knew as she was getting older she'd have to let go of her childish antics.

"What are you smiling about Darcy?" Stacy asked mockingly. She realized the excitement that occupied her chest had made its way up to her face. Jack made her happy and it showed.

"Nothing in particular, life in general and how I'm going to really miss this."

"Ahh Darce, you're such a liar, let's go."

Packing seemed to weigh differently on everyone. Everyone's sentiments and connections with the house were different. Daniel, thought of the first time they brought Darcy through the door when she was just one, their first Christmas there, watching Darcy become a young woman in that house. He poured himself a glass of whiskey and smiled as he walked down the hall. Seeing the empty spaces on the wall that once served as a shrine to his wife's vanity gave him a sense of relief. As he made his way into his bedroom his sentiments changed; he thought of all the lonely nights he'd spent in a cold empty bed.

As Darcy sorted through her childhood keepsakes and pictures, she had a strong feeling of apprehension. The only thing that ever brought her any kind of security was her home. She felt silly that an inanimate object could comfort her in such a way, but it was the only thing she could ever count on to be there as her personal sanctuary from life. She'd connected with it on nights when her parents weren't around to lull her back to sleep. It held all her secrets, her desires, the walls were riddled with private thoughts and emotions.

Jeanette wasn't too keen on having to pack or sort through anything, so she had the housekeepers take care of all that. The only item she had secured in her suitcase was Darcy's baby book. She looked through it before and realized how quickly time had passed. That house had been her personal prison, and although she always felt she'd been condemned to it by Darcy, she realized in fact, that Darcy was the only person that made her life worth living. All three of them agreed on one thing, it was definitely time to move on.

Christmas Eve was typical they had dinner together and after that her parents went off to one of their many annual holiday who's whos. That was a big part of the holiday appeal for Darcy, it was Halloween for her parents; it was the only time that even just for one night her parents pretended to be happy. Usually Darcy would tag along, but seeing as how it was her last Christmas at home, she decided to spend her last days with her sofa and annual holiday specials. The house felt sad and empty. As she sank further down into the cushions and began to sulk, she heard her doorbell. She usually had the privilege of ignoring the doorbell, but it was a holiday, so there was no housekeeper around. When she opened the door, she was pleasantly surprised. Amanda was there to offer some company.

"Hey Mandy!"

"Merry Christmas Darce," she handed her a small box.

"Aren't you Jewish?"

"Conveniently enough, why do you think I'm here with you and not off with my own family? Anyway, you'll be gone soon enough and I figured I wanted to spend our last Christmas together."

Darcy smiled, usually she had a smart remark to deflect any kind of genuine human sentiment, it was a defense, but at that moment she knew it was unnecessary. They sat and talked for hours, like they use to when they were younger and Darcy opened her gift. It was a watch with dual time, so she'd always know what time it was back home. It was a stellar night.

Darcy slipped into her pajamas and lounged on her chaise to watch TV. She looked around the room complacently. She knew that she'd be just fine. The assurance was a bit premature as she thought for a moment about all the nights she'd laid in her bed and drifted off to another world; a world of colors and hopes and fears and of course Jack. She wondered what would happen when she moved; would her dreams change, would Jack still come around? She had never brought up the move with him, mostly because she felt silly about doing so. After all, he didn't really exist outside of her mind, why should she have to. The whole collection of thoughts felt silly to her, so she turned over and let the darkness envelope her.

Darcy walked an excitingly unfamiliar path. She knew it was already past midnight and therefore Christmas Day was upon her. She continued to walk wondering where she was going, and wondering whether or not Jack would be there.

Jack was aware that any minute Darcy was going to break through the trees and reach her destination. He was beaming with anticipation; he wondered what her reaction would be. Jack knew what he was doing was wrong beyond anything else he'd ever done. He hoped that being as it was a holiday, none of the monitors would be on duty that day, because he would have to find a logical explanation for the activity that day. He wondered what the punishment would be if he simply admitted to messing around. That was the best excuse he'd come up with. When he was younger he and Max had done it before. It would certainly keep any suspicions away from Darcy. Whatever the consequences, they were worth it. Darcy and he had become so close and he wanted so desperately to get her something special for Christmas, this was the next best thing.

Darcy looked up at the seemingly endless waves of green and smiled. She heard the crunching beneath her feet and refocused; ahead she saw light in a clearing. When she saw him standing there, he seemed nervous, and yet his cool disposition kept him settled. He smiled as he approached her and she melted.

"Well," he started off and then paused.

"Well?"

"Come on."

"Where are we going?"

"It's kind of, well, a surprise." He took her hand and they walked off together. He was always careful to make sure she knew he had her hand, because although she could not feel the texture of his hand, his pulling her would still produce a physical reaction and she might stumble. They walked a little further and Darcy began to notice how empty the dream seemed. When they arrived at the steps of the old house she was confused.

"So this is…"

"Shhh, don't Darcy. Don't ask, don't make any smart remark, just keep going." They walked in and everything was as it always seemed. That is until he led her out into her favorite defunct courtyard. Darcy stood breathless. Where she half expected to see familiar shades of slate and dusk, there were greens and crimsons

and other rich colors only higher powers could produce. Somehow the courtyard was alive again and it looked incredible, the ground was no longer barren and the trees were reanimated. It also had not escaped her that tiny lights were delicately draped over the old widows walk and stretched out over the trees. She turned back towards Jack who stood by the stone bench arms crossed over his chest.

"You, how did you?" Words had become a commodity she could not afford.

"Merry Christmas Darcy." She smiled and as her eyes seemed to glow more than usual, his throat tightened and his chest ached. She felt her heart race and although every part of her body seemed to be tingling, she could not move. "Wait, there's one more thing." Jackson's eyes scanned the sky and as Darcy looked up a small white spec landed on her cheek. "You might not be able to feel it, but …"

"A white Christmas! Jack!" Darcy looked around as more and more white gathered and she closed her eyes and imagined the cold wet sensation. When she opened her eyes Jack was staring at her with a look she had not yet seen. The blue in his eyes shined brighter against the snow that made its way to his dark hair and Darcy could not contain her composure; she walked over and threw her arms around his neck. Not being able to feel him gave the hug an odd sensation, like she was hugging a tree, she could only feel an object, but she shut her eyes and tried desperately to send out any and all affection. Jack was caught off guard at first, then as he realized what was happening, he wrapped his arms around her. "I wish I could feel you. Do you feel me?" Darcy whispered.

"No." He felt her grip lessen and he knew it bothered her. "Well, not physically, but I feel you somewhere inside me."

"Me too," she pulled back and stared into his eyes. He smiled and walked over to a patch of snow latent grass and sat with his back against a tree. He motioned for her to walk over and she sat between his legs and rested her arms on his knees. He reached forward and intertwined his fingers with hers. She smiled when she noticed how much longer his were and she studied the veins that convoluted down his long forearms. They sat in silence and watched the snowfall. After a while Darcy heard Jack sigh and she felt his grip loosen. She stood up and he followed. He turned to face her and she saw the look of disappointment across his brow.

"Darcy…"

"Jack," she grabbed his arm, "this was the most incredible moment, I cant even, I don't want you to go." She buried her head in his chest and he rested his chin atop her head.

"I wish I could keep you, with me." He closed his eyes and tried to imagine the aromas that he could not conjure up. "Darcy…"

"Wait, before you say goodbye…" she pulled back and he looked at her in concern. He heard panic in her tone and assumed something might be wrong. Suddenly she tiptoed and pushed her lips against his. To no avail, her lips seemed to only feel the pressure, like being pressed against an inanimate object. She closed her eyes and desperately tried to hold on to him. Jackson was taken off guard. A strong mixture of emotions swept over his entire body, desire, elation, frustration. He watched Darcy as she kissed him, her eyes shut ever so slightly, lips pursed; he couldn't help himself. Before time stole away the opportunity, he pulled back and she opened her eyes.

"Darcy…"

"I know, its time…"

"Darcy," he reiterated in a more forceful tone. She looked up at him in surprise. "I love you."

As the sweet morning light swept over her face, Darcy sat up in a state of complete bliss. Usually she was in her living room in record time, to see what her parents had bought her. Daniel treated her like a child and never budged on his opening presents on Christmas morning tradition. Instead of rushing down, she got up, walked over to her bed and threw herself back. She recapped the entire night in as much detail as she could. She had no desire to celebrate; she had already gotten the best gift.

Jackson: Dominion

Jackson's holiday was short lived when he received his summon. He hoped it was just another assignment, but something told him it was much more. As he waited in the long hallway to be called in, he tried to fabricate the best story he could. He knew someone had recognized the activity, but he hoped no one had looked in. He was sure no one had crossed in, because he never saw anyone or felt the pocket. When he was moved into another room, he knew he would be going in against the Dominion. He had faced them once before, when he was younger and he and Max had gotten caught fooling around. All he had to do was keep his composure, appear apologetic and stick to his story. He tried his best before he arrived to appear well rested as to not stir any concern that he might not be sleeping.

He walked out of the building with bereavement and a new double night assignment. Someone must have sensed something and doubled him out as a test, but he had pulled off more exhausting tasks. As he walked along the water, the colors of the water made him think of Darcy; more specifically her eyes. He had never told anyone he loved them, and it felt good, almost even alleviating. For the first time in a long time, thoughts that had plagued him for so long, such as his purpose in life, or even the purpose of life all together, seemed unimportant, because for the first time in a long time, he wanted to live. He felt his eyes heavy and sat down on a bench; he buried his head in his hands and didn't even seem to notice the shadow that was cast over him.

"How'd it go?"

"Huh? Oh hey, what in particular?" Jackson tried to play coy.

"Summon…" Max raised his eyebrow in suspicion. "I saw you go in; go before Dominion?"

"Yup," Jack murmured as he stretched out. He didn't know how much he should share.

"Everything all right?"

"Yeah pretty much, just you know, got caught foolin." He was careful with his words. "Hey Max, d'ya ever wonder mate, like what's the point?"

Max sat down and lit a cigarette. "Point of?"

"Oh I dunno life, the universe, us."

"Whoa, this conversation seems to be a bit heavy for bench talk."

"No seriously, with everything we've seen and what we know and what we do…" Jack caught himself mid sentence because he should have known that Max had it so much worse. If anyone should be questioning the meaning of life or the existence of a higher power it should be Max. Max ran his hand over his forehead and rubbed his head.

"Look man, what's the point to anything? I just figure I'm here, I have to get something done and I just do it. I don't worry or wonder or any shit like that, I just exist because I have to you know? It's just a job and as for what lies ahead of me I'm probably better off not knowing but I just figure I'll find out soon enough."

"Yeah," Jack agreed as he took a cigarette from Max. He didn't really smoke, but figured now would be a good time to start.

"So what's really going on?" Max reiterated.

"Ha, obvious then?" Max shrugged his shoulders. "I dunno, didn't ya ever want… you know, like…" Jack nervously ran his hands through his dark hair "regular stuff, like a life, you know a girl."

"Shit." Max finally got what all this was about. He nodded his head and the crease in his forehead didn't give Jack much hope. "She why you were fooling around?" Jackson stared at the floor nervously. "Look man, we were dealt a shitty hand, you know. But you can't go messing around; jesus, if anyone knows about, you know, consequences, it's me. Just do yourself a favor and just let it go, forget about it you know. It's the best thing for her too and you know what I mean. I'm afraid to ask, but you haven't told her…"

"No, of course not, I don't want to kill her," Jackson spoke through a chuckle.

"No man, I don't want to have to, you know?" They both stood up and as Jackson faced Max, those words burned a hole in his chest. Max offered an unconvincing smile. "Jackson man, you're my best friend, just be careful alright? Do what I do man, find a couple nice one-nighters and just let it go." A strange and knowingly misplaced hatred began to make its way into Jackson's eyes. "You alright guy?"

"Yeah, yeah just tired you know?"

"Whatever man, take care. You know I always got your back right?"

"Yeah of course mate, me too." Jackson spoke through his teeth.

"Alright look, just get some rest and call me on Friday, we'll hang out and I'll hook you up."

Jackson nodded and Max walked away. Max didn't have too many emotions left, but he felt pity for Jackson. Thankfully Max had never fallen in love, but for a while he struggled with his indecorous place in the world. He hoped desperately that there would be piece of mind in Jackson's future and he prayed that he'd never have to fix any problem Jackson's capricious actions might conjure.

Jackson walked along the river with the realization Max's words had brought upon him. He thought about what he said about Darcy, then about Darcy. Her face, her voice, life had taken everything from him, he deserved this, he wouldn't give her up. The only person who really knew anything was Max, and all he had to do was wait a couple of days, go out with him, and assure him everything was copacetic. He'd wait a while before visiting Darcy again, and make sure he didn't pull any more stunts that would alert the monitors of any unsanctioned activity. He had the next couple of nights tied up and he figured he'd left Darcy with enough assurance to give him at least a week.

Darcy:
'Fraid of Changes

The trip overseas was long and unnerving. Darcy anticipated the worst and desperately hoped for the best or at the very least better. When they landed at Heathrow Airport, she felt the air return to her lungs. Oddly enough, as much time as both her parents had spent there, she'd never been to Europe. She was excited to see what the country had to offer up. When she stepped out of the airport and into the company car the idea that she was home finally hit her. She wondered how she'd feel in her new surroundings; she never really felt like she belonged in LA maybe things would be different.

"So where are we going?" Darcy asked whichever one of her parents would respond.

"Cranleigh in Surrey," Daniel answered as Jeanette rolled her eyes.

"Really, Surrey!?" Darcy cheered sarcastically. "I have no idea what or where that is." The driver chuckled at Darcy's reaction.

"I don't understand why we couldn't stay in London," Jeanette was never satisfied. "One of the most beautiful cities in the world and you prefer trees and grass."

"Well, I wanted Darcy to feel more comfortable and really wait till you guys see it. By the way Darcy, I pulled a few strings and I got you into the local private school in Cranleigh, its suppose to be one of the best, very prestigious."

"Dad, I'm supposed to go back and graduate in May, with my class remember? I already had enough credits," Darcy sounded annoyed.

"I know, but I just thought it would be good for you to go and maybe just audit the classes. It would be a great way for you to meet people your age and besides I don't want you to spend the next couple of weeks just staying in front of the damn computer or television."

"So what am I supposed to do just go in and crash the scene of some other group of kids I don't even know during their senior year of high school?"

"Sixth form," the driver corrected.

"What?!" Darcy snapped and when she caught herself she felt embarrassed.

"Sorry Madame didn't mean to intrude."

"No need to be," Daniel sounded angry; "Darcy, stop this petulance. You will go to school as I expect you to and that's all."

Already Darcy's new and improved life seemed dubious. As they drove further, she sank into her seat carrying the guilt of her snappy remark to the driver and the resentment towards her father's tone. Daniel had never been one to be so brash, but then again, Darcy wasn't prone to being difficult; the move proved to be trying on everyone equally. She closed her eyes and hoped it would erase most of the events of the last couple of hours.

When she felt the car finally stop, she carefully peeled back her eyelids. "Green," was all she could think. She couldn't help but smile at the seemly endless layers of flora. There were trees along seas of grass and shrubs and no light posts or busy streets or noise or even signs of life outside of nature. When she stepped out of the car, she felt loose gravel beneath her shoes and figured her mom would be furious at the fact that there wasn't even a real driveway. When she looked up she took notice of the house. She was surprised it was quite smaller than their LA home and very quaint. The home was laid partially in red brick, there was a three car attached garage, a large beautiful stained glass window next to the front door, and a couple of windows in what she made out to be a second floor; it reminded her of a cottage. She was drawn to it though and it made her smile.

Daniel walked over and placed his hand around Darcy's shoulder. "Its not so bad is it?"

"Well, its smaller that's for sure, Mom must be freaking out, but I kinda like it. How many Bedrooms?"

"Six."

"Six? Does it run underground or something?"

Daniel realized where Darcy was staring and he chuckled. "No Darcy, this is well what they use to call the servant's house." He placed his hand under her chin and turned her face slightly to the left. "That's the main house." He saw her jaw drop. "Welcome to Gidding's Hill." He gave her a nudge and walked off.

Darcy stood and stared at the house in disbelief. It was amazing. Laid in the same red brick as the smaller structure, it was trimmed with wood molding and the lower level had several giant windows that seemed to open outward. What caught her eyes most however wasn't the vastness of it, but way up close to the top, in what appeared to be the third level of the house were several small stained glass windows, much like the ones she'd been admiring in the smaller version. She was eager to run up and make out the designs, but instead she followed her father in for a tour of her new home. She quickly realized she'd been wrong about the entrance as well, unlike the loose graveled circular drive in front of the servants' house, the entrance to the main house was paved with a path of large embedded stones and rows of flower blooming trees. When they opened up the large wooden door and stepped in, she was even more awestruck. Although the house had clearly been modernized with all the amenities and stylings of the latest domestic architectures, the home still held many of its unique former qualities. The wooden floors and beams in the vaulted ceilings gave it a sense of old world that Darcy found comforting.

After conquering the first two levels of the house, Darcy convinced her father to accompany her to the third floor. When they opened the door she smiled. "Wow look at this space," Daniel declared. "At first I though it was an attic, but the ceiling is pretty high in here and the wood flooring is beautiful. With all this lighting this might make a great office. Though, I could do without those creepy windows."

Darcy observed the windows; there were five small squares and a larger one that arched over. "You know dad, this might also make a great bedroom?" She did her best to give him her pleading eyes.

"Oh I don't know; the idea of you being up here all alone. Besides, there's not even a closet or anything."

"Come on Dad, I'm not a baby, besides I'll buy a wardrobe thingy. Seriously I was even thinking about maybe taking over the little house, seeing as how we don't have servants, and this would be closer to you."

"Oh didn't I tell you?"

"Tell me what?" Darcy asked.

"It was one of the terms when I closed on the property, the grounds keeper and his family remain in the house and he keeps his job so long as it is done to our satisfaction," Daniel kicked around the gravel as he spoke.

"Oh, but dad, what does a ground keeper actually do?"

"Hell if I know, keep the grounds I'm guessing. Besides I got to meet Mr. and Mrs. Mackinnon, and they seem like good people."

"Any kids?"

“Yeah actually I believe they have a daughter about your age. Might be nice for you, but they’ll be gone until after the New Year as far as I know.”

“So dad, about the room…”

“Fine,” he knew he would have given in eventually so why drag it out any further.

“Yes!”

“But it comes with a few provisions,” Darcy rolled her eyes. “No more grief about the school thing, and I don’t want you spending all your time holed up in here.”

“Deal,” Darcy hugged Daniel tightly. “Now I just need a bed?”

“Come on let’s go, your mother’s probably already sitting in the car.”

Once Darcy had her room set up to her liking she stood back and stared at her progress. The room was much larger than her old one, so she bought a few more pieces than she had planned for. A large Cherry Wood wardrobe occupied almost an entire end; she bought a new lounger with a beautiful bohemian print, a long wood framed stand up mirror with a matching antique hope chest, a new desk, and two round night stands that she set upon either side of her bed. Her brass framed bed she set up against the larger of the stained glass windows. She recognized a few of the designs on the smaller ones from her Art class, the Madonna and child and the Reader. Someone had taken the time to duplicate the works in exquisite details. The one on the larger window was the most appealing to her although she did not recognize its origins. The painting appeared to be a child asleep in a sleigh bed and it gave the room certain tranquility. It had been a long day for Darcy, she slipped into her pajamas and went down to thank her father for everything and just to say goodnight.

As she lay in her new bed, she wasn’t very sleepy. This time however, she did not have the luxury of the television to lull her to sleep; it appeared the third floor needed rewiring. Instead she slipped away into her own thoughts. She thought of her new home, how much she felt at peace already and wontedly her thoughts drifted towards Jack. It had been four nights since their last meeting and even though it was special enough to keep her mind occupied, she still missed him horribly and she worried. What if he wasn’t coming back, what if he had just been fabricated to make her conventional life in LA more interesting. She looked over at her clock and realized that although it was 8:30pm, in LA it was probably an hour past noon, but jetlag took over and she drifted off.

The sky was clear except for a few puffs of white. As she continued on, the pungent smell of salt water infused the air. That was something new; Darcy had never actually smelled anything she hadn't had to conjure up in her imagination before, this time though the smell lingered. She walked across the wooden pier and realized it had no end on either side; it just went on over the melodic waves of the ocean. The sun was out but she also noticed that she felt a chill across the spine of her back, it was cold. She wondered if the changes in her senses in her dreams had something to do with the move. Then she wondered if she'd have other new abilities specifically if she'd finally be able to feel Jack.

He walked across the pier and spotted her standing, staring out across the foam riddled waves. The breeze blew her hair in every direction; he watched as she attempted several times to tame it back and then to no avail, she hugged her hands across her body. He continued toward her and knew he had never wanted her more and he would never want her less. He hurried over and took her by surprise when he wrapped his arms around her.

She smiled when she saw his hands interlock around her. Inside she felt disappointment when she realized she still couldn't feel his touch or his breath on the nape of her neck. "Jack," she turned to face him, "I've missed you so much." She jumped into his arms and realized that she could smell him and it was the most enticing smell. She buried her face in his neck. "Mmmm."

"What's this?" He chuckled.

"You smell so good."

He looked at her puzzled "like, as in I, you imagine, I might smell good?"

"No you just do, you smell really good."

"You can smell me? Like actually . . ."

"Yes, is that weird?"

"I'm not sure." He knew it wasn't impossible, she wasn't the first, but he'd heard of the consequences towards those who were known to be sensitive. As she nudged her face against his neck he felt his breath quicken and fire inside him. He closed his eyes and tried to imagine how her soft lips must feel against his skin. He was so wrapped up in a brief moment of exaltation, that he hadn't noticed when she pulled back. She giggled at the sight of him and when he opened his eyes

it didn't seem so amusing anymore. His eyes looked bluer against the sky and the sea. "Fancy a walk?"

"Sure, but I don't think we'll get anywhere."

"So long as you're next to me, I really don't care." They walked along the empty pier and made small talk through long resonant moments courtesy of the waves dancing. When the inevitable came Jackson took her shoulders, "uhhhh!"

Her eyes widened "what?"

"It's so frustrating I just," he looked at his feet for a second, "I wish I could at least kiss you goodbye."

She smiled, "I don't know, you have to admit there's something to all this you know, mystery." She blushed when she realized her innocent smile was laden with seduction. He returned the smile and nodded his head. "Who knows the way things are going with me I might be able to feel it one day or night, dream, whatever."

(tisk) "How long you willing to wait?" he snared sarcastically.

"For as long as I have to."

He felt his throat tightened and "hmpf." He felt guilty because he knew if he really wanted to, he had a way, but he'd never risk her. "Well Darcy," he looked disappointed and she knew it was more defeated than disappointed.

"Jack," she put his hand to her face and he looked down at her mouth when she spoke, "I love you too."

The next morning she sat up and looked around, she still couldn't believe she was home. She looked over and smiled at her sleeping friend. Then she walked down to face her day. When she finally made her way to the first floor, she was surprised to find her mother getting ready to head out. "Mmom," she always got nervous when she talked to her mother, "where you..."

"Oh good morning baby. I have a flight to catch I am sorry."

"On New Years Eve?"

"I told you I had to be in Paris. Besides, don't worry your father will be back in time to celebrate," she leaned in and kissed her.

"Where's dad anyway?"

"Went into the city for business, I know, I know even on a holiday; he's terrible."

"Well, maybe," she cleared her throat, "maybe I could come with you, I mean I've never been to France and you always said…"

"I know baby I've always wanted us to go to Paris together," she walked over and hugged her from behind, "take you to my home, see the sights together just us girls, just not today baby okay?" it was more suggested than asked. "I love you eh, je tame." Darcy wondered how such a beautiful accent could sound so cruel. "I'm in a horrible rush, but your father wanted me to remind you to go out and get some air and he could not get a technician to come out till after the holiday. You going to be okay," again more suggested than asked. Darcy smiled through her acrimony and nodded. "Okay then baby bye." Hollow kisses parted ways once again.

Darcy: Meet Cue

Darcy looked around and felt strange being there all alone. The house still felt more like a hotel or a vacation home. She decided to walk around the grounds and discover what she had not seen in their rush the day before. She decided that she would try to put the fact that it was New Years Eve out of her mind.

By noon, Darcy had been walking for over an hour and although she wanted to keep going, it was getting colder and her LA accustomed body was shivering in the 50 degree weather. She decided to go in and explore the channels on the TV. After about 5 times of going over every single channel, her stomach started to churn, so she headed down to the kitchen to get a snack. Darcy knew she'd have to get used to trudging up and down several flights of stairs daily. When she got to the kitchen something outside caught her attention; she flung open the small window above the sink and saw someone knocking at the servant's house.

It was a large, surly guy. He looked older than her but only by a couple of years. He stood there waiting for a response she very well knew he wasn't going to get. After a couple of seconds she decided if she was ever going to meet anyone, now was as good a time as any. She walked out towards the cottage and realized how big he really was. "Umm hi," she said half expecting to hear an accent on the other end of thr conversation.

"Oh shit, sorry you scared me. Umm I'm looking for…" he went blank. He wondered where she came from and who she was.

"Oh uh the Mackinnons right?" He smiled suspiciously and nodded. "They're out of town until after the holidays."

"Wow," he said taken aback.

"What?" she blushed as she put her hand up against her mouth afraid she might have remnants of the chips she had been eating.

"You're American," she smiled at him relieved. "So am I. Obviously, right?" he felt ridiculous stating the obvious. "Where are you from?"

"LA, I just moved here with my parents umm yesterday actually, you?" Darcy felt a little relieved that the first person she'd met actually had something in common with her; it was less intimidating. He was very handsome, but his eyes were sad. She wondered if he might be the Mackinnon girl's boyfriend, but he couldn't be if he didn't even know she wasn't there.

"Umm New York by way of Boston actually."

"And now Cranleigh," she said feeling wiser about her geography.

"Cambridge actually, I just came by to visit a friend," he corrected her with a strange eagerness.

"Wow, now I'm impressed."

"So if you moved here yesterday, how do you know…" he looked back at the cottage but before he could finish his sentence Darcy jumped in.

"Oh um I don't know anyone here. I live right there and so I guess that's how I know about them."

They both stood there in a brief moment of silence and he watched as she bit her lower lip nervously. He found it endearing. "I'm Max by the way, he offered out his hand and when she took it, they both giggled at the strong contrast in sizes. "So you actually live there?" Darcy blushed and he took notice. "No, it's really nice, just you know, like…"

"I know, it kinda freaks me out a little too. I'm Darcy, in case I forgot to …" the name he thought suited her. There was something innocent and ominous about her, she was beautiful, but he knew the attraction she radiated was much more than just physical.

"So, if I'm being nosy just tell me, but why are you not you know, out celebrating lie everyone?" As Darcy spoke she realized how ridiculous the question was, but she was so desperate for human contact.

"Ha ha, well, why aren't you?" Max asked playfully in return. "Well, I'm pretty much half way around the world from everyone I usually celebrate with, so I was coming by to see my friend."

"Yeah, me too, I mean I don't know anyone here and I already said that." She looked to the ground for a relief from her own nervousness.

"Well, then umm you want to maybe go find someplace to eat or something?" Max asked with indifference.

"You think anything's open?"

"I'm not sure, but at least we can take a tour of Cranleigh. After all, you're going be living here and the best way to learn your way around is to get lost right?"

Darcy smiled and after running in to get her coat, they set off. The start of the drive was mostly silent mainly due to the fact that Darcy was trying to memorize the drive and scenery and Max was lost in thought.

He wondered if he was acting "normal" and tried to keep his composure. It was getting harder for Max to relate to anyone and usually the only interaction he had with girls took place in the bedroom. Max had charisma, like a hunter attracting his prey, it was a skill he excelled at, but it was still work. With Darcy though, it felt natural and normal and those were two sentiments Max had lost long before. They found a Chinese restaurant and pulled in. They ate, talked and laughed.

Darcy found it refreshing that she had made not only a new friend, but one so easy to be around. Max was by all definitions a guy, but she never felt nervous or intimidated around him. She wondered if it had anything to do with the fact that by all accounts he was attractive, even more so than herself. She never got an awkward feeling about how he might be misconstruing the situation as was often the case with her, he was just genuine and she liked that. Something about him reminded her of Jack and she couldn't help but feel a little guilty.

Max was very surprised at how easy it was just being around her. He never thought he'd be able to have this type of interaction with anyone ever again. She had a lot to say and was equally interested in his opinions. She was funny, smart, and very easy on the eyes, but the more time they spend together the more he realized that he didn't want her as a fling or prospect; he wanted her as a friend. When they got back to her house the sun was just about to set and Darcy saw a light shinning through her living room window. Daniel was home in time to ring in the New Year with her.

"Well Max, I have to say, I really thought this New Years was going to suck, but it was pretty fun. Thanks." She wondered all of a sudden if it had been a date of sorts and how she should say goodbye without leading him on further if so, but then he spoke and her thoughts were laid to rest.

"Yeah it was and hey now at least you know, you know someone here right?" All of a sudden he seemed just as nervous and she realized he probably had the same fear, so she decided to bluntly clarify the situation.

"Yeah it's nice to actually have a friend here now." As she spoke, he looked up and smiled at her, it'd been a while since he had made a friend and never since he'd made friends with a girl. "So, I don't have a phone here yet, but…"

"You want to hang out again sometime, like maybe, umm day after tomorrow I could come by and see what's up?"

"Yeah, that'd be good. Thanks again," Darcy said with a genuine gratitude.

"No problem." He smiled and she opened the door and walked toward the house. He waited until she was inside before driving off.

Darcy was so happy to be spending New Years Eve with her dad. It'd been years since she was with her family on New Years and even longer since she'd had time with Daniel. He was probably more thrilled at the notion and even happier when he learned she'd actually gotten out of the house and made a friend. Even though time square celebrations were hours away, Daniel and Darcy rang in the New Year with the rest of London via television. They laughed and ate grapes and had a good time and Darcy knew that it was a perfect way to start off her new life.

She rushed up to bed and lay there thinking about the Mackinnons. She'd forgotten to ask Max how he knew them, and wondered about the Mackinnon girl. They had to be the same age if she was a friend of Max and in the same respect they must have common if not similar tastes. She hoped they'd get along just as well. Darcy couldn't stop the noise in her head, she had so many thoughts channeling through that she couldn't relax and sleep. She felt like a small child before the first day of school and then she remembered one Christmas she spent with her grandparents. She ran down and told her grandmother that Santa might not come because she was so excited she couldn't sleep; that's when her grandmother showed her a trick.

"Close your eyes and try to picture a plain white wall and every time something else pops in, focus on that wall," she remembered her grandmother saying to her.

It worked that night, and every other time Darcy felt too nervous or excited to sleep. She hadn't tried it in a while and it seemed like an opportune time. When the sun kissed Darcy's eyes that morning she sat up in a mixed state of ambivalence and disorientation. Her eyelids felt so heavy it seemed her body was fighting her will to wake up. There was no way it could be morning, it had to be a mistake. She thought back as early as she could but the very last thing she could remember was celebrating with her father; it couldn't be morning. Maybe she hadn't fallen asleep, maybe the light wasn't from the sun. She reached over to her watch, but it only affirmed that morning had come without warning. Darcy had never had a nights sleep uninterrupted by her dreams, how was this possible? She started to panic that perhaps something might be wrong with her, then she figured that she might have simply forgotten what she'd dreamt. That thought brought on an even more disturbing one, had she seen Jack? How could she ever forget even one moment with him, what if it happened again? What if she never saw him again? She lay back down and tried to go back to sleep, to no avail.

Jackson: Panic

Jackson awoke drenched in sweat and completely exhausted. There was no way he'd missed; he desperately tried to get a grip on the situation. Where was she? She seemed to be off the grid and from what he understood that only ever happened when... It was an impossible thought that he refused to culminate. He tried to think of any alternative he could. Then as the day progressed he became more desperate and began to weigh his options. He wondered how long it would take him to track her down and get to her. It seemed almost impossible, but it was the only way to make sure she was okay. He rushed over to his computer and before he could finish typing in her name, a dismal realization came to him, if by some miracle it was all just a mistake and she was fine, his brash, unnecessary actions might trigger suspicion and then possibility of death would be eminent. He decided to wait just one more night and then he would act. With only a couple hours left, he knew they'd be the longest moments in his life.

Darcy decided to try and occupy the grueling hours of the day with as much activity as possible. She ran down to meet Daniel in the kitchen. He stood with a small bag at his side. "Darcy, you startled me, I was just about to call up to you. I have to catch my flight, but I wanted to make sure you had everything you need." Then she understood the price of their celebration together.

"You're leaving?" She asked with an angry undertone.

"Just a couple of days, 5 at the very most, I have to go back and tie up some loose ends. I left you plenty of money, in case you need to catch a taxi or something. Plenty of food and stuff, emergency numbers, you have your new cell and I have mine, I programmed the numbers. Your mother is set to be back in a couple of days anyways."

"Dad, you're leaving me alone, in a foreign country, are you serious?" She felt a familiar feeling on displacement within.

"Darcy, it's hardly foreign and mom will..." he realized how absurd it was to assume he could rely on Darcy's mother for anything. "You're right, go on and pack a bag, you can go see your friends while I finish up." Darcy was about to run up until she thought of the grueling flight and how ridiculous it was that they'd only been there a couple of days and already going back.

"No, dad you go, it's too much. Why didn't we just stay until you were ready to leave?"

"Well, I had promised your mother..."

"Ahh of course, my mother."

"That and the owners of the house were moving and well it was just easier this way. Are you sure you'll be okay here alone? Now you have me worried," Daniel spoke as he inched further near the door.

"Dad I'm a big girl, besides I'm leaving in a couple of months anyway, I should practice." She smiled at him and guilt flushed through his veins. He wanted to stay in England. The thought of the long trip and the jetlag weighed heavy on him, but he knew he had to make sure everything was taken care of. After a fair exchange of I love yous and be carefuls on both ends the car arrived to drive him off. He reminded her before he left that in case of an emergency her mother was only an hour away by flight. By the late afternoon she sat staring out the window into the courtyard. She thought about everything and nothing in particular at the same time. She looked over at the empty cottage and wished the Mackinnons would return soon.

She stared down the stone laden road and secretly hoped to see Max drive up as he had done the day before. It was so strange because in LA she was alone quite often, but hadn't felt the cold hand of loneliness grip her shoulder until now. Perhaps LA was always so full of people it was almost impossible to feel alone, but now left alone with her thoughts she realized how empty her life would be out there. Finally after about what seemed like an eternity, twilight gave way to dusk and the night was officially welcoming. Completely aware that she would not be seeing much of Daniel anymore, Darcy made her way up to her room. She changed into her pajamas and crawled into bed. She turned and ran her fingers across the child seemingly sleeping at the top of the head of her bed. Darcy loved that the night brought the pictures in her windows to life, without the fading rays of the sun burning through it was easier to make out the details. She hoped to share the same fate as her dormant friend.

Darcy was relieved when she found herself walking through the crowded streets. She walked along searching through the faces for the indigo that always seemed to have an almost anaphylactic effect on her. As the neverending parade of 'what ifs' made its way into her head, she decided to push them back and just focus.

He entered with a determination he had never felt in his life, the pull came directly from his chest. He hated when Darcy's dreams were crowded. It wasn't long before he saw her standing with a familiar frantic look on her face. Usually he lingered at arms length to admire her for a while, but this time instead of stopping it still in his chest, the sight of her made his heart almost burst out completely. The feeling carried him over to her with a resolute he had never had.

Darcy stood and took a deep breath. He'd be there, he had to be, he always would be. The assurance was beginning to break off until she felt a strong restraining pressure around her waist and a pressing at the base of her neck. When she looked down and saw the arms that wrapped so tightly around her that the tendons flickered, relief ensued. She reached up and realized that it was Jack's face pressed so tightly against her neck. She couldn't feel his breath but she could hear how hard and fast it was moving through him. She closed her eyes and felt the damp cold rush as a tear slid slowly from the corner of her pressed eyelid down the side of her cheek.

His voice cracked "Jesus Darcy, I thought you'd died, I thought I was never going to see you again." For the first time he hadn't been careful about his choice in words.

"I know, I was afraid you were gone too."

"Never, what happened last night? I mean..."

"I don't know. I just, I fell asleep I guess and all of a sudden it was morning and I can't remember."

"But you slept?"

"Yeah I did, maybe, I figured like with the move and everything, maybe I was just exhausted or I honestly thought maybe I did dream and I just couldn't remember. What if I wouldn't be able to remember anymore, I freaked out a little..."

"No you weren't even..." he caught himself. He couldn't figure out what had happened. How did she do it? How was she off the grid like that? "But you're okay?"

"Now," her voice cracked and he let her loose long enough to turn her around. With tears still inexplicably making their way to the surface of her eyes she blushed and lifted her hand to her face. Before she could brush them away, he put his hand

to her cheek and did it for her, hoping he'd be able to feel the moisture beneath his skin to no avail.

"I don't think I've ever been scared of anything in all my life, until yesterday." She looked at him and wondered what that even meant, she had so many questions, but it was not the time. Jackson pulled back and regained his composure. "How does that feel?" he asked.

"What?"

"Crying," he wiped the last lingering tear, "I can't remember the last time I ever cried. I don't even think I could if I tried."

"I cry for everything; it's stupid." She smiled and his heart ached. He wanted to ask her more about what she'd done differently the night before, but it wasn't the time.

Darcy: Max

When Darcy woke up she lay in bed and thanked the stars for Jack. She knew she could never lose him so easily. She heard a deep unfamiliar ring and looked around her room. As she tried to find the source, she ran down the stairs. It took a while before she realized it was the door. Apparently and to no surprise, she was the only one home. More than anyone back home Darcy missed their housekeeper. She'd spent more time with her than her own parents; she'd cried for her more than anyone else the morning they left. Darcy wanted to take her along, but she had a family of her own and she should have retired years before, but she stuck around for Darcy.

When she opened the door she was greeted by a tall, lanky, man with a small mustache. The technicians had arrived to work on the house. Darcy let them in excited that she would soon be blessed with the technology she'd been missing so dearly. She ran up and brushed her teeth and pulled her hair back, since she figured she'd be spending the day alone again, she decided to lounge around in her pajamas. She'd just settled into a groove in the sofa when the bell once again interrupted her. Thinking that the technicians had gone out and needed to come back in, she ran down annoyed.

"You don't have to ring the bell every time you want to come back in, just..." When she opened the door she was taken back.

"You really shouldn't be so trusting, especially since you don't even know anyone here." Max smiled a devious looking half smile.

"Hi, no, sorry I thought you were um" she pointed upward at no one in particular, "technician people."

"Oh, I see, well, I stayed nearby with," he paused and cleared his throat unknowingly "a friend last night and I wondered if you might want to ride with me back into London. You know, so you can look around and stuff."

"Umm yeah, sounds interesting." She closed the door behind her excitedly.

"I'm not really into fashion and if it's your thing I really don't care, but you know you're wearing..."

"Oh my god, how embarrassing, I forgot. Let me go change. Umm come in please, I won't take long." She let him in and up into the living room. "Here watch TV I'll be right down."

"Down, you mean you're room is higher up?" He asked still taken aback by the vastness of the house.

"Yeah, long story, hold on, be right back." Darcy ran into her room and in record time threw on some jeans and a sweater. She was so wrapped up in getting ready, that she didn't seem to notice that she'd had company all along. "Jesus!" she yelled out to no one in particular.

"Um no, Colin mum." The small round man stood in a state of awkwardness as he fiddled with the wires in his hand.

"Sorry, I totally forgot you guys were here." She ran back down to Max with the blush of embarrassment still apparent on her face. "Sorry I forgot about the men, do you want to rain check or would you mind waiting just a bit till they're done? I mean it's up to you I would understand if you have things, like..." he found her nervous nature amusing.

"Darcy, its fine I can wait, no hurry, besides it's early. I mean we can't even go have lunch yet." Darcy knew Max couldn't be older than twenty but his eyes looked much older. They were a beautiful shade of green, but they looked worn.

"So why are you going into London? Do you live there? I thought you went to Cambridge, is that in London?"

"Wow, I've never heard so many questions in one sentence. Um I go to Cambridge, but I live in London. It takes me about 45 – 50 minutes daily by train, so no, it's not in the same place. Technically I'm not suppose to live more than a couple minutes past the university, but I have special circumstances that..." he stopped himself before he would say too much. "Whatever, I go to Cambridge, but I work out of London," he said curtly. She caught the sound of annoyance in his voice.

"Sorry, I ask a lot of questions." She bit her lower lip and focused on her untied shoelace. He felt bad for being so brash. There was something about her a fragility that he felt protective of.

"No, sorry it's nothing, I really don't mind, I think I'm just tired." She smiled at him dubiously. "Really, look, ask me something, anything. Come on Darcy, please." He shot her a pleading smile that was impossible to deny.

"Okay, what's your major, like or if there are majors here, I mean."

"I know what..." he chuckled to himself feeling sheepish and as he scratched his temple, she couldn't help but smile at his boyish demeanor, "Art History."

"Art?" she looked surprised and half smiled as she raised an eyebrow.

"Why are you giving me that look?"

"I just didn't… why art?" She couldn't do much to hide the amusement as she asked.

"I don't know, I guess I just always connected with it. Like it's easier to appreciate what's inside some else's head when it's laid out like that for you to see. I mean we all walk around, you know, normal for the most part, but inside us we all have thoughts, questions, opinions, you know about life, religion, death, creation, purpose, meaning, and I think art, not just pictures, but like words, books, music, lyrics, they're just outlets. You say all the things you need to get out of your head without you know, saying them and sounding crazy. It gives me hope or it used to anyway that it was all for something, we're all here for something or because of it anyway." When he was done he felt uneasy about having expressed so much. She brought that out of him, she seemed to reconnect him with bits of humanity it had taken him years to callous and he hadn't decided if it was a good thing or a bad one. When he looked up at her she smiled and grabbed his hand.

"Come here, I want to show you something." His hands felt rough in hers and he let go and hid them in his pockets. He followed her up into her room. "See, this is why I chose this room." He stood there admiring the art that had been meticulously recreated on each of her windows. "This one is my favorite, but I don't know it, do you?" He stood there and smiled, it had been one of his favorites for a while too. He nodded.

"Gauguin. 1881 Paul Gauguin painted the Young Girl Dreaming." He had stared at the painting before wondering what awaited her on the other end of her sleep. Wondering what it'd be like to just close your eyes and slip away apathetically. As they both stood there admiring the window they were interrupted.

"Well, we're all done and you know set to be off," the lanky man reappeared.

"Oh okay, umm thank you," Darcy smiled and they followed the men out. "So, hungry?"

"Starving." They talked most of the drive. Max tried to point out the few bits and facts he actually knew about London. After lunch he drove to his place to drop off his car and they toured the rest of London on foot and by taxi. They walked and laughed and did all the touristy things Max found annoying. Time seemed to fly by so quickly and before they knew it the night was well underway. Darcy was amazed at how much prettier the city seemed at night.

"I should get you home; your parents are probably worried."

"Doubt it, they're out of town. My mom is in France and my dad is in LA or New York I forgot to ask which, but I should get home."

"Your parents left you alone, here?" He sounded concerned and stunned.

"I'm used to being alone. My parents are, well, eccentric."

"I mean, I'm not judging, shit, I was adopted, I'm just saying. This place is beautiful but it can be scary you know." He thought hard for a moment as she stared at the river with admiration in her eyes. "Come on lets go." They walked into the building and up two flights of stairs until they reached a green door.

"Where are we?" She asked nervously.

"You're going to stay with me tonight."

"What, no it's fine really; you probably have plans and stuff." By the stares he was receiving on the streets surely he had a date. Darcy knew that she had nothing to fear from Max, he never made her feel uncomfortable or like his intentions were anything other than noble. He seemed to ignore her refusal and lead her in. She was very impressed. His place was a lot bigger than it seemed from the outside. It was very neat and it smelled good. The hard wood floors glistened under the feet of his furniture.

"You can stay in the bedroom," the bed was the only thing unmade, "I'll, umm change the sheets and if you need anything, or do you want to go back and get some stuff from home?"

"Max you don't have to really I'm fine."

"Darcy, its fine really look I don't want to wake up tomorrow and hear that you were kidnapped or mauled by a bear out there in the forest where you live," he joked and she giggled.

"I hardly know you, how do I know I wont get mauled here," she joked, but he only let out as small smile. He broke the discomfort he felt from the unintentionally ironic comment.

"At least here someone will find you. Please, its fine I'll sleep in the living room. So do you want me to take you back to get stuff or do you want to do some shopping? I'll even buy."

"If I'm staying, I'm buying. Is there really bears…"

After picking up a few essentials, clothes, and some takeout, they were back at Max's. They ate and watched a movie. The night passed as they talked about their lives back in the states. It had only been a couple of days, and yet somehow it already seemed like another life. Before too long it was well into the hours of the early morning and Darcy excused herself to change and ready her self for bed. Max was quick to change the sheets while she was gone. While doing so he felt bad that she'd have to sleep on a bed where so much indecency had thrived. She walked in and he excused himself.

Darcy threw herself down on his bed. She felt awkward only having known Max a couple of days, but it actually felt good and secure to fall asleep near another person. However, a guilt that had been absent all day made an unwelcome visit. She wondered how Jack would react to know she was in a strange man's bed, even if she was there alone. She had no desires toward Max and he didn't seem to hold any towards her. Jack would want her to be safe; still she should let him know. She felt funny about referring to Jack as a real person, because even though he was very real to her, she had to remind herself of the situation. As she drifted off, she convinced herself that she should probably be committed.

That night Jack wasn't there, but she didn't worry, because her dream was as lively as ever. She wondered where he was on the nights he was away or if he even went anywhere. There were so many questions she was always too afraid to ask, even herself. After breakfast and light conversation Max drove Darcy home. He was reluctant to leave her, but he had things to take care of and he'd be by to check on her later.

Max: Dominion

Max walked down the long hallway until he reached the double doors of Dominion, he knew it was a matter of time before he'd be summoned. He hadn't been called to task in the few weeks since he'd moved over seas and although he was grateful for the rest, he wondered if perhaps it wasn't time. After all, with everything he'd been going through especially with Darcy he wondered if he wasn't regenerating his humanity. As Max stood before the conspirators, he wondered what the task was, it wasn't just a routine assignment, because he was summoned; he became excited at the idea of a challenge. He had only been before the conspirators twice before, when he was recruited and when his condemning fate was revealed to him so cruelly. They were an intimidating group, by any standards. All thirteen of them sat in a horseshoe configuration like a panel of judges. He never knew their names and they spoke in a series of whispers too fast for him to make out and in a language he did not recognize. The only one who ever addressed him directly was Dominic; he was the only one who ever spoke to anyone from what Jackson and Max could make out. Dominic sat at the center and never took his eyes off you from when you entered until you exited the room.

"Max, nice to see you, I do hope this change hasn't been too difficult for you." When he spoke the words flowed out of his mouth through pressed lips and he held a monotone so as to never reveal any sincerity in his words. His black eyes were piercing and the white in his eyes barely showed at the corners. The black and silver hair on his head was short and never changed. He didn't look old, but his hair added years to his face and his demeanor was that of an older man. You never spoke until he let his hand down because you could never tell when his sentence was over. "I can see you have had some light nights for a couple of weeks now. Well, we feel it is compulsory that you resume your duties. Now another matter at hand, as we are aware you are familiar with one of our muses," a short hardly audible whisper shot through the silence and he spoke again "forgive me, he is in fact an advisor, well, that makes it all the more prudent." As the conspirators paused to exchange information, a strange thought entered Max's head; his next target was going to be a colleague. He wondered which one and was sure it would be a challenging and enticing task. As quick as he cut off, Dominic spoke once more. "Ah yes advisor 653712, I believe you refer to him as Jackson."

Max spoke before he could stop himself. "You want me to kill Jackson?!" Dominic glared at Max in amazement as his hand was still up. "Sorry, I just…"

"Should it be asked of you, you will target whomever we desire, however, no. As advisor 653712 is one of our most promising, we are not prepared to relieve him of duty just yet. Jackson is still somewhat vital to us; we just need to be sure he stays out of trouble. The monitors tracked some unsanctioned activity a few days ago, just the once of course and that was taken care of. That is not what concerns us so much. Something in his presence has changed and of course we've taken that into consideration, if it's something happening outside our area of composure, we will handle that but if it is within our realm we must be made aware. As you are the only one that we are aware of that he interacts with outside our confinements, besides your usual tasks, you will be made responsible to find out exactly what it is that he seems to be so preoccupied with. That will be all, oh and you will be tasked on your way out." He lowered his hand and as Max turned to walk out something unusual happened; Dominic spoke again. "Of course as an assassin should more drastic measures become imperative like I stated before it will be in your commitment as no one else must be made aware of the current situation." Even though Max couldn't see it in his vacant expression or hear it in his apathetic words, he got the feeling Dominic was happy about the sadistic idea.

Max walked out of the room in a mixed state of disbelief, anger, and disappointment. He should have known better, when he saw Jackson looking so bad. Perhaps he didn't want to believe it; if he didn't know anything, he'd have nothing to report or deal with. "Fuck, shit, fuck," he realized he was cursing out loud. How could they ask this of him, as if it wasn't enough that he'd been robbed of a life, a soul, now they were asking him to give up the only real friend he ever had. He calmed himself down with the notion that he still didn't know what he was really dealing with; maybe it was nothing. Maybe whatever it was, he could help Jackson get back on track. After all, it seemed Jackson had somehow made himself somewhat indispensable and at least he had that in his favor. Max had been tasked, but for the next day, he figured he should call Jackson and meet with him, to see if he could figure this out. He let the phone ring on and just as the call was about to go to voicemail, the line was interrupted. It was Darcy, she was just calling to let Max know she was fine and she was going to sleep. Max hadn't realized so much time had passed, and offered to go up to her house, but she assured him she'd be alright for the night. He felt a little relieved as he didn't feel up for the company.

Max walked into his apartment and sat at the edge of his bed and buried his head in his hands. He knew Jackson was in trouble and he knew what it was about. He remembered the conversation on the bridge, the one he tried so hard to redirect, it was about a girl. It wasn't an asinine notion, that they could still have something genuine in the world. Especially someone in Jackson's position; he was still connected with all the emotions that made life copious. Max wondered what it must be like to have affections for someone in that respect. Max's appearance guaranteed that he'd never be in short supply of physical affections, but the vacuous copulation he so frequently engaged in seemed lacking at times. As he lay back onto his pillow, a sweet aroma of soap, water, and berry made his throat burn. Usually after a girl slept in his bed the sheets were infused with the stench of nauseating perfumes, this particular fragrance was more natural and alluring. Darcy was enchanting in every respect. Picturing her he thought of Jackson for some reason. He could see the appeal of risking everything for a girl like Darcy. He reached under his pillow and pulled out a t-shirt, the one she'd slept in. He folded it up and placed it on his nightstand. As he lay back and drifted off the sleep, he found himself looking over to it every so often.

DARCY

Darcy spent the night with Jack. As usual they spent most of the time just talking and walking through another one of Darcy's scenic concoctions. Something strange happened that evening. After Jack excused himself with a tender goodbye, instead of waking up slowly as she usually did, she was pulled out of her sleep by a loud thud. She sat up in panic. Although it was already morning, the sky was still kissed by the bluish black colors of early dawn as the sun had not yet graced the sky. She stood up and grabbed her phone, she had no idea who she'd call that wasn't hours away. The thud made itself heard once again. She screamed out and jumped up onto her bed. She thought about calling Max, but she knew he'd go out there and she still had no idea what was going on and she didn't want to make him drive all that way out for nothing. Remembering her knew connections to the outside world, she grabbed the remote and flipped on the television. She turned it high enough to drown out any noise that might make its presence. She decided that at least until someone else got there, be it her parents or the Mackinnons, she'd be staying with Max.

The next day she waited until well passed noon to call Max. She told him about the noises and how scared she was. He found the story amusing, until she asked him if she could stay with him. It wasn't that he didn't want her around, on the contrary, but he knew he had been tasked and he wasn't sure how that would go. Through the grit of his teeth he agreed. He couldn't turn her down after all, it was his idea in the first place; somehow he'd make it work. Besides, she'd be in another room. He offered to go out and pick her up, but she said, she wanted to try and make it out there on her own, and if she got lost she'd just call him.

Darcy liked the idea of seeing London on her own, not because she hadn't had fun with Max, but mostly because Darcy enjoyed spending time alone. She liked the idea of doing and seeing things at her own pace. Walking through the streets of London made LA seem so empty. The streets were filled with voices and faces that looked and sounded alien to her. It reminded her of one of her dreams. She took advantage of the time alone and visited the places she'd made plans to see before she got there. Ordinarily she would have felt nervous about being in such a foreign place alone, so far from anyone she knew, but the thought of Max being a phone call away gave her a sense of complacency. She had no idea why, but she knew that for some reason he'd be there for her if ever she needed him. That was just one of the ways he reminded her so much of Jack.

Max paced through his apartment uneasy at the idea that at any moment Darcy would arrive. He sat at the edge of his sofa and took a deep breath. He had never had anyone anywhere near him when he carried out his stint. He thought back to his very first task, he was seventeen and the next morning when he walked down to see his parents, they sat unaware of the bereavement that lingered under his finger nails and he knew he had to leave them. He felt like a monster and knew it wasn't fair that something so depraved should unknowingly plague their lives. That was the last night he ever shared a home with anyone. When he heard the knock at the door he nearly jumped out of his skin. When he opened the door her couldn't help but laugh a little. "You look like a snowman."

"Not used to temperatures below 70 degrees." Darcy stood there in her jeans, an oversized coat, scarf, hat, and gloves. It still didn't take away from her painful attractiveness. The thought made him swallow hard and he let her in. "So tell me the truth am I being a pain," she bit down on her lower lip and looked up at him, "because I feel like I am and I've been thinking and I'm pretty sure I can survive another night. I mean it was probably like just an owl or something."

Max smiled and rolled his eyes. "I have a feeling you're a pain in the ass, even when you're not trying to be," he joked. "Its fine Darcy, or do you want me to say something like, I'm really glad you decided to come by, I was really looking forward to it." She just stared at him nervously. "Seriously I'm kidding I want you to stay, please."

"Good, because I'm pretty sure I'm scared of owls, anyway."

"Just one thing, I have to turn in early tonight though, I have something to do early."

"That's okay, look, I'll sleep here in the living room and you sleep on your bed."

"No, that's not…"

"No really, that way I can at least watch TV." He agreed halfheartedly and she got up to go change. He sat and watched as she flipped aggressively through the channels. She finally settled on a sci-fi movie and he was impressed at her taste in film, she really was perfect. They talked and as time seemed to be speeding by he was careful to make sure to keep to his schedule. He excused himself and went into his bedroom. He sat at the edge of his bed and rubbed his face. He hoped for the best and laid back. At least she was safely in another room.

Darcy curled herself into a ball on the plush sofa and nestled under a blanket. She looked around and then in the direction of Max's bedroom, it felt nice having someone else close by again. She couldn't fall asleep, so she stayed up flipping through channels. Just as she was about to doze off, she was stirred from her sleep by a grunting sound. Startled she stood up and for a few seconds forgetting where she was. When she refocused she realized it was coming from the bedroom and more specifically from Max. She figured he must be having a nightmare. At first she decided to ignore it, but as it progressed she became worried. She cracked the door and he was sleeping face down; at first she just stood at the doorway watching him toss and turn and then the grunting stopped and gave way to heavy almost panting breaths. She decided to try and subdue his discomfort.

When she got closer she noticed as he lay on his stomach how broad his shoulders and back really were. Under his clothes his frame was big, but now with every detail of his muscles defined it seemed more intimidating. Something else caught Darcy's eye, his body appeared to be riddled with scars. As her eyes adjusted better to the dimness, she noticed that up his back closer to his shoulder were a series of scratches. As she studied them she figured out that the four red gashes resembled those that would be made by fingernails, very determined fingernails. At first, she thought that they might have been a souvenir from a more intimate encounter, but as she squinted through the darkness they appeared to be bleeding as if they were fresh, but it would be impossible. She lifted her hand and ran her fingers down the gashes; just then she felt an agonizing pressure around her forearm. Her eyes widened as she realized that Max had a forceful grip on her, and he seemed to still be sleeping. He mumbled and squeezed harder, Darcy wanted to cry out in agony, but she was afraid in his sleep he might hurt her or worse; instead she used her other hand to pry his fingers off and ran out and back onto the couch. She knew he hadn't purposely hurt her, but her arm was throbbing. She curled back up and fell asleep.

Darcy sat on the park bench and put her elbows to her knees. She thought about Max and it made her sad for some reason. She knew there was something sad about him that she couldn't place. She thought back to the empty apartment, the lonely holiday, and now the nightmare. She ran her hand over her forearm and studied it, he was a big guy, but he had been amazingly strong. It wasn't too long before a long shadow was cast beside her.

"Swing?" She looked up and Jack smiled playfully.

"Sure, I think I remember how." She got up, followed him to an old swing set and took the seat beside him.

"What's wrong?"

"What, why would something be wrong?"

"Oh, I don't know, you looked a bit," he struggled to find the right word, "concerned."

"Oh, no, it's nothing just," she paused a moment, "I met this guy…" he gave her a look of jealousy and concern "no, not like that. I told you I just moved and so far he's the only person I've met. He's just been really nice and he's been looking after me, especially since as usual my parents have been gone and I'm basically miles away from everyone I know. I was meaning to tell you, but I hadn't gotten a chance, but he let me stay with him so I wouldn't have to stay alone." His brow furrowed and his eyes looked intensely at her. "Jack come on its really not like that trust me, there was a thud…"

"Then what are you worried about?" he asked somewhat impatiently.

"I don't really know there's something about him. I don't really think he has anyone in his life, I mean he seems normal, but I feel like he's just so sad. I just feel bad for him is all."

Jack smiled and stood up. "Well, now at least he has you."

She could sense the small hint of sarcasm in his tone. "Yeah, but not like you have me or anything," She stood up and pressed her lips to his cheek and he smiled at the notion.

Admittedly he was still a little jealous, but mostly toward the fact that it whoever this person was, he at least had a possibility of actually being able to be with Darcy in any respect. He also felt uneasy about the fact that she had stayed with him, although he was grateful that she was safer, he knew what really lingered in the heads of men and wondered how noble this guys intentions really were. He opted not to know anything about him including his name because it would be too tempting for him. He decided that at least for the time being he had no other choice but to take Darcy at her word.

As he held her wrist in his hand he ran his finger over her forearm ineffectually. He had done this before and Darcy had always thought it was another attempt to awake some kind of physical connection, but she noticed what she had not before, he was tracing the outline of her veins with his finger. "Why do you do that?" Jackson looked at her confused. "Trace my veins, I've seen you do it before, but I never really paid that much attention."

He smiled, he knew he did it, but he never really noticed when he was doing it. "I don't know, I guess they intrigue me." She gave him a speculating glance. "I mean it's like computer wiring under your skin. No one really pays attention to them, but they're so vital. They carry our blood, oxygen, and all the other stuff we need to stay… alive." Darcy couldn't help but smirk and he blushed. "Don't laugh I just think its an amazing thing you know?" He smiled and kissed her wrist then traced the veins up her forearm with his lips and suddenly, it wasn't so funny anymore. "Significant insignificance," he whispered. She longed for titillation.

Darcy seldom overslept, but she had stayed up a little later than usual. Max opened his eyes in exhaustion; the night had proved trying, evidently he was out of practice. As he rolled to his side he felt a slight burn in his right shoulder. He ran his hand over the scrape and as he reexamined his hand to look for traces of blood, he noticed a bite mark on the top of his left hand as well. Usually he treated whatever mishaps he came upon and dismissed them lightly as a part of the job, but that morning as he studied his hand he could see the desperation. The unwavering desire from someone willing to do anything to hold onto whatever remnants of life they could was there pressed into his hand. He ran water over both his hands and splashed some onto his face. Remembering a pact he had made with himself long ago to permanently suppress any such feelings, he realized this was all coming about for some reason and such as he was about to pinpoint he felt a strange soft touch on his shoulder and looked up.

"That looks pretty bad are you okay?"

"Yeah wow, you always scare me," he jerked back and turned around. "I thought you were still asleep."

"Sorry, I was just going to see if you were done, because you know the door was open. So what happened?" She asked as her voice fell well below the normal octave.

"Oh I just I ran into, there was a loose you know, from the bed…"

"A spring?"

"Yeah, when I rolled over to get up it sliced my shoulder." He walked out of the bathroom and uncomfortably pulled on a t shirt. She started brushing her teeth with a vague feeling of apprehension. He sounded colder than usual and she got a strange feeling of resentment from him. He felt bad for being so crass and walked back into the bathroom to try and rectify himself that's when he noticed a long contusion peeking from underneath her sleeve. "So what happened to you?"

Darcy gave him a puzzled look and he redirected his eyes down to her forearm. She quickly grabbed the edge of her sleeve in her fingers. "Oh um I guess the other night when I got scared, I jumped up and hit my arm. She didn't want to make him feel bad about what he had done and she also didn't want to let on that she'd watched him sleeping. "Listen I really appreciate everything, but I'm honestly starting to feel bad about it, so I'm gonna go."

"Don't," he hesitated, "like feel bad about it. It was nothing, seriously and it's been kinda nice having you around," he cleared his throat nervously and smiled.

Darcy couldn't help but to offer up a smile as well. "Thanks Max, for everything, but anyways, I should be getting back I actually have to get stuff ready. Day after tomorrow I have school and stuff."

"School?" he gave her a look of confusion through a playful smile.

"Yeah like I'm basically done, but my parents thought it'd be a good idea to like audit some classes, you know meet people and stuff."

"Oh I see, well, then I guess with your new friends I probably won't be seeing you as much…" he teased.

"Shut up, I seriously hadn't thought about how nervous I'd be about it."

"Nah, you'll be fine seriously, from what I've seen if there's anyone that can handle anything it's you." He immediately choked on his words and looked away. "As long as there's no owls or bears around," he winked and his attractive nature broke through. Darcy blushed and walked over to get the rest of her things. He walked her out to her taxi. "You know you can call me if you need anything right?" As she rode away, a rush of opposing emotions swept over him. Although he was relieved that he could focus better on the crucial matter at hand and that he would no longer have a connection to the proverbial soul, he felt sad to see her go.

Darcy was relieved to get home and find that her mother was back. She walked in and after a brief exchange she went up to her room. She dropped to her bed and stared at the sleeping girl as she ran her hand over the cold glass she couldn't help but wonder what it was like to sleep forever like the girl immortalized in the painting. She wondered what she was dreaming of and then she thought of Jackson. It was hard not to imagine if that's what death might have been like. Would she just never wake up one day, and find that even if her breath left her body she'd keep dreaming? She hoped with every breath in her body that she'd dream an eternity with Jack.

Darcy: Beginnings

Monday morning came with a rush that Darcy found inconvenient. Her father swept into her room with an annoying excitement. He had already made all the necessary arrangements and the school was expecting her. He also hand delivered her new uniform. Darcy had never been one for plaid but she figured clothes were just going to be one less thing to worry about. She changed and quickly made her way down the two flights of stairs and out into the courtyard. As she waited for the car to pull around, she was greeted by a tall, slender man. "Morning, you're looking very sharp, but feeling a bit nervous I gather."

She smiled, she found the man's tone endearing. He had white hair that peeked out from under his hat and his baby blue almost translucent eyes were welcoming. "A little, it doesn't show too much does it?"

"No, you look just fine. You must be Darcy." He held out his hand and as she took it, he had a strong grip, but she could feel the veins in his hands. "I'm Thomas Mackinnon, Gidding's Hill groundskeeper and occasional professional golfer," he winked and she couldn't help but smile. "Shame you missed my boy, he could've given you a ride, although you might find the school close enough to walk, only a couple miles. He's bout your age, also in sixth form, same school and everything."

"Boy? I thought my dad said you had a daughter."

"If only," he giggled "sure the wife would've appreciated that, sure she would've been a lot less trouble." Darcy smiled and just then, the car came around.

"Well, it was really nice to meet you, I probably shouldn't be late and I guess I'll be seeing you?" He smiled and waved and she was off to face her day. Mr. Mackinnon had been right; it seemed seconds had passed before the car was slowing down in front of a vast red brick building that looked more like a cathedral than a school. She stepped out of the car and studied the plaid procession as it moved in through large, worn wooden doors. She took a deep breath, braced herself and headed up the stairs. Before she could reach the less then welcoming opening, a well dressed, overly perfumed woman made her way to the door.

"Darcy Whitten?" Her accent was thick and her hair seemed to be pulled up so tightly atop her head that it gave her a small eye lift.

"Yes, I'm Darcy," her voice hadn't been that shaky since her first day at elementary school.

"Eleanor Wickerstaff, your father came by and made all the necessary arrangements for you. Very nice man Daniel Whitten, quite clever as well." She was walking so fast Darcy had to struggle to keep pace. "Welcome, I have arranged for Clem Dancy, another student much like yourself, sixth form, last term, to take you under her allegorical wing. As Da…your father mentioned you were interested in business, I've taken the liberty of seeing to it that you audit classes befitting your interest. As a guest here I hope you will find it meets and exceeds all your expectations as well, I expect you will follow the schedule of the rest of the academic body. Of course should you have any questions or concerns, I am always at your disposal, feel free to come to me with anything. Ah well, here we are. Good morning Miss Dancy," she forced a smile through her cracked crimson lipstick, "this is Miss Whitten, I leave her in your very capable hands. Have a nice day girls." Before Darcy could get in a word, the only thing left of Ms. Wickerstaff was the faint sound of her four inch heels.

"Hi, Darcy right? I'm Clem," the girl offered her hand and Darcy took it with a bit of apprehension. "Don't worry, aside from the dodgy food and less than sheik fashion, it's not so bad." Her accent was different, but Darcy could not place it. Clem was tall like Darcy, but not as voluptuous, with her sandy hair and milky brown eyes, she was rather attractive, but what really stood out to Darcy were Clem's thick pink lips that quivered a bit when she spoke. "So, you're American then? Well, this ought to be pretty interesting then."

"Why?" Darcy asked in a mixture of surprise and sarcasm.

"Small town, everyone knows everyone, except you now, and plus you're foreign, so…"

Darcy laughed "that's crazy I'm not forgh… oh well, I guess I kind've am. Look, I know you were sort of assigned to take care of me and all, but I'm pretty sure if you just point me in the right direction I should be okay and you can get back to your life" Darcy smiled.

"Well, aren't you friendly," she winked at Darcy and smiled.

"No, I'm sorry I didn't mean it like that, I just didn't want to be like a pain in the butt."

"Sure, well I have the smallest suspicion that you're going to be one either way. Besides, I have a feeling I'm gonna like you and if Wickerstaff thinks I've bailed out on you there'll certainly be hell to pay." They both giggled and continued on to their first class.

"She seems nice," Darcy joked.

"She's a cheeky one; you know half the boys in school are dying to get into those knickers," Clem winked as they both giggled.

Thankfully, Clem seemed not only nice, but someone Darcy could actually enjoy spending time with. The day went by faster than she'd anticipated and at the end of the day, Clem offered her a ride home.

Jackson and Max

Jackson walked out of Dominion with his routine assignment feeling relieved that everything appeared to have blown over. As he walked down along the river he stopped to breathe deeply. Max eyed his friend from a distance for just a minute. Inside he could feel his throat tighten and his breathing became shallow. He focused and stepped forward. "Happy Holidays?"

"Oh hey, yeah I guess so and yours?" For some reason, Jack became inexplicably nervous.

"Actually better than I expected. So what have you been up to, anything good?" Max smiled as he offered Jack a cigarette.

"Just you know family and stuff," he choked on his own words when he remembered Max probably did not know, "a bit boring really. I'm sure whatever you were up to, was much more exciting." There was something different about Max that day, Jackson couldn't place it but it sparked his curiosity.

"You'd be surprised," he really would be. "So what happened, you know with that girl? You get that stuff taken care of?" Max studied Jackson for any undertone his answer might reveal.

Jackson stood there and tried desperately to maintain his composure "Yup that's all done with." He couldn't believe Max even remembered that.

"Good to hear, so what do you say to a pizza or something?"

"Sounds good." Max decided not to press Jackson. He hoped there really wasn't anything else going on, and figured that he would have better luck getting what he needed by simply hanging around rather than holding him to an inquisition.

The dinner didn't seem to get past catching up and small talk. It seemed they were both so busy trying to read one another that they could never extract anything useful. Jackson felt there was something underlying in Max's sudden interest in his personal life. The last time he had tried to lean on him for advice he all but shut him up and now he seemed more prying. By the end of the dinner, Jackson made the decision that he'd have to keep Max at hand. It wouldn't prove too difficult; Max was often inviting him out, so all he had to do was be more accepting.

Max got back to his place frustrated and slightly suspicious. This Jackson thing was going to drive him crazy. He wondered whether it wouldn't be easier to just tell him the truth, that if he was involved with a girl, he should break it off before Max was forced to intervene. He wondered how Jackson could put everything on the line for a girl. He had heard of love, but he knew it was an idea that appealed more to girls. Countless girls had professed their love to Max, but he never believed them, mostly because he couldn't understand the concept. His sentiments were shallow and easily dismissed. Until now his attraction to women had been mainly physical, then again, there was Darcy. His interest in her wasn't the same as it had been, he felt for her. The funny thing was that as attractive as he found her to be, he could not bring himself to imagine a physical relationship with her. Just then he remembered her first day of school and picked up the phone to make sure she had been alright, but mostly he missed her.

DARCY

Clem and Darcy sat up in Darcy's room talking and laughing. "This house is absolutely absurd. Okay, you're officially my very best friend. And you practically live here by yourself."

"Not always a good thing," Darcy snapped back.

Clem shrugged her shoulders in disagreement. "This doesn't freak you out at all? I mean you don't' find it the least bit creepy?" She pointed in the direction of the windows and Darcy shook her head. "Well, it sure creeps the hell out of me, especially this one." She gestured towards the head of the Darcy's bed. "Let's try this." With a swift movement she lifted a latch and pushed the oval window outward. "There, a little fresh air."

"I had no idea that window could even do that."

"And what do we have there? Is that a guest house; oh my god do you know the kind of trouble you could stir up in there?" Darcy gave her a doubtful look. "Well, do you know what kind of trouble I could stir up in there?"

"Ha ha, I'm sure you could but people actually live there. A family, the Gr... Mackinnons, yeah, the Mackinnons. They have a son our age I think, but I haven't met him."

"Shut up! Mackie, lives a stone throws away? You lucky bitch."

"You know him?"

"Who doesn't, he is the most gorgeous boy on the planet, well one of five hundred, top thirty at the very least." Clem leaned herself a little too far out the window for Darcy's comfort. "You think he's home? Probably not, probably off on some hot steamy date with some hot steamy bird. Have you seen him yet?" Darcy shook her head.

"Well, don't worry, you will. Probably all the time jogging, topless, sweaty like and panting," Darcy raised her eyebrow. "Sorry, easy to get carried away."

Darcy noticed her phone ringing and she excused herself to answer it. It was Max calling to see how her first day had gone. She explained to him how different and boring everything seemed and proceeded to tell him about Clem, who stupidly cheered at the mention of her name. They agreed to talk at a more convenient time and hung up.

"Never mind, looks like you have someone to occupy your time already. Good, that'll leave Mack all to me, and besides he changes girlfriends every week or used to anyways, these days he's usually alone, but anyway, by my calculations you're just another probability I can live without. So who's this Max character than? Boyfriend?

American? Hot?"

"No, yes and no, and I'm not sure," Clem furrowed her brow in confusion. "Just a friend, he's American, but he lives in London and I guess by normal standards, he's pretty hot. Actually by anyone's standards he'd be hot, but I just..."

"You just don't see him that way blah blah blah. Then I hope there's someone who you do see that way or I'm going to start to wonder about you." Darcy blushed, "ha there is, I knew it. Hmm better for me, now you can introduce me to this Max and I'll have more options." She shot Darcy a devious smile "so pick you up for school tomorrow then?" Darcy agreed and walked her out to her car. As she walked back towards her door she looked up the window in cottage and hoped for a glimpse of the already infamous Mack.

The next morning Darcy awoke with the same bereavement that usually follows the end of a great night with Jackson. She opened her eyes and jumped in the shower. Just as she was finishing up her buttered toast, Clem was out front honking inappropriately excessively. Darcy ran out almost directly into Mr. Mackinnon.

"Oh I see you already have a ride to school, would you like me to send away your father's car then?"

"Oh yeah I'm so sorry I forgot to tell him last night." It had completely slipped her mind.

"No worries, I'd ask my boy to drive you, but I can never tell what he's up to these day and I can't guarantee you'd even make it school. By looks of it he's running late again this morning, over slept." Darcy smiled when she saw Clem making the most inappropriate and obscene faces. She excused herself from Mr. Mackinnon and was off. Clem took a long unnecessary detour to buy time for a morning smoke. When they arrived to school Clem walked Darcy into a building she was not familiar with yet. It looked like a chapel.

"Where are we going?"

"Cummings Hall, I know right, but really that's what it's named," she snorted. "Sixth form assembly, we have them every so often you know make sure we've decided on a future and ensuring we're prepared for whatever bloody thing lies ahead. Boring as hell, but it beats a day of lectures and sometimes we get an early dismissal. Now walk a little less lively, I want to ensure a seat near the back."

Darcy slid into the wooden pew and Clem nearly slammed into her. She looked up at the beams in the vaulted ceilings that lay horizontal and met at a peak in the center and then she eyed the rest of the students. She was amazed, in LA there were about 300-400 students in her graduating class alone and here there appeared to be about 100 at the very most. As a faculty member she was unfamiliar with reached the wooden podium set on a platform resembling a pulpit, a wave of silence and stillness swept over the students. Suddenly Darcy felt a sharp jab in her side and when she looked down she realized Clem had all but stabbed her with her elbow. She was mouthing frantically and pointing to someone in front of them. "What?" Darcy mouthed.

"It's him, Mack, in front right there, between the blondes," whom according to Clem's very distracting hand gestures also appeared to be large busted. She managed the entire statement without letting so much as a whisper escape her lips. Curiosity got the better of Darcy and she shifted until she spotted the back of a head between two blonde girls. Both girls seem to be leaning in as close as they could and each kept whispering into his ears every so often, but he never moved his head in either direction. The only thing that she could make out was his dark colored hair and the back of his neck.

Throughout the rest of the presentation, for some reason, Darcy found herself looking in his direction, but to no avail. She was drawn to him, but she couldn't figure out why. When the presentation was over, Clem was right, they were dismissed early. Thanks to Clem's almost superhuman swiftness, they were amongst the first out the door. As Clem stopped in the school courtyard to discuss where a group of students were going for lunch, Darcy kept looking over her shoulder towards the door. "Is that okay Darcy? Darcy!"

"Hmm what?" She wondered how long Clem had been talking.

"Jesus Darcy are you still with us? Pizza, you know pizza, food is that okay?"

"Yes, I know pizza, that's fine." She heard the door and quickly turned around.

"Pfh don't mind her, ditsy, American," Darcy was trying her best to ignore Clem, but she managed to crack a smile. "What in the world…oh I see. It happened, you saw Mack didn't you? I told you he was cute, not cut yourself off from the world cute, but fit enough yeah."

"What, what are you talking about? Please I barely saw past the back of his head."

"Well, then hold on right quick, and lets get this over with."

"Where are you going?" Before she got a response, Clem had skipped out of sight. Darcy felt the chill of the wind; she shivered and pushed her hand into her coat pockets. She felt a bump and turned to face Clem. "Back so soon?"

"I just wanted to check something out."

"What..."

"Mack! Hey, Mack, come here right quick I want you to meet a friend of mine."

"What are you doing?" Darcy whispered. "Oh my god I hate you," she felt herself blush. She never did well with confrontation; she took a deep breath and turned around.

"Darcy, Mack, Mack, Darcy." As Clem smiled Darcy gathered the courage to lift her eyes off the floor for an infinitesimal second and felt her heart stop still in her chest As he stood there staring down at her, his blue eyes widened. It couldn't be possible; she had to be hallucinating. She placed her hand over her mouth in shock.

He squinted his eyes and spoke coldly, "right then," he spoke through his teeth as if the words pained him, "yeah well, gotta run, good to meet ya I suppose" he shrugged his shoulders and he was off.

"Wow, someone's in a foul mood or something. Unless," she studied Darcy "you look all right to me. I can't... well except for that stupid face your making; maybe you freaked him out. Darcy? Darcy! What the hell is wrong..."

"Umm I'm sorry I have to rain check on the pizza, go on without me, I'll call you later." Darcy felt bad leaving Clem so inexplicably but she had to make sure.

Jackson couldn't walk faster without bursting out into an all out stride. He felt his breathing become shallow and his chest was so tight he couldn't swallow without feeling the pain of the course breath pass through. How could this happen? He thought hard; he should have asked or been more attentive, he was sure Darcy had mentioned something. Seeing her standing there in the flesh almost killed him, but he knew if anything went wrong it would most certainly kill her. He couldn't figure out a solution. There had been countless times before when he wanted to tell her the truth, but he just couldn't. He had to stay clear of her; it was for her own good. He was sure she'd recognized him, but she might be unsure, after all Clem had called him Mack. All his thoughts seemed to be culminating collectively and it was as if there was an auditorium full of people in his head. He reached his car and fumbled in his pockets for his keys.

"Hey, wait, hold on a minute." He felt every muscle in his body tighten and he knew he was stuck. He turned to face her still unsure what he would do. "Ha! I wasn't sure because of the accent and hair style, but your face…" she put her arm on his forearm and he quickly jerked back.

"What about my face?" he asked curtly as he painfully kept a straight face and averted his eyes to the floor. She was more beautiful than he'd ever seen her. Her demeanor quickly changed.

"It's… but you're… you're…I" he shot her a look of annoyance and put on his sunglasses.

"What? What is it?" He stared at her with contempt and she studied his face in desperation.

"No… it was just… your smell and…" She had spoken before she could think and now she wanted so desperately to take back her words.

He knew she was nervous and by the way she stammered through her words that she had realized the impossibility of what she might have thought. "Excuse me," he snorted, "did you just say I smell?" He chuckled and knew he was being uncouth, but he had no choice. Just then one of the blondes came over to where they stood.

"Hey Mack could you give me a lift?" She turned to face Darcy as if she hadn't noticed she was standing there, "Oh, who's your friend?"

"Friend?" he asked sarcastically. "Darcy, I think is her name, right?" he gave her a nod as if she were mentally challenged and needed to be reassured of her own name and she felt stupid. "But apparently she's having a bit of trouble articulating today. Must be an American thing," he smiled wickedly. "Nice to meet you Darcy," he got into his car and drove off.

Darcy stood there dumbfounded and humiliated. She felt crazy and it scared her. How could this have happened? It was Jackson; his hair was styled differently and of course the accent was unfamiliar, but there was no mistaking his eyes or his smell. But no it just wasn't possible. Darcy decided that the walk home would help her clear her head.

By the time she reached Gidding's Hill, she was almost frozen and out of breathe. She ran towards her house and noticed that she didn't see Mack's car outside anywhere thankfully. She went up to her room and threw herself on the bed. She felt physically sick almost faint. In an attempt to stop the room from spinning, she closed her eyes tightly and placed her hands over her face. As the cold air that lingered in her lungs attempted to escape her lips, her chest burned. She wasn't sure how much time had passed before she sat up again. It seemed like days had passed, her vision was still blurred and her head was throbbing, but the sun was still pretty high up. She walked down into the restroom and splashed cold water over her face. She reminded herself to get a grip and walked down to see if anyone else was home. She found her mother talking on the phone and from the make of her licentious laughter it wasn't a conversation Darcy wanted to hear or interrupt. Instead she called Max. He agreed to pick her up as soon as he was done with his classes.

When Max arrived to Darcy's he was surprised to find her home so early in the afternoon, he slowed to admire her from the distance. He couldn't help but notice how classic she looked even in jeans and a sweatshirt. Her sea colored eyes looked red and slightly swollen. He stopped the car and she climbed in. "Long erm short day?" she shot him an unwelcoming look. "So, are you hungry?"

"Starving," she smiled and he felt relieved. They drove into London near his apartment where he swore they served the best pizza, and he was right. Max kept the conversation as light as he could throughout lunch. Darcy was visibly bothered by something, but he didn't want to pry. "Hey, I have an idea; do you want to go for a walk?"

Max grimaced at the thought, "not really, why do you?" Darcy bit down on her lower lip and shook her head no. "You're a bad liar; come on let's go," he said willing yet not so much wanting.

"Do you always give in so easily?" she teased him.

"I hope not." He paid the cashier and she noticed the girl's reaction to his husky voice and sinister smile. Undoubtedly Max was attractive, but Darcy knew that his appeal was something more. There was something insidious about him; it was a dangerous allure. They walked out without direction or agenda and as they kept on, Darcy stopped short when they came to an old cathedral. "What? Why are we stopping?" Darcy gave Max the same look from the pizza parlor. "No Darcy, seriously I don't do church and stuff, no. Besides, I don't think it would even be open on a Tuesday afternoon."

Darcy rushed up the cement steps and Max followed reluctantly, she grabbed a hold of the wooden handle and pulled open the door with a strength she had to dig a bit deeper to find. "Darcy what are we doing here?" Max whispered.

"I just need…" she searched for the right response, "reassurance." They walked into the church and although there was no sign of life, they took a seat in the back pew. It was very dim save for the faint light flickering from the candles set on either side of the lectern and the bit of sun that snuck in through the clerestory. Darcy leaned over and whispered to Max, when she spoke her breath traveled lightly and tickled his neck and the delicate scent of cherry from her breath infused the air. "Max, do you believe in all this?" The crease in his forehead deepened. "Like, do you believe in fate, heaven, God, destiny?"

"I don't know, but if God exists, I doubt he has anything to do with destiny. Well, let's hope he doesn't or we're all fucked." Darcy gave him a disapproving nod. "Sorry, I meant we're all in trouble." They both sat in silence for a brief moment.

"Well, I know they exist."

"Oh yeah, what makes you so sure?"

She paused for a moment and thought of Jackson, "There are too many beautiful moments in life. They have to come from somewhere amazing."

Max swallowed hard, "what about the bad stuff?" She looked at him pensively. "Where does all that come from?"

"Maybe," she bit down nervously on her lip and flashes of Harley swept over her, "that's just us. Maybe, we're broken. Some of us cracked, but still repairable, and some of us just shattered." Darcy smiled and he couldn't help but think how naïve she was, dangerously unaware. She stood up and stepped out the pew, walked forward and began admiring the windows. As he watched her float through the church he knew that she was right. She was so beautiful; it would only make sense that only God himself could have created something so enchanting. He sat and stared straight down the aisle at the altar. He wondered why he hadn't deserved exoneration, why he had been condemned. He bowed his head in shame at the fact that he duplicitously sat in a sacred place, a place that cherished life and secretly he wished for an absolution from the sins committed and those foreordained.

When they walked out of the church, there was a thick silence between them as both were lost in thought. Before they reached Max's car, they stopped to admire the water. "Colors," Max could barely speak and he cleared his throat.

"What?" Darcy was confused.

"The only thing that assures me or leads me to believe that God might exist, colors." Darcy smiled and he blushed. "Seriously like..." He stared at the hues of the thin line of shade that seemed to smudge the water and skyline together. "Never mind; come on lets go."

Darcy lay in her bed staring up at the ceiling. Most of the anger she'd been feeling had dissipated. While she was sitting in the church she thought of how beautiful life could be and that's when she was most certain Mack simply couldn't be Jack. Her Jack would and even more appropriately could never hurt her. It was all just an ecumenical coincidence. She put on some music and slipped away into ambiguous lyrics.

Jackson felt nervous when he saw Darcy staring into an empty department store window. He wondered how she would react when she saw him. He went over several scenarios in his mind, but no matter what, each seemed to end in certain peril. He decided to tell her everything. It was certainly the best way he could figure she stood a chance. He'd explain everything and let her know why he could never see her again in any form of existence. Heartbreak, as far as he knew, had never actually killed anyone. Besides, by the way he'd treated her, he figured she probably hated him already. He stuck his hands deep into his pockets to repress the ever present desire to reach out for her and walked over.

Darcy stared at the worn mannequins in the empty department store. Through the hazy reflection of the glass the white faceless figures appeared ghostly. As she looked around the store at the empty racks, she noticed inside one of several empty display cases sat an abandoned locket; it made her smile and morose at the same time. Then her vision shifted as she saw through the reflection the vision of pure and absolute propensity. She turned around smiled and flung her arms around his neck. He was taken aback at the fact that she hadn't even brought up the grotesque behaviors of the previous hours.

"I missed you so much," Darcy said.

"What?" He wondered if there was an angle and what it might be.

"I had the worst day, and seriously for a while I thought I was going crazy. I know how this sounds, but I met some guy and for a couple of minutes I swore..." she thought carefully about what she was about to say and the ramifications of sounding lunatic. "It's just, I never realized...never mind. I just really missed, you." She turned back in the direction of the window and pulled his arms around her, as he stood behind her, he swallowed hard and felt cascades of guilt and self loathing. He loved her more than he had known; revelation would not come to pass that night. There had to be another way and he was determined to find it. He placed his chin over her head and knew how unfair he was being. She deserved love in its purest and he had robbed her of it, just as he had been unjustly robbed of any chance at a life with her.

The next few days seemed to fly by for Darcy. She hung out with Clem and was able to steer clear of Mack Mackinnon. As she reached the end of the week, she was actually excited about her first weekend with her new friends. They had all made plans to check out some music from a local band in London and she was eager to see what the nightlife was like. Clem occupied most of her free time, as she seemed to have practically moved herself in to Darcy's house. Friday afternoon however, Clem had to run a couple of errands and instead of having her father send a large rather embarrassing car, she decided to walk home.

Jackson did everything he could to remain as covert as possible. He knew he had to be very careful without raising unwanted suspicions from anyone. The week dragged for him as everyday seemed to run longer and became more unnerving. Max had called Jackson about four times and in an attempt to keep him at bay, Jackson had finally agreed to go out with him on Friday night. Friday afternoon gave him a sense of false relief. Just as he had settled on the notion that he had gotten through the week without running into Darcy, he noticed a familiar figure walking down the road. His immediate desire to stop and grab her was difficult to subdue. She was wearing a long coat and knit hat, but she was still unmistakable. He reasoned with himself and drove by slowly leaving her unaware and hoping where ever her destination was that she was close. Jackson knew Darcy was tough and that she could take care of herself, but after a few minutes he had a need to make sure she was safe. He decided to double back and check if she was still walking. He was surprised that as he drove out of the private road leading up to Gidding's Hill, she was walking in. He panicked and wondered if she was on her way up to see him. Perhaps she still had doubts and had gotten his address from someone at the school, probably from that annoyingly nosy girl that had caused all this trouble to begin with. He thought about his options and decided to face her before she reached his place. Having her close to his house and especially near his family was too risky. He pulled the hood of his jacket over his head and put on his sunglasses.

Darcy had just reached the cobblestone road leading up to her house when she realized she still had a ways to go. She seriously thought about calling her dad to send a car. As she paused to check and make sure she still had some feeling left in her frozen hands, she saw a familiar car coming down the road and she moved over to let it by, surprisingly it stopped instead. The passenger window rolled down and she walked over, but still kept her distance.

"A little cold out to be stalking someone eh?" He asked in a snooty, unappealing tone.

"Stalking? Is that what this is? Shouldn't you sitting behind a bush somewhere with binoculars then?" Darcy tried her very best to sound annoyed.

"What me?! Shouldn't you, I mean clearly you're the one that seems to be seeking me out."

"That's the stupidest thing I've ever heard, what makes you think I'm "seeking" you out?" She did her best impression of him and he honestly couldn't help but laugh.

"Well, aren't you?"

"No." She started walking and he followed slowly in reverse.

"Then what are you doing here?"

"Where?"

"Here, Gidding's Hill."

"I live here," she said dryly.

"What live here, as in..."

"As in it is my home, where I live." She sounded crass and Jackson found it amusing, at the same time he felt his worlds collide and he knew he had to make sure she'd stay as far away from Mack as she could. He felt bad, but he was left no options, he'd be forced to be cruel and unbecoming.

"Well, then I guess that makes us neighbors."

"I guess so." Darcy stopped and walked towards the car, but the mortar had worn thin and as a rock let loose she tripped and scrapped her knee. He immediately felt the desire to run out and comfort her; keeping his composure was grueling, but necessary.

"I suppose a good neighbor would offer you a lift, you know in this cold weather and what with you being injured?" Darcy looked up at him and half smiled still unable to get to her feet. He bit down on his lip, "Unfortunately, I'm in a bit of a hurry, but enjoy the rest of your walk. Be more careful, oh, and that looks like it hurt, might want to put some ice on that." He gave her a half smile and drove off.

She wondered how she could have ever thought that he could be Jackson; he was so vile. She hobbled back to her house and decided to let her knee heal a little before making the journey up to her room. Her night hadn't even begun yet and already it had fermented. She was about to call Clem and back out of her night out when she heard her phone ringing; it was Amanda and Stacy. It had been a while since she'd heard from her friends; the eight hour time difference didn't help. When she hung up she realized how much she missed them and decided she needed a night out after all. Darcy had never really thought too much about fashion, but on her first night out in London she was a bit nervous. By the time she heard the honking out front she'd gone through several versions of herself in front of the mirror.

The streets of London were alive and for a brief moment Darcy felt as if she was dreaming. They parked the car and met up with a few of Clem's friends. "Mind ya eyes boys she's taken." Clem winked in her direction and although at first Darcy felt a little uncomfortable, they all seemed nice enough. They walked for a while until they reached a dark corner. "Well then, welcome to Plectrum." Clem sensed Darcy's nervousness, "come now it's hardly cause for butterflies just stale pints, hot sweaty blokes, and good music." Darcy smiled and they walked in.

… And One Night

Jackson got to Max's in a haze of annoyance and shame. He felt bad for Darcy but he knew he had to shake it off and act normal. He had never been to Max's place and he was pretty impressed. He must be good to have earned such luxuries. Jackson reminded himself what being good at what Max did really entailed and it send a shiver down his spine. "So what are we in for tonight eh?"

"Well, I met this chick and she seemed pretty cool. I told her we'd meet them up if that's okay?" Max asked a question he really didn't expect an answer to.

"Them?"

"Yeah she's got a couple of friends. I told you I'd hook you up," he winked at Jack.

"Right, friends, they've always got friends haven't they. I mean they travel in packs like dogs."

"Prey dude, more to pick off from right?" Max joked, but his choice in words made Jackson uneasy. With that they were off to conquer the night.

When they walked into the pub Jackson squinted his eyes through the darkness and smoke to be able to see where Max was going. Practically blind, he couldn't help it when it bumped into someone. He tried to focus and looked down and to his annoyance it was Clem. "Oh sorry excuse me."

Clem rolled her eyes, "yes well, watch where you're going next time eh." Then under her breath she mumbled "ya bloody bastard." Max over heard and turned back to see what had happened and she met his gaze. "Oh no, not you, sorry, I was talking to someone… excuse me." Max smiled and rolled his eyes. He was the most attractive person she'd ever seen and she couldn't help but wonder who he was.

Jackson wondered if Darcy hadn't gone out with Clem, but he lost her in the poor lighting. It wasn't very long before a tall statuesque blonde was hanging off Max's arm. "Jack this lovely woman is …"

"Hi I'm Ella and these are my friends Emily and Scarlett."

"Nice to meet you, I'm Jackson er Jack."

The five of them found a table and sat discommodiously as strangers often do. As the night progressed Max was more and more lost in a shallow and pretended conversation with Ella. Emily and Scarlett seemed to be putting their best efforts forward as they rivaled for Jackson's attention. Emily excused herself to take a call and Scarlett went in for the proverbial kill. "I love this band really, I think I'm gonna go upfront for a while, you want to come."

Seeing as his options were none he obliged and walked toward the stage carefully keeping his eyes focused to spot Clem. He hadn't really taken notice when the girl grabbed his hand as they were walking. Then he saw Darcy across the crowd. She was standing by the bar with a group of people, a couple of guys that he recognized seemed to be talking her up, but she was more focused on the music. He smiled when he realized how uninterested she seemed in any of them.

As he stared at her Scarlett seemed to be talking about everything and anything she could think of. Jackson felt bad that he could not keep his attention on her. Especially since she actually seemed like a genuinely nice person. He hadn't immediately noticed but she was attractive as well. Petite with light auburn hair that sat just below her shoulders, the name suited her. She spoke in a soft flowing voice and her face was luminous. She deserved better company, but he couldn't give up his alibi. He tried to refocus and looked up at the band. After a while he noticed the singer seemed to be preoccupied and when he followed his gaze and made out what it was he was staring at he became annoyed.

A couple of songs later their set ended and another band took the stage. Jackson noticed that as the singer made his way off the stage, he headed straight towards Darcy. He took Scarlet by the hand and she became excited. "I could use a drink, how bout you dear?" She nodded as he winked and made his way to the bar, where the guy had successfully struck up a conversation with Darcy.

"...so you really liked it then, you're not just trying to be nice are ya?" The eager musician subtly fished for approval.

"No, it was good, seriously, I like you're lyrics, they're," she paused and bit her lower lip as she searched for the right word and Jackson clenched his teeth. "sort of deep and ambiguous."

"Cool, that's kind of what I try to do, like get them to mean different things to different people. Well, are you gonna be around cause we have another set in a bit and I'd love to play you something," the musician kept on.

She was taking a sip of her drink when she was about to answer and with

Scarlett in tow Jackson discreetly yet purposely bumped into her sending the drink all down the front of her shirt. "Oh so sorry," it took Darcy a while to make out the voice. "Darcy right, excuse me, you really do have the worst luck don't you?" he laughed a little and walked up to order his drinks.

"Is she alright?" Scarlett asked as they started off.

"She's a bit clumsy is all, should have seen her fall earlier. Eh two pints please and perhaps some napkins for the young lady there. You really should be more careful."

Darcy grabbed a handful of napkins and turned to face Mack but he could not bring himself to look directly at her. "Oh hey are you alright then?" The musician interrupted before Darcy had a chance to respond to Mack.

"I'm fine thanks, sorry I…"

"Sorry? What are you apologizing for?" As he helped wipe some drops off her cheek, he smiled and it was clear the faux musician was smitten with her. Jackson was very annoyed.

"Hope you brought a jacket or a clean shirt, cause you're kind of…" Jackson sarcastically pointed out that her blouse was now transparent from the liquid gathering over her chest. "Unless, that's the look you were going for," he winked and playfully nudged he mystery frontman in the side with his elbow.

"Excuse me." She felt the color rise up to her face; humiliated she walked away and made her way to the ladies room. When Darcy finally reemerged, Clem saw how bummed out she looked and offered to take her home. Despite her embarrassing spill Darcy had enjoyed her night out and she was sure to let Clem know it. That night she was thrilled to see her Jackson.

Darcy walked past a pond and sat beneath a tree. As she put her hand to the ground she felt the crunching of moss beneath her fingers. Jack walked across the field with his hands in his pockets and a condemned look on his face. He stood next to where she sat and hung his head. "Is everything alright?"

"Yeah why?" he lied.

"Well, I don't know, usually you're happier to see me."

He sighed and she felt something inside her freeze over. He sat down next to her and placed his hand over her knee on the phantom gash. He knew that he should be able to see it or at least feel the broken skin beneath his hand. "Darcy?"

"Yes?"

"What are we doing?" He bit down on his lips. "Like I mean what am I doing?" He put his hands on his head and ran his fingers through his hair in frustration.

"I don't know what are you doing?" She had a vague feeling where the conversation was headed. "Are you like breaking up with me?"

"What no, but you see how absurd the notion is?" Darcy nodded. "I mean we're not even together, I mean you know not in the conventional way. All I'm doing is denying you."

"What are you talking about; what does that even mean? I love you, more than I… actually I've never loved anyone. Conventional or not and what, what are you denying me?"

"Everything take your pick, a life, a real life, affections, connections, your sanity, the truth." He buried his head in his hands.

She hesitated for a moment as she stared at him. "Really, what are you talking about? No one will ever love you like I do and do you honestly think anyone will love me…"

"Darcy, you're easy to love, trust me."

"Like you?" her voice trembled and he knew she was crying.

"No, no one will ever love you as much as I do. I promise."

"Then? Then why do you want to leave me?"

"I don't, I just don't want you to miss…"

"I wont, I can't miss anything if I have you Jackson please." She let go of all her restraint and knew she had to plead, to beg, to do anything to keep him.

He hated seeing that side of her, supplicating, lessened. "Darcy I could never leave you I swear it, but I want you to promise me that you'll never let me stand in your way." By this time they were both on their feet and she clung to him tightly. He looked down at her face and pressed his lips to hers.

Falling

The next few weeks Darcy saw less and less of Mack and she had settled into her new life. She had finally convinced her father to let her have a car and between Clem and Max she was finally making her way around on her own. Her father was going to Switzerland to a funeral for one of his business partners and her mother had decided she'd rather go to Paris for the weekend. Jeanette had been acting strangely and more enigmatic than usual. Darcy made sure to tell her as often as she could how much she loved her before she left. That was the only thing Darcy ever felt she could offer up to her parents. As little as she saw them, and as disagreeable as they could be, she always made sure they knew how she felt. She knew she had a tendency to be closed off emotionally, but she needed them to know. With her parents away, Clem had taken it upon her self to throw a party at Darcy's house and in exchange Clem had to take Darcy out for pizza. They ended up at the parlor near Max's house as it had quickly become one of Darcy's favorites as well. They walked in and ordered. "Oh my god it's him." Clem quickly grabbed a napkin and wiped her chin.

"Who?"

"The guy, remember, at the pub, the one I told you about?"

"Oh, the man of your dreams, so go talk to him," Darcy responded in an annoyingly disinterested tone. Clem rolled her eyes and gave her an inquisitive look. "Go, maybe its fate."

"Ugh but he's here with our favorite person." Darcy didn't want to turn back and see Mack. Her day had been going so well, and he still made her feel stupid whenever he was around. They finished up their pizza and headed to the cashier.

Jackson hadn't noticed Darcy pass, but he found it strange when Max excused himself so suddenly. Max went up to the counter and caught Darcy off guard.

"Hey, Darce," she turned to face him, smiled and gave him a hug. Clem nearly stopped breathing.

"Max, what are doing here?" She asked rhetorically.

"Really, that's your best opener? Makes you sound kinda dumb," he said playfully.

Clem elbowed her. "Oh Max this is Clem, Clem, Max." He shot her a smile and nodded knowingly.

"So you're still going to be alone for the next couple of days?" Max asked somewhat concerned.

"Well, actually Clem is going to stay with me tonight."

"Great, but what about tomorrow?" Darcy gave him an inquisitive look. "Expect you around 8ish?" He rolled his eyes sarcastically and she smiled. She wondered why he was being so high spirited.

"You here alone?" Darcy asked suggestively half expecting to find him the company of a lady friend.

"No, I'm here with a friend; Well actually it's…"

"We know Mack," Clem interrupted rather loudly.

"Oh right, Mack." He had forgotten about "Mack". All three of them looked in Mack's direction and he looked up at the mention of his name. That's when he saw Darcy. His eyes widened in horror when he saw her talking to Max. His breath became shallow and he struggled to keep from hyperventilating. Darcy seemed to be the only one to notice his reaction and for a brief moment she swore she saw Jack again. Max studied Darcy's face, "not your favorite person?"

Darcy took in a deep ineffective breath, "well, something like that."

"No that's basically it," added Clem. Max shrugged his shoulders and as the girls excused themselves he headed back toward his table.

When Max returned to the table Jackson hid his shaky hands in his lap. "How do you know that girl?"

"Who Darcy? Oh she's a friend." Impossible, Jackson knew all too well the types of relationships Max had with girls and friendship was never one. He gave him a suspicious look with hints of resentment. "No really," Max giggled, "I know what you're thinking, but it's not like that with her. She really is just a friend. The only girl I've ever had as a friend, it's weird for me too."

"But you'd want more?"

"With Darcy, no, she's different. I feel like protective of her, she… its just different." Jackson gave him a look of doubt. "Dude she's slept in my bed and shit and I swear I never even wanted to try anything." Jackson felt the contents of his stomach rising up his throat. It was so much worse than he thought. He was the guy Darcy had told him about. He clenched his teeth almost to the point of breaking. "Why how do you now her?" Max asked, interrupting Jackson's inner monologue.

"School," the word screeched out of his mouth. "So, how'd did you even meet her, I mean she's like younger and she lives way out."

"I know, it's your fault actually, so thanks." He gave a malicious grin and Jackson furrowed his brow. "Yeah, I went off looking for you on New Years Eve and she was there alone so we got together and just went from there. Why, you like her or what?" The idea gave Max a weird feeling. If anyone should be with Darcy, Jack was the best choice. Not only was he his best friend, but as well he was genuinely a good guy. However, Max knew that he would never allow Darcy to be with someone like them, where a future was impossible, where the risks were too high, but under normal circumstances, Jackson would have been ideal.

Clem walked down to Darcy's car in an elated state of mind. Something inside her was turned on she couldn't concentrate; everything about Max was burned into her. It was a brand she feared would remain etched into her insides. She had felt it the first time she saw him but now, it had amplified and she knew that her only hope for remedy was to have him anyway she could. She looked to Darcy in desperation "well?"

"Well?" Clem rolled her eyes. "Oh my god it was Max. Max was the guy! Max was the guy?" The word flew out of Darcy's mouth, but she wasn't really sure why she was so surprised.

Clem slid into Darcy's seat "yes and I want him. Like as in I really want him." She whined and looked over to Darcy.

"What?" Darcy asked, still wondering why she was so surprised.

"Please, you have to help me."

"How, what do you think I can do or what? I mean I will, do whatever I can, but seriously what?"

"I don't know put in a word or invite him tonight or something, anything." Clem would not let him get away so easily.

"Okay, I'll try, but I don't really think he wants to hang out with a bunch of kids." Darcy had no reservations about the possibility of Clem and Max, but she had a feeling she wasn't right for him and equally she didn't want Clem to get hurt.

Jackson was relieved when he overheard Max turn down Darcy's invitation over the phone. It was too late though, conclusively and unrelenting destiny had defeated him. He knew it was time to let her go. He had no choice. The idea of Darcy being anywhere near a brute like Max was unbearable. But he knew that if it was true Max could keep Darcy safe, he could keep track of Max and with that he could still watch over Darcy. Jackson did his very best to keep his composure while Max was still around. "You okay?" Max asked as they walked out.

"Oh yeah, why?"

"You just got quiet. Shit man, I forgot everyone calls you Mack. No offense but that's a pretty shitty nickname."

"Yeah no I agree with you there. It's not very appealing to me either, but it just kinda stuck you know?"

"Oh and man I don't know what you did to that other Clem chick, but I don't think she likes you." Jackson just shrugged his shoulders. "So, you going to that party at your neighbor's then?"

"Party? Um nah I actually I have a date," Jackson lied badly. "What about you?"

"Hell no, I can take hanging out with Darce, but not like a whole bunch of kids dude."

The fact that he had a pet name for Darcy rubbed Jackson the wrong way. "Kids," Jackson chuckled, "you're like a year older than me mate."

"Whatever man, have a good time and take it easy. Call you later in the week alright."

Jackson got home that night and lay on his bed. He thought about all the time he had spent with Darcy. About how he had seen her grow over the years, about how beautiful she was and about how much he was going to miss her. He knew Jackson would never see Darcy again and in a couple of months when school was over, he'd move and she'd never have to run into Mack either. The thought killed him. Outside his window he could hear the commotion from Darcy's house. It made him smile to think she was having a good time; she deserved that much but as he looked out the window, an angelic figure in the courtyard caught his eye. There she was, sitting alone on a wooden bench, staring up at the sky. As he watched, she looked just as she had in all her dreams, and he wished he could run over and take her as he often did, but this time with every sensation his body would allow him. He watched a little longer until someone came out and called her in, as she got up to walk in after them, she looked up at his window and although she didn't see him, he knew he would never see her look at him with the love and absolute affection she did in her dreams. The light inside him burned out.

Darcy walked through, down the coble stone road with a smile and a stride that carried her lightly over to the familiar house. She stood at the entrance and looked back in anticipation. It had been a week since she'd last seen Jackson and although she was starting to worry, she knew he'd be there that night, he had to be. After a couple of minutes a cold breeze shot through the air and carried with it the scent of decay. Darcy went into the house in an attempt to escape it. When she walked in, she was shocked, all the furniture in the house was gone and as she looked around it looked more defunct than usual. She got a stale feeling in the pit of her stomach and ran out to the courtyard. As she looked out, everything had disappeared. The ground where she stood was cold, stale cement and as she looked around all she saw was the endless pallid grey sheet. She turned back toward the house and it was gone. There was nothing left, no trace of the bench she had shared with Jackson dozens of times or the ground where she swayed in his arms the first time he professed his love. Then the affirmation that he was gone knocked her to her knees. She buried her head in her hands and wept.

No Long Goodbye

The next morning her eyes refused to open. She knew if she opened them it was only going to bring forth what had already happened. She sat at the edge of her bed and pushed her hands over her eyes. She felt numb; she lay back onto her bed and tried to shake off the pictures that flashed continuously in her head. After about an hour, as she was about to stand up, a rush of nausea came over her and she ran down to the restroom. She slinked to the floor and rested her forehead on her forearms clutched tightly around the cold porcelain. Suddenly an intense and inexplicable fear overwhelmed her. She felt her heart race and an ache in her chest. She felt the need to stand up and rush out of the house. She stood looking down the road, trying to catch her breath and searching in desperation for directions to a nonexistent path that might lead her to Jackson.

Daniel was not thrilled with the fact that Darcy spent the rest of the weekend in her room. He knew that if she didn't come out for school on Monday, he was going to have to intervene. Darcy wanted nothing more than to sleep. She tried to sleep as long as she could. When Clem called her on Saturday night, Darcy told her she had a cold and would call her back when she felt better. By Monday morning, her whole body ached and the effects of her self-induced coma were visible on her face. She really didn't feel like interacting with anyone, but she didn't have the energy to deal with her father. When she walked into class on Monday Clem noticed the dark circles that shadowed her crimson coated eyes.

"pst Darcy," she whispered "are you okay? You really look like shite."

"I'm fine I just haven't been feeling well."

"Well, pull yourself together girl, we've got a week and a half left before extended leave." Clem was quieted down by a symphony of shushing.

"Hmm?"

"Yeah, after next Thursday we have a week off and you can't be sick because I've made plans." Clem winked as she spoke in a not so quiet whisper. Darcy let show a cracked smile.

The next couple of days were mechanical. When she got back to her house on Wednesday afternoon, she sat at the edge of her bed and ran through her previous encounters with Jack. He was gone and as she recalled from her youth it could have been years before she saw him or she might never see him again. So many questions had been left unanswered but one in particular pulled at her insides "Why had he left her?" The desperation and longing she felt manifested into a dark physical yearning. She sighed and took solace in the fact that she had just one more week of school, then, she'd have a break. She knew she needed to get away so she began making plans to go home and visit her friends. She felt bad for Clem, but she needed an escape. Just as she felt the hot tears sting at the corners of her eyes, which were already raw from the corroding saline that had made it's way down nights before, she heard the door bell ring.

The house keeper called up to her, but she felt too nauseous to respond. She figured after a few minutes whoever it was would just go, but then she heard loud footsteps thudding up the stairs followed by small taps quickly behind. Suddenly her door flung open and she laughed when she saw Max trying to walk and reason with the housekeeper at the same time. She was a tall thin foreign woman that Darcy made it a point not to get to know, mostly for fear that she was defiling the memory of her old housekeeper.

"It's okay he's my friend," she said as she sat up.

"Wow, I guess I don't have to worry about you being here alone. You have one mean guard dog and she's not too easy on the eyes either."

"Don't be mean." He hadn't really noticed it right off, but there was something different about her. She was still as beautiful as ever, but her eyes looked worn and when she stood up to hug him, he noticed her shoulders were drawn in.

"Everything okay?" A weird, inconveniently unfamiliar feeling stirred within him. She stared up at him and he noticed through her broken smile that her lips were shivering. What, if anything, could ever be so cruel as to make something so beautiful so sad, he wondered.

"Yeah, I just..." he gave her a doubtful expression and admitting defeat, she hung her head and began to cry. She was amazed that she was still able to even produce tears. She flung her arms around his neck and buried her head in his chest. Darcy had hugged him before and once she had kissed him lightly on the check, but he never returned her affections. Max's kisses and embraces were hollow and meaningless and he never wanted to deceive Darcy the way he deceived most of the women he shared them with, but this time it was different. This time it didn't feel obligatory, something inside him wanted to take her in his arms and comfort her, the thought made him uneasy but without hesitation he swallowed hard enough that she heard and cradled her gently in his arms. His insides came alive for a few brief moments.

"What does that feel like?" he spoke as he pulled back after a few minutes.

"What," she asked as she sniffled and lifted her hand to wipe her eye.

He caught the tear under his thumb before she could and she smiled. "Crying, I can't remember ever crying, but girls cry all the time." It was true; crying was usually brought on by feelings of loss, sorrow, guilt, anger, elation, which were all a result of love, a sentiment Max never held.

"Wet, and embarrassing," Max chuckled, "but relieving. I feel stupid because I do cry for everything, but sometimes I feel like if I don't, my heart might burst." She went over and sat on her bed and he walked over to the windows.

"Wow, when the sun goes down, they really look amazing." Darcy nodded in agreement. Max never asked her why she was crying and although she thought it was a bit strange, she didn't mind so much, because she would not be able to offer him the truth. Max knew he was better off not knowing, because temptation was something he knew not of, if Max got an urge to do something, he just did it without care or consequence.

"Want to watch a movie?" Darcy felt a shift in the friendship and she just wanted to feel slightly familiar again. He smiled and nodded. "Max," she looked up him "will you stay with me?"

He looked at her perplexed "on a Wednesday?"

"Please, I'll wake you up early and you won't be late, besides I have to be up for school also." Max still had a way of making her feel comfortable and her body needed it.

"...and your parents?"

"My mom's still in Paris and my dad usually stays in the city during the week, please, I just feel so crappy." He breathed deeply and shook his head in opposition to the words that seem to automatically escape his lips...

"It's so unfair that you use that eye thing against me. Make me feel bad." Darcy smiled victoriously and ran over to put on a movie. She figured with Max around she might be able to tolerate the night.

Jackson pulled into the circular drive way and before he turned in for the night, walked over to make sure the Whitten house was secure. He never went in or even let himself be seen, but it was his way of still keeping Darcy safe. He often walked around her house to make sure all was well especially when she was alone. It was a sorry attempt at making up for hurting her the way he had. When he rounded the corner of the house he was stunned to see an all too familiar car in the Whitten drive. He felt his teeth clench when he saw Max was there. He walked up to his room and looked out the window. After seeing Clem hang her head out for cigarette breaks on several occasions, he gathered that Darcy's room was on the third floor. He looked up and saw a faint flickering coming from the windows and he wondered. How could someone like Darcy see anything in something like Max? He lay back in his bed and thought about the conversation he had had with Darcy when she first met Max. Max had preyed on Darcy's sentimental nature and Jackson hated him for that. Then he reminded himself that Max was an unknowing pawn in the twisted existence he had created.

Max was so cold, there was hardly anything human about him, but when he spoke about Darcy, Jack noticed something inside him seemed to reanimate. How could it not? Jack closed his eyes and tried desperately to avert his thoughts.

Darcy hadn't even remembered falling asleep, but as she walked through the market place it seemed everything was moving slower than normal. The people seemed happier than usual and a serene ambiance provided the rhythm for the pace. She felt a breeze blow through the streets, and as she walked on, it progressed to a windy day. She stuck her hands in her pockets and felt something cool and plastic under her fingers; it was her I pod. She put it on and realized it was only uploaded with one song, but it was one of her favorites so she let it play on as she kept walking.

Jackson was well aware he would not be sleeping that night. Every second dragged on endlessly and minutes seemed like hours. Every time Jackson peeked out he hoped the car would finally have gone and he could relax. When he finally saw the lights die down through the bedroom window, he felt his heart sink into the pit of his stomach. As the clock read 2:30am and after taking one last glance out the window, Jackson succumbed to desperation from deep within him and without thinking he closed his eyes and drifted.

When Jackson entered in he smiled when he saw the market place. It had only been a little over a week, since he'd last visited Darcy under those circumstances, but he truly had missed spending time with her in her thoughts. It was the only place they were both at their most pure, no pretenses, no influences, just them unscripted, raw. Also, the idea of having a place that was just theirs made it easier to feel normal for Jackson. He walked on and as he came to a familiar figure, his heart sank. There she was, standing before a girl sitting on a stool behind a stand covered in dolls. She had the most engaged look in her eyes as she stared at the girl. He knew he'd hurt her and that the damage was irreparable. He was afraid; by now she'd probably be upset with him, rightfully so. He didn't want to shake her from her serenity so he called out her name, but she didn't so much as flinch and as he walked closer he noticed her ear buds were in place. He had never encountered someone who could disconnect like she had a tendency to, but then again there was a lot Darcy could manage. It gave him a second chance to stand back and consider what he as about to do; he could only imagine what she had been through in the past couple of days. What he had put her through, what he would stir up in her all over again. He decided to let go of his selfish ambitions and leave her alone. He turned and began to walk away.

Darcy felt the shift in atmosphere and a doubtful, yet unrelenting hope infused her. Then the little girl looked up and smiled at her. Confused Darcy looked back over her shoulder, but there was no one there. She returned her attention to the girl who was still fixated on her. Then the girl looked past Darcy and winked, when Darcy followed her gaze, her heart made its way to her stomach. He walking away, but by now he was unmistakable. "Jackson!" she screamed with every breath she could summon. "Jackson wait!" She started after him. He stopped and took a deep breath, he turned to face her with a pained look on his face and as he saw the pleading agony in her eyes, he turned and was gone. "Just wait, please…"

Darcy sat up in the dark with tear streaming down her face. Just as she felt her heart race and a rush of anxiety sweep over, someone grabbed her shoulder.

"Shh, shh, lay back, you're having a bad dream. It's okay." She focused her eyes and remembered it was Max. He leaned his back against the backboard of her bed and cradled her head against his chest. "I'm right here, I'm here." Darcy closed her eyes and as her breathing became labored. Max felt grateful. Once her breathing became more rhythmic, he was careful to place her head back on her pillow. He walked over to the window and as he looked out his throat tightened. He couldn't understand or make any sense of how or why it happened. Max looked back at Darcy sleeping so peaceful and painfully unaware and it made him angry. His own affections for Darcy were still alien to him.

She was beautiful and earlier in the night when she shifted in her sleep her t-shirt was folded over exposing her bare stomach and the bottom portion of her breast. It was a sight that would have enticed any man, but instead Max's usual dissolute instead gave way to affection. He too had noticed that rather than remaining fixated on the seemingly perfect contours of her body or the flawlessness of her skin as he half expected to be, he immediately proceeded to gently roll it back down. He still had to clutch the cotton tight within his fingers to keep his finger from brushing her skin, but he had no idea why he felt to the need to keep her covered, shielded, protected.

Max snuck out at around 5:30am and left Darcy still half sleeping. He stepped out the front door into the bruised sky and lit a cigarette. He walked down to his car and was startled to see someone standing by it. "Holy fuck, you scared me." Jackson nodded and swallowed hard. Max saw the look of spite in his eyes and he felt a strange wave of guilt and despise.

"Nice night?" Jackson asked sardonically as he cocked his head to one side and raised his eyebrow.

Max handed him a cigarette. "Nice enough I guess." It took Max a while to divert his gaze from the cold stare Jackson was giving him. "Why do you ask?"

"No reason," Jackson's voice trembled when he spoke and Max felt empathetic.

"Everything alright man, you seem…weird. Hey, why are you even up this early anyway?" As the words and smoke simultaneously cascaded out of Max's mouth, Jackson's distaste grew.

"Couldn't sleep," he let his tone fall a little.

Jackson noticed Max's jawbone flicker as he clenched his teeth. They both stood in a moment of awkward silence, until Max threw down the remnants of his cigarette. "Well, I have to get going..." he turned to get into his car.

"I just..." he rubbed his head methodically, "you and Darcy eh?" Jackson managed to crack a smirk.

"Oh," he managed rubbing his eyes that now burned from lack of sleep "um nah wasn't like that, she just needed, she doesn't like to be alone so..." He wondered if he should've lead on that it might have been a possibility, but he decided against it.

Inside Jackson felt a helplessness that had never been there before. He had never had the unrelenting desire to cause someone physical pain as he did there before Max. He hated that Max got to have her in any respect that was normal. He'd stayed because she needed him and that was still bad enough. "Very cool of you," he said as he winked.

"Dude, shut up," he chuckled "call you later. We're still on for this weekend," he shouted from his car. Jack nodded and rolled his eyes.

Jackson looked up at Darcy's window and leaned against the wall of his home. As he was getting lost in thought he looked up again and saw a pair of unmistakably striking eyes looking down at him. He panicked and averted his eyes down and ran in to get his keys. Darcy caught Mack looking up at her window and something inside her stirred. She grabbed her jacket and ran down. By the time she reached the door Jackson was practically at his car. She felt the icy floor beneath her feet and felt a shiver run deep up her spine. He looked up at her for a half a second and climbed in the cab. "Wait..." she reminded herself to remain composed.

"What the hell, are you insane? Do you have a death wish; it's freezing out here," she couldn't tell if it was genuine concern or annoyance.

"Wait, I just want to talk..." her voice was shaking and he could tell she was on the verge of tears or perhaps she really was freezing.

"Maybe later, I've got to be off." He looked back and began reversing.

Darcy and Daniel: Parting is such sorrow

Defeated she walked back into her house. Just as she came down for school, she was surprised to see her father at in the kitchen. "Ddad, wow, you scared me, what are you doing here so early?" He gave her a look she had never seen before and at first she panicked when she thought that he might have seen Max leave and gotten the wrong idea, but then as she gave him a second glance she realized that it was a face that could only have been brought on by pure dysphoria. "Dad, what is it, what's wrong? Did something happen?" Daniel could not speak for fear that he might choke on his words. "You're starting to freak me out. What is it?!" As tears made their way down his face, her worst fears were realized. She had never seen her father cry and figured it had to be the worst thing she could ever imagine. "Did someone ddie? Oh no, Grandma." Darcy put her hand over her mouth and as the tears began to build up in her face, Daniel finally spoke out of necessity.

"No Darcy, not grandma." Darcy looked up at her father and something inside her knew.

"No dad, no." Daniel reached over and took her. "No dad," she cried and he felt every bone in his body turn to stone. "No, not my mom, I need her dad," they both fell to the floor. "I need my mom."

The next few days felt as they went on without her; she watched from a distance like her dreams used to feel. The service was private and held in France. Due to the nature of her mother's self-inflicted travesty, Daniel, made sure it was as tasteful and discrete as possible. Darcy found it ironic that her mother had always promised her a trip to France, and she had finally fulfilled her commitment. It was one of those places she'd always wanted to see, but she knew she'd never want to go back. There were many strangers around claiming to be related to her and claiming to be at her emotional service. "Where were you before…" she couldn't help but wonder. She never spoke to anyone; she didn't care to or she didn't want to care.

Daniel knew Darcy's grief had given way to an even deeper anger when she found out that Jeanette's death had not been accidental, so he wasn't too surprised when she told him she wanted to be home as soon as possible. The problem was that nothing felt like home to Darcy anymore. However, when they reached Gidding's Hill, they both felt a small sense of relief.

The days bled over and Darcy had been having troubled nights. By Sunday night, her dreams started becoming more and more erratic and disturbing.

She never saw Jackson, but faint whispers of his name would shoot through the conversations around her and every once in a while she could see her mother walking through the crowd, but she could never reach her. She had lost control of her own thoughts and felt like she was starting to go insane. Monday morning arrived with deciduous anticipation.

After getting dressed she stared at herself in the mirror, she came to the conclusion that she couldn't take anymore. Her insides ached like nothing she'd ever felt before, she knew her mother would always be with her one way or another, but decided to do everything she could to forget about Jackson. She would not sleep until she was sure she would never see or think of him again. She went to school that morning in a state of unwillingness. Daniel was going back to work, but he told Darcy she could stay home for as long as she needed to. She didn't want to displease her father but more so, she was starting to feel more and more lost and she didn't want him asking any questions. She did her best to avoid everyone and Clem figured she was still mourning, as the effects were still visible on her face.

That night didn't prove too trying, she spent most of the night chatting with her friends back in the States thanks to the merciful difference in time. They were good at keeping Darcy's mind as far away from her mother as possible. They knew her well enough that there were no apologies, no pity, no emotional inquisitions. When the sun kissed the sky that morning, she was worn, but amazed that she was still functioning. Wednesday night was far more difficult, she found herself nodding off in bits, but was still able to steer herself to a state of consciousness. In the moments that sleep would pull her in, she would see her mother's face beautifully sad and distorted. She had to force herself to find relief in vigilance. That morning, she could seriously feel the physical effects and was thankful that all she had to do was get through one day and then she had an extended leave for a week.

Unaware as to whether or not it was another side effect of the sleep deprivation, when she saw Clem in the parking lot on Thursday morning she felt unusually chipper. "Hey Darcy, look at you all peppy this morning. What's going on eh, something good, did you get laid, is it drugs?" Darcy rolled her eyes. "Stop smiling then it's annoying so early." Clem giggled. "Well, as your best mate I have to tell you, you still look like utter crap, but

I'm glad to see you at least resemble a human being now." She hugged her and Darcy felt glad to have a physical connection to humanity.

Darcy noticed a large parade of students making their way down to Cummings Hall and this made her feel even better. "Is there an assembly today?"

"Mmm hmm, mid point, need to make sure we're still thriving and such. Thank god because I've got a serious hankering for food about now and I don't think I could have made it through an entire morning of sessions."

They walked in and sat at the back with a couple of friends. As Darcy was trying her best to pay attention to one of the guys next to her enthusiastically telling her about his vacations to America she couldn't help but overhear Clem whispering to another friend, "ooh yummy." She looked up and saw Mack slide into a bench nearby and as Clem caught Darcy's eyes she quickly mouthed "oh sorry I mean blah," and Darcy couldn't help but chuckle when Clem made a motion as if she were throwing up and the boy became annoyed with Darcy. During the speeches, Darcy could feel her eyes growing heavier and she knew at any moment she could simply pass out.

Jackson sat as uncomfortably as he usually did now that he knew Darcy was around. Jackson was looking forward to this extended leave as much as anyone. He was feeling worse everyday and he needed to just lock himself in for a week or so. He was drifting off in his own thoughts when he felt someone squeeze his thigh. He looked over and Leila, a girl with whom he had become very familiar during his first year in secondary leaned into his ear.

"Careful, if they catch you day dreaming, I'm sure there will be wicked consequences." As she tried to make her voice sound soft and suggestive, it just came off as bothersome. He smiled politely and averted his attention to the front; she however did not find it necessary to remove her hand from his leg. He looked over and spotted Darcy, he hadn't realized how close she was and he could see her perfectly. It was still inexpressively hard to see her. His longing was almost as unbearable as hers was, she was wonderfully lucid, but he also couldn't help to notice the dark circles that had taken up residency beneath her eyes. He felt awful, but he couldn't peel his eyes away from her.

After a couple of minutes Darcy got the strangest feeling and looked over in his direction. She met Mack Mackinnon's eyes and it was the first time he did not look away, she smiled at him and as he returned the smile, it was not with the sly connotation his smiles were usually laced with. It seemed genuine. They held gazes until she noticed the hand on his thigh, then she rolled her eyes as she shook her head and turned to look forward. Jackson suddenly realized what had transpired and sat up quickly prying Leila's fingers from his leg.

As the procession made its way into the courtyard, Darcy felt queasy, her vision had somewhat doubled and her head was throbbing. She excused herself as quickly as she could and told Clem she was going home to change and she'd meet them up later. She walked as quickly as she could to her car without arousing suspicions. By the time she'd reached her car, Jackson was in his. He watched her fumble for her keys and get into her car. Something told him that she wasn't necessarily okay. She sat for her few minutes with the ignition running, folded her arms over the steering wheel and rested her head on her hands. After a few seconds she put her car in drive and drove off. Jackson decided to follow behind her and make sure she got home okay.

Darcy opened her eyes wide as she tried to hold on to the pattern of the road. She could feel the heaviness on her eyelids and her focus fading. She turned the music up and switched the heater on to the highest setting to try and make her self as uncomfortable as possible. It was no use; her body was fighting her and succeeding. She heard a loud honking and realized her eyes were closed. She quickly jerked up and by the time she was able to refocus ahead, it was too late.

It took Jackson a while to figure out what exactly was happening. When he saw Darcy's tire make its way off the road, all he could do was honk madly and hope she'd react, but as he saw her car hit the tree, he felt his heart burst.

Darcy tired to take in a deep breath, but she felt compressed. She looked around and in a haze made out the scene. She immediately felt the impact take its toll on her body, and she thought of how people always said they couldn't feel the pain until later, they were so wrong. Everything seemed to be going in slow motion; she examined her body and all her limbs were still attached. She could hear ringing in her ears that began to give way to a faint tapping. She turned and through blurred vision she saw Jack, no it was Mack, staring in at her.

"Darcy, are you all right?"

"I'm stuck," she was speaking as loud as she could, but somehow it only came out a faint whisper. He went around the passenger's side, thankful she was alive and as he could hear the sirens in the distance he pulled her out of the car. She kept coming in and out of consciousness, unsure if it was a product of the accident or if she was just tired. He held her and although it was the moment he'd been dreaming about, he was so preoccupied he couldn't focus on what was happening. He could see her fighting to sit up.

"It's okay, relax, I've got you. You're gonna be okay."

"Don't…" he looked down at her as he cradled her in his lap. "I don't want to fall asleep."

He swallowed hard in an attempt to pass the guilt down his throat. The ambulance arrived and he waited patiently while they secured her inside and climbed in with her. On route he heard the tech say that she needed to relax. He leaned over to her ear, tried to cut back as much as he could on his accent and whispered in her ear. "Darcy, please, just sleep, I'm right here, I won't let anything happen to you." He pressed his hand to her face and saw a tear roll down her eyes as they were pressed shut.

"Ja…" in a few seconds she was out.

He looked up at the EMT with traces of guilt still lodged in his throat. Jackson called his father from the hospital and made sure Mr. Whitten knew what had happened. He never went in to see her, but he waited until he knew she was going to be okay. He heard the diagnosis, the injuries she suffered from the accident had been minor, but she was suffering from severe exhaustion. On the drive home the culpability was immense as he knew he was probably the reason Darcy hadn't been sleeping. The fact that he might have blown his cover didn't even bother him anymore. His only concern was her safety and he knew he wanted to be with her at whatever cost. He could keep her safe somehow, but he couldn't live without her and she shouldn't have to either.

Clouded Clarity

On Friday she woke up in a fog but with a new perspective on things. She thought hard about everything that had happened. As she tugged at the IV cord in irritation, she studied the fluids that were entering her body unnaturally and thought about what Jackson had said about her veins and smiled; then a flash of her mother interrupted the thought. She remembered studying her as she lay in her casket, thinking how beautiful she looked. Wondering how someone so beautiful could have such ugly intentions, she noticed the thick flesh colored paste that surrounded her wrists, and as she closed her eyes she imagined the flush of life spilling out from underneath the made over slits in her mother's wrist and the paradox that resulted from the rosary she clutched in the same hands that had committed the worse of all sin. It was a moment she never wanted to remember, but she knew she could never forget; kneeling beside her mother's lifeless corpse in a wooden box, waiting, secretly hoping she might sit up and the infusion of flowers and chemicals that surrounded her. Darcy would never again be able to appreciate or even stand the smell of fresh flowers.

Darcy quickly dismissed all thoughts of her mother and refocused on her own wrist. She could only remember bits and pieces from the accident, but she did remember Mack. She smiled at the thought and realized that she'd been so stupid. She thought about how insane she'd probably been acting, how absurd the entire Jackson thing was, she knew everything would change. It was no wonder the poor boy tried his best to keep away the crazy girl. The thought amused her a little.

When Jackson awoke on Friday morning, he felt unbalanced. He turned over and noticed it was half past eleven. He couldn't remember the last time he'd slept in, he also couldn't remember the last time he had slept with out having to cross over for business or personal reasons. He could feel his head throbbing at the temples and the emotional exhaustion of the events from the day before made his stomach uneasy. He heard a knock at his bedroom door and jumped up, startled for no reason. "Jackson dear," it was his mother, "are you up?"

"Umm," he rubbed his eyes, "more or less."

"Great, I've made some sandwiches and when you're done, your father needs you."

He opened the door and poked his head out. "Erm, I'm not really hungry, I'm feeling a bit dodgy actually, but give me a couple of minutes and I'll be down."

When he reemerged still shaky, his father asked him to run an errand Mr. Whitten had requested. Apparently the housekeeper, Anne, had packed a bag for Darcy and he asked Mr. Mackinnon to please have it sent over to the hospital. Mr. Mackinnon was never thrilled at the notion of having Jackson home with nothing to do; he didn't believe in school breaks, because he figured in the real world they were so keenly being prepped for, there was no such animal. Jackson made it a point to never have to deal with his father, as their relationship had always been vacuous of any kind of emotional connection. Jackson grimaced at the idea, but figured he'd rather face his own emotional anguish from possibly seeing Darcy, than face his father's reaction to being refused.

Jackson ran back in to change his shirt and grab his jacket when on his way out he was stopped by his mother.

"Jackson dear, are you going over to see the Whitten girl?"

"Darcy mum, and I don't believe I have much choice in the matter."

"No, I suppose not," she stared down at her feet. "Poor girl, I don't believe she'll ever recover."

"The doctors said she'd be fine…"

"Oh no sweetheart, I mean you know the emotional aspect of it all. Losing her mother the way she did, and now this."

"What, her mother? Wha…"

"Oh you hadn't heard?" Jackson nodded and wondered what he could have missed. "Apparently she" it pained her to say it and her voice dropped two octaves lower and she clutched tightly to the crucifix around her neck, "took her own life a couple of days ago. The poor…" She kept on nervously, but Jackson had drowned out the sound of her voice, only barely audible faint muffles seem to graze his ears. He couldn't believe it. He felt even worse for everything Darcy had had to go through and worse that he hadn't been there to comfort her.

Jackson made his way to the Whitten house in a pensive state. He hadn't been inside the main house since he was a boy, when the Grandes still resided there. Mr. and Mrs. Grande had lived there for as long as he could remember and that was also how long he could remember them being old. They had never had children of their own and often invited Jack over to do odd jobs or just keep them company. Anne had also been with the Grandes for a couple of years and now she was working for the Whittens. She was Polish and it took some time for Jackson to easily interpret what she was saying. He rang the doorbell and stood there discomposed. "Yackson," he smiled at her accent, "come, go up, the bag is on bed." He walked in and followed her to the stairs and she held up her hand expressing the number three. The third floor, Darcy's room, he felt nervous all of a sudden, even though she wasn't in there, it was still a little too close for comfort. He looked at Anne.

"Couldn't you maybe fetch it for me and then I'll just..."

She smiled, "you big boy, you go and get." She winked and waved him off like one might a puppy and walked away. Jackson looked up at the stairs and began laboriously up them. When he got to the next set, he swallowed hard and continued.

When he walked into Darcy's room the first thing he noticed was the smell. Her scent lingered and it was the most inviting scent. He felt his breathing become shallow as he walked through her room, it felt wrong like he was invading her privacy, but at the same time, he'd missed her so much any piece of her was appeasing. He noticed the windows and he flashed back to his youth. He remembered Mrs.Grande meticulously and passionately painting each one. It took her all of two months to complete them. She sat with a big art book, duplicating each one and she asked him to choose one and he remembered flipping through the book until he came upon one that caught his attention the most. He was glad to see that Darcy hadn't done away with them, but then again, it made sense that she wouldn't. As he stopped to admire his artistic contribution, he smiled at the fact that she slept over Darcy's bed. He ran his hand over Darcy's pillow, bent down, and kissed it gently. Whenever she put her head down on it, his kiss would grace her cheek. He grabbed the bag and walked out of the room.

When he walked into the hospital he got chills. The thought of disease just reminded him of the frailty and ephemeral state of the human body. He thought about looking in on Darcy, but he knew it was a bad idea. He walked over to the nurse's station and asked how she was doing. After the reassurance, he left her bag and as he turned to walk away, he caught a glimpse of her through the half opened door of her room. She must have heard him talking because she was looking right at him and she mouthed out a thank you and smiled. He returned the smile and walked away with a weight on his heart. He also noted that she no longer looked at him with the hint of suspicion she usually did.

Darcy had heard the familiar thick accented voice, and although she initially believed she might be hallucinating, when she heard her name she sat up in curiosity. Mack had gone, probably on her father's urging to leave her things. She had no recollection of what transpired in the ambulance, but she recalled him coming to her rescue at the scene. She felt stupid for having misjudged him. Maybe he wasn't a bad guy. Thinking back on how weird she had acted during their first meeting, it was no wonder he was avoiding her. He must have thought her a lunatic, and she probably was. That night she still hurt for Jackson, but she fell asleep amid her tears and with a new sense of sentience.

Darcy walked through the neighborhood in amazement. The houses were beautiful. It was a place she'd never been and she appreciated the change in scenery. As she walked further along admiring the cherry blossoms that surrounded the pathway, a shift in atmosphere broke her tranquility. It was almost like the change she felt when Jackson would appear, but this time, it made her feel uneasy. She kept going, but had the strangest notion she was being watched. No, not watched, stalked. She swallowed hard and summoned up every bit of rationality she could and kept walking.

As she continued down, she sky began to dim and she noticed the foliage that framed the houses began to turn. The pink on the trees going down the path became less and less until the trees were eventually barren. In the distance she could hear a faint whispering. She could not make out who it was or what they were saying, but then in the far distance she saw him. It was strange because he was standing so far from her. It looked like Jackson except that he was hard to make out. She had to focus really hard just to make him out and even then he was blurry. She stared at him for a minute and although he was looking in her direction, it was almost as if he really couldn't see her, like his gaze was going past her or through her. Then he spoke, but in a scratchy deep voice that sounded misplaced. "Does it still hurt?"

She was tempted to answer him or ask him where he'd been, anything, but then as she was about to speak, she noticed something else. His eyes, the blue had faded to an almost grey hue. She had never seen his eyes look that way almost as if it wasn't him at all. Instead, she turned around and started off in the other direction. As she walked she began to feel fearful, as if she were being chased, but when she turned back there was no one there.

THE GANG IS ALL HERE

Over the next few days, Darcy rested and recovered. She was glade to be home on Monday with the knowledge that she'd have the entire week to lay back and get her head straight. On her drive home, she was forced to promise her father that she'd slow down and get some rest. She obliged unarguably as she had decided to try and make amends with her sanity. The disappointment from missing her trip to America was short lived, she was just happy to be alive. The weirdest cognition was that it was the first time Gidding's Hill felt like home. She wanted nothing more than to be up in her room surrounded by her faithful images and enveloped in the warmth that radiated contrarily from the cool wooden floors.

Jackson sat up and rubbed his eyes, extended leave was always his favorite time of the year. It was the only time he got to catch up on his sleep. He had been working almost every night; he couldn't remember any other year he was commissioned so much. He couldn't complain too much because it was good excuse for not having to go out so much with Max. His phone rang and he grimaced; it was Scarlett. Saturday at Max's urging they had gone out with the girls yet again and it seemed as though Max was pushing Scarlett on him. Jackson was not very happy at the fact that he had even gone so far as to give her his phone number even after he'd insisted on not being interested in her. However, Max was acting so strangely that Jackson did not want to aggravate the situation any further. For example, when he asked him how he had spend his Friday night and Jackson had told him about the accident, after pressing on about Darcy's state, he got a strange look Jackson had never seen on him before. It was almost a look of guilt. Jackson was also surprised to find out that he hadn't heard of Darcy's mother either.

He heard the car roll up the road and he ran to the window. Darcy was back and Jackson felt a mix of opposing emotions. He still wasn't sure how he would approach Darcy, as Jackson or Mack. He wondered if she would remember that brief encounter in the ambulance. Jack had prematurely made the decision he would tell her the truth at whatever cost, but now he wondered whether or not he'd go through with it. He saw her walk into her house and felt a wave of relief.

That same afternoon, Darcy had been in her bedroom all of three hours and was already feeling anxious. She went down and sat in the sill of a bay window that looked out over the landscapes in the back yard. It was the most beautiful place she'd ever seen; it was still hard to comprehend that it was hers and she wondered why she didn't spend more time out there. There were so many green nooks that harbored benches and small garden tables; it seemed like the perfect place to go out and get lost in. She couldn't help but wonder how her mother could have still been so unhappy in such a magnificent place. She gazed out onto the lush vegetation and noticed Mr. Mackinnon pruning some small shrubs and shouting at someone. Darcy giggled when she looked over and saw Mack on a ladder with his head practically buried in a tree. The more she stared at him the more she wished she hadn't been so stupid. Perhaps if they would have met under normal circumstances they could be friends. She still couldn't remember everything from the accident, but he had helped her and she had yet to thank him. After a while Mr. Mackinnon threw down his gloves and walked around to the front. Mack reemerged from the tree and sat on the ground for a while. Darcy figured it was her chance to catch him alone and thank him. She figured she could also do with some fresh air.

Darcy stood and walked towards one of the back doors, but as she was about to open it, she heard the doorbell. Her heart jumped up inside her chest and she couldn't help but wonder if it was a possibility. She ran to the door before Anne could reach it and flung it open. "What no black eye? I expected at least that much; makes the whole story more dramatic like, oh, or maybe a cast, just around the arm or one leg." Darcy lifted her arm and revealed the bandage wrapped tightly around her hand and wrist and Clem blushed.

"Hey Clem," Darcy smiled, "who told you?"

"Hi sweet heart, you know I'm only joking, your dad filled me in. Wow, your lip is busted, I hadn't noticed. But it doesn't look too bad really, gives you a nice Hollywood plump."

"Yeah well, my body is still unforgiving, but it could have been so much worse."

They walked back over to the bay window and sat. "So what are we doing then eh?" Darcy chuckled as Clem peered out of the glass. "Ah lovely view, do we still hate him?"

"No, I guess I'm kinda over it," Darcy admitted.

"Well that's great, because I quite enjoy you when you're not acting like a lunatic." It was nice having Clem around. Darcy knew that she had been lucky to have met her so soon. Clem was different than Amanda and Stacy, not necessarily better, but different. She was more in tune with who Darcy really was. She had even been tempted to tell her about the whole Jackson thing before it ended so abruptly. They withdrew to Darcy's room, to catch up and just hang out for a while.

It hadn't been too long until Darcy heard the stomping footsteps and all too familiar debate between Anne and Max. "Geeze lady calm down, I have no idea what you're saying, but you've seen me like a million times so what's the big deal." Darcy smiled at Clem and poked her head out of the door.

"It's okay Anne, come on up Max." Clem's insides crawled at the mention of his name. It was conflicting, she wanted with all her being to see him, and yet the very thought that he was about to walk in the room gave her a feeling of dread.

Max walked through the door with a look of contentment as he had once again eluded the housekeeper. "Hey," he cupped Darcy's face and examined it the way a doctor might examine a patient. "How you feeling?"

Darcy smiled and pulled her head back "I'm fine Max."

He smiled and hugged her playfully. "Good, you had me a little worried, but then I remembered how hard your head is and I figured you couldn't have done too much damage."

"Thanks a lot. How'd you know anyway?" He rolled his eyes towards the window. "Oh, right"

They stood there in a moment of silence and that's when Max noticed they were in company. "Oh, hi, I didn't see you there."

"Oh yeah, no worries, me either." He shot Clem a confused look and smiled as she blushed when she realized how stupid she sounded. "Hi, I'm Clem," she had no idea why, but she was extending her hand for him to shake.

"Yeah, I remember you, you got some mouth on you," he raised his eyebrows and smiled as he shook her hand. "So how've you been?"

"Great, fine, fantastic."

He chuckled, at the notion that he made her nervous. "Well, I guess you're good then." Darcy couldn't help but chuckle a little too as she winked at Clem, whose face changed a deep purple hue.

"Yeah well, I'm just gonna step out for a spell, let you two catch up."

"What, no, where are you going?" Darcy asked Clem as she made her way to the door.

"No worries, I'm just going out for a smoke, I'll be back." Clem walked out feeling flushed as the heat from her body was radiating to her face. When she reached the second floor, she was out of breath; she opted for the back door instead of having to trudge down yet another staircase.

"Your friend is …"

"Awesome." Max raised his eyebrow in doubt. "Seriously, she's really cool, she just, well, I think you make her nervous," Darcy explained.

"Why in the world would anyone ever let someone make them nervous? What's there to be nervous about? That's why relationships are so hopeless; girls make things so complicated. Seriously, there's nothing to be nervous about its all chemical, but you all confuse attraction with emotion."

"So you're telling me a girl's never made you feel intimidated before?"

"Girls have made me feel a lot of things, intimidation, not so much."

"Maybe you're confusing emotion with attraction." He giggled at her appeals. "Really Max, you should be careful, one day you might be sorry."

Max was convinced that it was impossible. Apologies were derived from compunction and Max had surrendered his conscience long ago, or so it seemed. "So how are you doing really?" Darcy looked at him confused. "Why didn't you call me?"

"Well, I was a little drugged…"

"Not then," Max said somewhat forcefully and she finally realized what he was really referring to.

"Who…" Max looked toward the window and Darcy nodded in understanding as she bit down on her lip. "Wow, I didn't even know he knew, but I guess, duh makes sense. Look, I just, I don't want to talk…" Max just nodded, one of the things that drew him to Darcy was how alike they were.

Clem lit her cigarette and sat on the cold stone steps leading down into the garden. She didn't notice the shadow cast beside her. "Do you think I could maybe bum one of those?" When she noticed Jackson Mackinnon standing next to her she felt the heat begin to rise up again in her face. She handed him a cigarette.

"So, how's the patient doing?" He asked as he lit up.

"Wow, you actually sound sincere, erm concerned even." He looked at her in confusion. "It's just, it seems you quite literally go out of your way to act like a total knob when she's round."

"Hmph yeah I guess I have been acting like quite an ass. Does she hate me yet?" he cracked a half smile.

Clem started to notice something in his smile, an underlying longing. "Sadly no, Darcy is…" she sighed in search of the best approach, "I don't know what she its, but she's quite genuine and good. Yeah, good, I've never, girls usually aren't so nice. Besides, I think you redeemed yourself with the whole white horse thing." He felt his face flush over. "Very heroic…"

"She," he hesitated, "what did she say?"

Clem was taken aback by how curious he was, but something in his eyes made him seem vulnerable. "Um, well, she doesn't really remember too much, but she says she saw you help her out of the car and she remembered hearing you tell her to hang on or something and pretty much after that everything's gone. She can't remember how she got to hospital or even anything after the accident until Saturday morning." He was nodding and took a long drag from his cigarette. "Do you," he looked down at her as she spoke, "you fancy her don't you?" She smiled playfully, "well, well Mr. Mackinnon, don't worry, I won't tell anyone. But I'm afraid well, maybe you might have a bit of competition."

"Who Max," he asked sarcastically, "nah I wouldn't worry too much about that. Besides, as I see it, it's a bit of a concern for you as well." Clem blushed. "Look, I know you don't really know me, and it's not like I've done much to win over your affections, but let me give you a bit of, oh I dunno take it as a suggestion," he swallowed hard and she looked up at him, "he might not be…"

"So, we thought we'd lost you out here, but I see you're in good company." They both looked back startled. "Hey Mmmack, so what's up man?" Max trudged halfway down the steps cooly.

"Oh, not too much just a bit of girl talk." Jackson joked as he flicked what was left of his cigarette to the ground and he winked at Clem. Her insides flared as Jackson was almost equally as good looking as Max.

"I'll bet," Max snorted. "Darcy was getting hungry so I told her I'd go out and get something."

"Company?" Clem asked surprised at her own overenthusiasm.

"Oh um I'm good, but I think I was actually sent out to fetch you for her." He winked at Clem and she couldn't help but smile. "I'll see you girls in a bit." She turned and skipped up the stone steps.

"So do you take orders or should I call one in?"

"Shut up MACK," he taunted back.

"This nice guy thing, it really sits well with you, but what's up with her?" Jack asked genuinely pensive as he nodded in Clem's direction.

"Her?" Max furrowed his brow. "You think I was harsh or something? I thought I was pretty charming." Jackson rolled his eyes.

"Well, I can't argue there, but what I meant was like she was fishing you know, why didn't you ask her to go with you? She's obviously interested." He knew it was unlikely Max would ever turn down a sure thing and he wondered what his angle was.

"Dude, she's pretty and all, but too easy, too clingy. Like, I can tell she's into me, but those are the ones we should steer clear of. I mean she seems like a nice girl, not these one-nighters. She wants a relationship and I don't have to explain it you man, you know how we operate. It's not like we can fall in love or anything." Jackson was surprised by the mere fact that Max was even talking about the concept of love and he wondered if it had anything to do with Darcy. The very thought aroused something dark him. Max caught on as well, "besides she's a friend of a friend and that never works out."

"Yeah I guess our lives are different eh?"

"Lives, what lives? Life is an aberration; we just exist." They stood in silence and Jackson had never heard Max speak that way; his humanity was seeping through.

"Hey," they both looked up as she spoke. She smiled when she caught Jackson's eyes, then averted her attention to Max. "What happened?"

Max looked at her puzzled for a second. "Oh shit the pizza! Sorry, I got distracted."

"Don't worry about it," truthfully she had begun to feel nauseous from her pain medications and she just was starting to feel more and more lethargic. "I'm just gonna eat some cereal or something."

"No, no I'm on my way." He turned to walk towards the stairs and she grabbed his forearm and he grabbed hers back. Jackson looked away as he felt his throat tighten and his fist clench at the sight of them in any kind of embrace.

"No seriously, besides I'm tired and Clem had to go, so it'd be a waste. Oh and don't be mad at me okay?" She bit down on her lower lip.

"What, why, I hate that face. What did you do?" Max asked her.

"I kinda told her we'd all go out sometime, you know after my body stops throbbing." He rolled his eyes at her. "Anyways, I'm really getting tired, so I'm gonna go up and try to sleep." Jackson heard her and the temptation pulled at his stomach. She was so magnetically beautiful. He just wanted to grab her and hold her like he had done so many times before.

"Yeah, great I love set ups. So when did you say your dad was shipping out?" Max was surprisingly concerned as far as Jackson could see.

"Oh, um tomorrow afternoon."

"So, still bummed out about not being able to go?" Max asked her seemingly interested.

"No, not at all, he has stuff to take care of and besides I really don't think I'll ever want to go back to France again. Anyway, I'm sort of looking forward to doing nothing. Besides I think Anne is staying a couple of nights. My dad got paranoid."

"I'm glad he did," As Max and Darcy spoke Jackson stood there awkwardly. "Well, I'll call you or call me or whatever." Darcy nodded. "Later Mackinnon, I'll give you a call man." He walked towards his car and Jackson turned to go towards the cottage when Darcy ran down the steps.

Just as she was about to call out to Mack, she felt an arm on her shoulder. "Darcy wait; before I forget," Jackson slowed down to try and hear what Max had returned so desperately to say. "I just wanted you to know," he looked to the ground for pride, for the motivation to do something he'd never done before, "I'm really sorry."

Darcy smiled, "for what?"

He hesitated "just for everything that you know, happened to you." She swallowed the lump that built up in her throat. She walked over and kissed him on the cheek. His face lit up and his benevolence stirred. Jackson stood heartbroken and as he watched Max walk over to his car he thought about the hollow inexplicable apology. What did Max have to be so remorseful for? Was it even a possibility? He knew Max had surrendered his conscience long before. Jackson reached for his doorknob and felt a tap on the shoulder. When he turned around, his heart stopped still in his chest, she looked enchanting.

"Umm Mack, look, I know we kind of ..." she stared down at her feet. "I know I've been kind of weird and maybe like a little rude, but I'm, really not like that." She sighed and he knew how difficult it was for her to say what she was trying to. She didn't have any means to apologize and letting her continue on seemed criminal.

"Darcy," she looked up at him and he let her stare straight into his eyes, straight into his soul. "I'm" he hesitated "I'm actually..." he looked at her face and realized he loved her infinitely, "I want to apologize if I've been well a bit of a shit. I mean there's really no excusing it but it's just, well I've been a little out of sorts and..."

She was surprised by the fact that he was apologizing, but she saw something profoundly beautiful in him. "So let's start over, Darcy Whitten," she extended out her bandaged arm with a smile. He took in a distressed breath and his teeth clenched as he took her hand. The guilt robbed him of any words, so he offered up a nod instead.

"Well, Darcy Whitten, lovely to have met you, I sincerely hope to see you around," he said in a deeper orchestrated voice as he smiled. "That's what I should've said the first day we met." They had never exchanged enough words for her to notice how quickly he spoke and how thick his accent really was.

The night sky seemed more amethyst than usual. When she looked up, the stars glittered beyond their usually capacity. It had been a while since she'd dreamt of the night sky but it was refreshing. Disillusioned she sat at the end of a pier and gazed out onto the desert sands beneath her. As much as she missed her fallacy, there was something about being tangible that felt contended. She took a deep breath and felt a chill slither down her backbone.

Prey.

He stood watching her, careful not to be revealing. He swore he'd never visit her again, but he needed the confirmation. With every breath she took, he grew more and more susceptible. How could someone, anyone change his whole world?

He thought back all the way to their first meeting and he wondered how he let it get to where it was. He was beyond restitution. Darcy Whitten, just a girl, fragile, temporary, ordinary. As he prepared to leave he took one last look in her direction and there under the tints of a dimly lit bruised sky, he knew exactly how and why. Vindication.

Perhaps

By Wednesday she was going stir crazy. Clem had gotten held up mysteriously and Max hadn't called and with Daniel out Anne wasn't offering up too much company. She grabbed a pair of cotton pants and a t-shirt, pulled on her tennis shoes and with music in her ears she stepped out for a jog. Her body still wasn't healed, but she hoped it would show some mercy. She ran through the lush vegetation and with a melodic stride and an unaided determination she pushed her body as far as it would take her. She ran for 45 minutes, until the burn in her throat became anaphylactic and her knees finally buckled sending her to the floor. There, folded over she put her head in her hands and wept. It was a loud waling splurge. She felt every ounce of pain both physical and emotional break out of her body. She turned over and lay in her back staring up into the crowns of the trees for hints of the sky. "Bird watching?" She looked over and saw the pair of cobalt eyes looking down at her.

"God, you scared me," she confessed.

"No, not god, just me, but sorry for the confusion," she giggled at sat up. "So what brings out here?" Jackson asked somewhat surprised.

"I just needed space I guess and a little bit of nothing." She sniffled and he could tell she'd been crying.

"Ah I see," he said. "What were you looking for up there, birds, monkeys?" Her eyes widened a bit and he smiled. "No I was joking, no monkeys."

"I know." She sat in silence, then spoke "I guess I was looking for… hope, answers," her voice became soft almost inaudible, "revelations."

He furrowed his brow at her choice in words. "What is it you need to know exactly?"

She felt a little embarrassed, "I don't know, once I asked someone if he believed in a higher power and his answer was so simple. I guess I expected… he said his assurance was just colors, but as I watched the green against the seemingly endless blue in the sky I couldn't help but wonder, like is our faith based on what we see?" He wasn't sure if the question wasn't rhetorical. "Because, I'm not sure, I've seen some beautiful things that never really existed." Jackson could see that she was struggling to come to terms with herself. "Doesn't make sense huh?" She felt embarrassed, he was probably remembering how weird she could be, but she couldn't help talking, the weight was too much to bear alone.

"Conviction doesn't come from seeing something and being reassured. Like how do you know everything you saw or felt never existed? How can you be so sure?"

"Because, it just didn't, I mean it was fleeting and it just changed, disappeared. I think it's all a delusion seriously. For a while I thought I was going crazy."

"Everything is a fleeting delusion. Like your green, it's momentary; it'll soon fade to brown and eventually ash. The leaves will shrivel and dry and disappear. And well, as for your phantom blue sky, it's actually colorless atmosphere that gets it hue from bits of sunlight moving through and reacting to molecules and stuff." He sounded so scientific she couldn't help but giggle and he blushed. "Who knows what's real, maybe it's all a lie, but that doesn't mean it's not real to you. It might not be ideal, but life is not ideal it's just brief and dissipating." She stared at him and he bit down on his lip wishing he had had more restraint when he spoke to her.

"Thanks."

"For?"

"Listening I guess, and everything else." She still hadn't thanked him for the accident. Her apology made him uncomfortable.

"It's getting pretty cold out." He offered her his hand to help her up. She got to her feet, stuck her hands in her pockets and began to follow him back home.

"You probably think I'm even more insane," she suddenly wanted to go back and simply give a silent nod rather than her usually verbal splurge.

"No I just think," he pulled a leaf out of her hair, "you think too much." The sensation of the silky strands beneath his finger tips were almost too much for him to withstand. He swallowed hard and she noted his reaction, at which she felt her stomach react.

That night he had an epiphany that brought him the smallest hint of solace. Darcy was always going to be his and perhaps if he couldn't have her as Jackson, he could have her as Mack. Clearly it wasn't ideal, but he had said it himself life wasn't ideal. The physical separation had proved much worse than he had anticipated and it was getting harder to keep from reaching out to hold her. He lay back and closed his eyes lost in an emotional euphoria.

Darcy thought about everything that night, her life in general, her new existence, her friends, her mother, Jackson, her loss, and Mack. It was scary to think how life could change instantaneously. She thought about their conversation earlier, the way he looked at her, the way her body shuddered when he touched her hair. He reminded her so much of Jack, but it wasn't just his appearance it was the way he made her feel inside; a penetrating desire that pulled at her core. She tossed and turned and realized Mack was right she thought too much. She decided to use her grandmother's trick once more and with the white wall in her sight she slipped away.

When the dawn snuck through her window, she sat up in disbelief. That was it. That day she had missed her dream it was because of the white wall. She felt a strange nostalgia. She wished she could share it with Jack. Then she sat back and reminded herself to absolve any thoughts of him.

Thursday Darcy found ways to keep herself busy, but every so often she caught herself peering out the window secretly hoping for a glimpse of Mack to no avail. She was so eager when Clem invited her out to the pub again. She was really excited about the band that would be playing, but mostly she felt suffocated. Her body was still giving her grief, but Anne was finally out of the house and with the time change her dad wouldn't be calling; it was finally her chance to get out of the house. She readied herself with a pace and eagerness she had not had in a while. She pulled the black sweater over her jeans and pulled up her hair. She looked out her window and saw Mack's car in the drive, just the she got an idea and quickly grabbed her phone.

Max was surprised to learn that Darcy was going out already and even though he advised against it she insisted. He wanted to find a way to turn down her down, but the desire to see her wouldn't allow it. She let on that it wouldn't be so bad, because it wasn't just Clem going, there were other friends as well. It wasn't until she suggested that he take Mack along that he really did regret having agreed. Having Jackson and Darcy so close made Max feel somewhat uncomfortable, but it was too late to back out and refusing to invite Mack would seem suspicious. He decided that when he called up Jackson he would leave out the fact that Darcy was going to be there and hope he'd get turned down as he often did.

Jackson stared up into Darcy's window with a lust that pulled at him. When she walked by the window he noticed she was getting ready and he wondered where the night would take her. He was shaken out of his bemusement when the phone rang. He was reluctant to answer when he noticed it was Max, but then he had a hopeful epiphany, maybe he'd find Darcy out that night. It was a slim chance but one he was desperately willing to take, so much to Max's annoyance, he agreed.

When Clem got to Darcy's she noticed a strange look on Darcy's face, a mischievous glare in her eyes. "Hey," Darcy said a little too cheerfully.

"Okay what you do? I know you did something, because ya have on that stupid grin," Clem asked annoyed.

"Nothing," Clem gave her an unconvinced look. "Nothing you didn't ask me to do."

"What?! Surely I have no idea what you're talking about."

"Oh surely you don't; then why is your face turning purple?"

"Damn if you weren't disabled I'd ask you to drive so I could ready myself properly," Clem was excited and it showed in her tone of voice.

"I'm not..." Darcy laughed. "Move over, I can drive."

"Why do you let me go out looking like a complete slag?"

"What, what does that even mean?" Darcy giggled, "you look just fine."

Arriving at the Plectrum, there was a mutual feeling of apprehension. Darcy knew the possibility of seeing Mack was almost irrefutable. The atmosphere in the building proved as hazy as it had before. The girls met up with their friends and walked into the unwavering mixture of music and simultaneous conversations. Clem appeared nervous and Darcy found it somewhat refreshing. She'd always been the braver of the two and it made Darcy feel less delicate. Almost an hour past and Darcy had lost herself in the music and excitement, while Clem was beginning to worry that Max might not make his anticipated appearance.

Jack was surprised that Max was so quiet on the ride over to Plectrum, usually he had a lot of small talk and smart remarks waiting for him, the silence was unnerving. "Hey man, is everything all right?"

"Hmm, what, oh yeah why do ask?"

"Oh I dunno, maybe because usually I can't get you to shut up and now its like," Jackson was careful, "like you're nervous about something."

Max chuckled "what, really, I hadn't thought about it, hmm I guess I kinda am." Jackson was almost shocked to hear those words escape his lips. What was Max so nervous about, it couldn't possibly be Clem, there had been so many girls before. Then it occurred to Jackson that perhaps it wasn't Clem that made him nervous and even worse it was probably Darcy. That would be the worst thing that could ever happen, too bad for Jackson to even conciliate.

"What about exactly?"

Max wasn't even too sure himself, but he figured he should at least try to give up a good enough explanation. "I don't know dude, I guess it's that whole Clem shit. I mean I'm trying to figure out how I'm gonna let her down without making it weird with Darcy." Jackson was almost as unconvinced as Max was.

When they walked into the smoky hallway Max looked around, but had a hard time finding the girls. After a couple of minutes Jackson excused himself to get a drink. He got to the bar and ordered a beer.

"Music is pretty good don't you think? I love this song." The sound of her voice behind him made his heart flutter. He responded without turning to face her, for fear his true appetite would reveal itself.

"Yeah, I like the lyrics," he turned to look at her and mockingly said, "they're dark and ambiguous." Darcy blushed slightly but it illuminated her face in the most appropriate way. "Sorry, I was just having a laugh; if you want I can just sod off."

"That's so embarrassing; I can't even believe you remember that." She held back a grin; he smiled and felt the heat in his palms rise. "Wait, you should be embarrassed, evesdropper."

He chuckled, "yeah I suppose I should, but I'm not really, embarrassed that is." They stood in a moment of underappreciated silence, "so where's everyone?"

"I have no idea," she said looking around. "Hey and where's Max?" His name escaping her lips pierced his ears.

"I dunno around somewhere, dodging your friend I think."

Darcy couldn't help but laugh a little, "oh no, I was afraid that would happen."

When Max was finally able to zero in on Darcy, he tried not to be visibly upset that she was with Jackson. He assumed there was nothing else to fear from Jackson, but he began to wonder. Max had never been in a situation where he did not have complete and absolute control. He could maneuver any situation and he knew what he had to do to get it back. Just as he hung up his phone Clem approached him and directed him to the table Darcy, Jackson, and a few other friends were now occupying. After about an hour of hollow almost painfully scripted conversations, Darcy excused herself to get some air and even though Clem offered to go with her, she preferred to go alone. Before she got up though she gave Jackson a strange look and he tilted his head subtly in comprehension. A gesture that was still not subtle enough to escape Max who was studying every interaction between the both of them. Just as Jackson got up to follow far behind her, he was surprised to see Scarlett walking straight towards him. His eyes widened, he knew he couldn't have her anywhere near Darcy. He turned back at Max who gave him an unknowing shoulder shrug. He thought as fast as he could manage and he was grateful Darcy was by now probably standing over by the door expecting him.

"Hey Scar, what, what are you doing here?"

"What you're not glad to see me then?" She spoke suggestively and Clem couldn't help but gag a little at the display of assumed affections.

"Um yeah, but..." he frantically searched for a cohesive thought, "you know what, I was kinda feeling a bit anxious actually, needed to go out for some air."

"Erm, why don't I come with ya then?" She had presumptuously taken it as an invitation. He knew if he blew her off in front of everyone Max would know his whole necessary faux courtship had indeed been a front.

Defeated Jackson asked "You know what; do you maybe want to get out of here instead, my parents are off on holiday for the weekend?"

"That was fast," Clem muttered to no one in particular.

"Um sure," she responded eagerly, "oh wait, but what about Ella?"

"Oh, I'm pretty sure Max, you can...'

"Yeah man, go on ahead." Max smiled in contentment that Jackson would be off with Scarlett and away from Darcy plus Ella would be the perfect wall between Clem and him. When Darcy got back from the restroom she was surprised to find the table had disbanded and Clem sat with two other friends smoking frantically.

"What happened? Where's Max and Mack?"

"Well," Clem motioned toward the bar where Ella was hanging on Max's neck, "that happened to Max and Mackinnon at least had the decency to carry out his indiscretion in the privacy of his own home, tossers." Darcy raised her eyebrows and bit down on her lip.

"Oh Clem, I'm really sorry, I just thought..."

"It's not your fault Darcy, they're just like dogs, the lot of em', very cute, but not very loyal. I'm really surprised at Mack though, I thought..." she looked at Darcy, "nevermind."

She felt bad for Clem; she knew how much she had been looking forward to spending time with Max. It was the first time she actually felt a bit disgusted by Max, and as she met his distant gaze she made sure he saw it in her face. She was also a bit disappointed that Mack had gone off with someone as well. But she figured she shouldn't be too surprised and felt foolish for having flirted with the notion of him being interested in her. She wondered if she hadn't been too obvious and hoped he hadn't noticed; she felt stupid.

Not too much time passed before Clem was ready to call it a night. Darcy apologized continuously for what had happened with Max and Clem found it amusing that Darcy was so guilt ridden she felt responsible for other people's actions as well. After reassuring her for the fourth time, she dropped her off at Gidding's Hill. Darcy walked up the drive and instead sat on a stone step on her porch. She looked up at the stars pensively and found it amazing that they could be the exact same stars she coveted as a child back home. Focusing in on one in particular, she wondered if she'd seen it before, if she'd ever wished on it or looked to it for comfort, she wondered how many wishes it kept, how many promises it held, how many times it had been claimed or given away, how many broken hearts it belonged to, and as it sat there shinning unaware that it meant so much to so many, something so insignificant, she wondered...

Revelations

"Do you know them?"

"Oh my god, you scared me, again." He stood a bit far off in his doorway, but she could still make out his beautiful face and she got nervous.

"Sorry I guess I do that a lot." Jackson spoke without restraint.

"Know who?" She asked trying to keep on with any conversation for reasons unknown to her. He looked puzzled for a moment.

"Oh, I meant the stars, constellations…I just thought because you seemed so entranced."

He was so beautiful she couldn't help but feel for him. "No, I wish I did though. When I was little I really wanted to be an astronaut, but the one time I rode Space Mountain I freaked out and threw up, so I figured it was probably not going to happen." He laughed sweetly. "'I don't know I just wanted to see something prolific, it's just so amazing the idea of being so close to the Heavens, to be out amongst the nothing, to be part of something so limited, knowing most people will never see it in their entire lifetime."

"What do you think it would feel like being up there," Jackson asked genuinely.

She thought for a moment "criminal," he gave her a confused look. "Like being somewhere I shouldn't be, it's unnatural, like peeking behind the curtains you know, but impossibly great I'm sure." He couldn't take anymore, as he clenched his teeth, he knew he had to have her.

She looked up at him, as she met his gaze as chill ran down her spine. She stayed staring at him across the drive and as he was about to make his way from the cottage to where she stood, the door opened behind him and Scarlett walked out towards him. She cupped his face in her hands and kissed him forcefully. Darcy averted her eyes downward and felt a familiar ache in her chest. Jackson pulled down on Scarlett's arms and pulled his head back. That's when she noticed Darcy standing there.

"Oh how embarrassing, I didn't know there was someone else out here. Jackson, are you ever coming back in, the movie's starting," she whined. Darcy had already turned to walk in, but as she heard those words, she stopped and turned back. That's when she caught him looking at her with horror in his widened eyes?

She tried to swallow, but her throat was too tight. She felt faint and sat on the step; she placed her hands over her eyes and thoughts ran across her mind unmercifully. Memories of Jackson flooded her eyes and even a jolt of what had transpired in the ambulance. Jackson ran over to her with Scarlett following close behind. "Is she okay? Isn't that the same girl from..."

Darcy reached her feet before they reached her. "What did you call him?" she asked Scarlett somewhat breathless.

"Jackson, that is his name," she said mockingly.

She looked to Jackson's face for explanation, "Jjackson?"

He swallowed hard and defeated replied, "Jackson Mackinnon. Um they call me Mack from Mackinnon." He had a pitiful look on his face, he wanted to be able to offer up an explanation, the truth even, but with Scarlett there it was impossible.

With her hand placed disgustedly over her mouth, Darcy was nodding, "no, no, nuh, uh, no."

She ran in and slammed the door. Her face was riddled with heat and tears were endlessly streaming down her face. She felt the same rush of panic from before; desperate she ran to her father's study and grabbed the keys from the desk drawer. As her car was still out of commission, her father had left his keys behind in case of an emergency. She ran out to the garage and as she was climbing in the car, she felt a cold touch on her arm, "Darcy wait let me explain," with Scarlett securely out of the way it was his chance for reparation or at the very least revelation.

"Don't touch me, Jackson," his name escaped her lips with contemp. He let her go, but did not move. "Just tell me one thing."

"Anything," he said pleading.

"God I feel crazy."

"You're not crazy Darcy."

"This is going to sound completely insane, but how long...how long have you known..." she had to ready herself in case she really had been crazy all along, "how..."

"I've known you since you were a girl Darcy. It was all real, the dreams, the walks, the..."

"Shh stop just," she sniffled.

"you were so beautiful, you are the most beautiful...all these years, I just..."

"I have to go," Darcy snipped.

"No wait, where are you going?" Jackson asked pleading.

"What do you care, you have company anyway."

"Darcy please, don't, just wait please," then he thought of something. "Are you going to see Max?"

"Bye Jackson." Fear infused his whole body.

"Darcy, please don't say anything, please don't go see him." He was shouting after her. "Just wait, let, give me a chance…"

"I already feel crazy, do you think I want him to think I'm crazy too? I have no idea what to think, but I just can't…"

"Darcy please, please don't leave me."

She was crying inconsolably "I, I loved you and you left me and worse, you stood by and watched me fall apart!" He stood paralyzed by guilt.

"I couldn't, I just couldn't…" She pulled the car out and drove off.

Darcy and Max: Comfort

She tried her best to stop crying, but she couldn't. The realization that the rejection had been real was overwhelming. Why couldn't he love her? Why couldn't Harley? She reached Max's door faster than she could comprehend how she had even gotten there. She knocked frantically. Max opened the door and as he stood there in the doorway without his shirt on, he blushed when he saw Darcy. Then he noticed she was crying.

"Darcy, are you still mad about…" before he could finish she stood on her tiptoes grabbed his shoulders for support and kissed him. At first, he grabbed the doorframe to keep from falling over but when he realized what was happening he let go and wrapped his arms around her. He had kissed so many, but she was the first. With her eyes shut painfully tight she kissed him in search of atonement. After a minute, Max pulled away.

"Darcy, I can't…"

"What, no, don't say that, yes you can…" she reassured him desperately.

"No Darcy," he said with regret in every word, "I really can't. I mean why now? What happened to you?"

She was crying and he felt unfamiliar pangs deep within "Yes you can, you have to, because if not then…"

"Darcy, listen I don't…" he interrupted and just then a set of honey colored eyes appeared from behind the doorway. Of course he wasn't alone, she felt humiliated and defeated all at once. She raised her hand in an effort to silence him; she really couldn't stand to hear it and began to walk away quickly.

"Darcy, Darcy!" Max felt helpless for the first time, but he knew it just meant he had to think everything through. He cared for Darcy more than he had ever cared for anyone. And although the kiss was the best thing he had ever experienced, it still felt wrong; cheated, like it didn't belong to him. He ran and when he finally reached her she was slinked on a stairway.

Darcy immediately felt contrite and disgusted for having done that. She knew her friendship with Max was over and she also was aware that upon breaking the news to Clem she would be compromising that one as well. She just needed someone, anyone to assure her that she was capable of real affection. She hated herself more for being so insecure. Her apology was not very fruitful, she did not offer up an explanation, she simply told him she was sorry and she'd tell him more about what was going on later.

"Darcy, look, whatever is going on, you know..." she looked at him with sorry eyes and he decided on a different approach. "Look, just come in. Want to watch a movie?" he asked in an attempt to break the tension. She smiled through her desperate sadness. "Please stay, come on Darcy, you don't even have to talk to me all night."

"No I don't want to interrupt," she said through her sniffles.

"Darcy she's just, we're just watching a movie really. Please don't make me feel bad Darcy, I can't, I don't know how..." He patted his chest with his hand lightly over his heart. He offered her his hand and she couldn't hurt him and she really didn't want to be alone, so she took it.

Ella left earlier than she'd probably expected to and when Darcy finally fell asleep Max walked into his bedroom. He had thought about carrying her over to his bed, but he was too afraid to touch her. Every time he would look at her, he thought of her mouth, her sweet breath, her lips. He was frustrated by the unrelenting desire for her. It was the only emotion he could not control. It worried him to no end.

Jackson: Confessions and Reparations

When Jackson reached his driveway, he could hardly breathe. A hatred, a fear, a rage rose up from a dark place hidden within him. He could not contain the physical manifestation. He walked into his room and punched the wall until his hand lay raw and blood soaked. With his hands on his head he slinked down the wall defeated and when he reached the floor, he noticed his hands were trembling. He closed his eyes and rested his head against the wall. He thought of Darcy from girl to young woman, every smile, every embrace, every tear, and finally the one image he had so desperately been trying to erase. He had run into Max's building in a hopes he could reach Darcy before she went in, he had even gone so far as to leave Scarlett outside with cab fare, but when he reached the hall his heart stopped when he saw them kissing. Max's arms wrapped tightly around Darcy's delicate frame killed him. As he held his head in his hand and rubbed his forehead in an attempt to clear his mind he got up and instead walked over to the Whitten house.

In all the commotion, Darcy had forgotten to lock the door. He made his way up to her room and sat on a chair in the corner of the room. As he waited, he stared at her bed and at the girl above and threw his head back against the wall. He hated himself, his life, his existence, his god, for everything, he hated Max and with that thought he felt crushed. With his elbows on his knees, and his head in his hands he wept.

When Darcy reached the drive she decided not to park the car in the garage, as it was attached to the cottage and she'd chance running into Jackson. She pulled up onto her lawn. When she opened her front door, she felt disconnected. She had snuck out before Max had even woken up. Consumed by emotional exhaustion, she struggled to make her way up to her room. She walked in and was startled to see him sitting in the corner of the room. He stared at her with a frown and deep creases in his forehead, his blue eyes crimson laden. He was still beautiful; he was still hers.

"Nice night?" he managed sarcastically.

Darcy closed her eyes and shook her head, "Jackson, what are doing here?"

"Did you," he swallowed hard, "you didn't sleep with him."

She just looked at him; he let out a sigh closed his eyes and tears rolled down his beautiful face. It was too much for her. "Jackson, do you really think...who do you think I am? You think I'd do...no, I didn't." He opened his eyes in relief and stared at her.

"I'm sorry for asking, it's just..." he couldn't speak, he just put his hand over his chest, over his heart just as Max had done, but this time with more conviction.

"Besides it's my understanding that you're already taken anyways."

He was taken back, but he knew he had no right to ask without offering up his own innocence. "It's not like that, nothing happened. I mean she likes me but, I don't even, I mean I ...

"What are you doing here Jackson, Mack, whoever you are. I mean what do you want?" Darcy spoke in a colder tone than she ever had to him.

"You know who I am, I just, I'm...yours."

"No, you're..."

"Yes I am, I've always been, I'll always be, even if you're not mine." Tears made their way to the corner of her eyes as he stood over her. She wanted so desperately to hold him; he was so beautiful. "Please you've forgiven people for a lot worse."

"Worse? There has never been worse. You let me fall in love with you, you lied to me, then you abandoned me, you let me torture myself thinking I was crazy, I crashed because of you and I even..."

"Please, let me, I'll do anything, what do you want, anything."

"The truth," she said assertively.

He stood back a minute. "Are you sure, at any cost?" He was unsure, but she nodded a bit confused about what exactly that meant. "The truth is, Darcy, I can't," he clenched his teeth and balled a fist. She gave him a look of disappointment. "I just don't want to put you in danger, to hurt you, I just..."

"The truth or nothing..." she insisted.

He sat back down in the chair at the corner of the room. "When I was eight years old, I started having nightmares, or I thought they were nightmares as I was usually afraid, terrified. I was always being watched, stalked by a group of people, only they weren't like people, they were more like animated corpses. They watched how I reacted to seeing different things, horrible pictures; morbid, dark things. If I flinched they would show me more or worse in nature, I started to notice a pattern, the more I reacted, the worse they got."

"What were they?" Darcy asked nervously.

He was a bit disappointed she'd interrupted as he wanted to get through the explanation as quickly as possible. "Just like dismembered bodies, tortures, death, people killing themselves, each other, children, my family…" he shook his head. "Anyway, when I finally caught on to how it worked I just taught myself to ignore it, to look past it somehow. It wasn't until I was about twelve or so, that I was recruited. One of the people, the watchers we call them, finally spoke to me. I was going to Dominion, I had a purpose." He looked up at Darcy who appeared confused. "Look, you know the world as everyone else does as a series of random events that lead to progress, war, life, death right? Well, I know how the world really works. It's not cause and effect, it's all controlled."

"What like everything is predetermined, destiny?"

"No, no look let me… I'm trying my best to explain it to you. It's more like a game, we're all pawns and Dominion, well, they're the players." She looked at him dubiously. "I know, it sounds far fetched but it's true. People like me we're recruited to sort of work for them to…"

"Who are they; and there are more of you? Like people that can do, what exactly do you do?"

"I'm an advisor, I, we all work through dreams, the state of unconscious, this is when people are open for suggestion, this is where your ideas and future plans are laid out, when you make most of your decisions. We all do different things, muses are used for inspiration, the watchers are like guard dogs, advisors like me we work on a more political level, there are more, but we aren't really told that much."

"Political as in…"

"As in wage wars, advice leaders, alliances, weapons …"

"genocide?" As Darcy interrupted again, a look of shame swept his face. "So then what would be the point?"

"To what?" He asked shamefully.

"Living?"

"That's been the worst part. Once you know, it's like there is none, I swear there were times I thought if I died it wouldn't matter, because nothing really mattered." She tried to figure out what she should be feeling. "But then," he looked up at her "I was fooling around, just practicing, and I saw a girl. There was something about her and I just couldn't help but return to see her and... then it mattered. I wanted to live I didn't care if it was all for nothing, I just wanted to be near you, to be with you."

"I just, you know how this all sounds, you're basically telling me that everything I do, everything I feel, my whole life is just..."

"No, you, that's not how it works," he looked frustrated. "You're not a receiver, like you've never been a target, so everything you are and your life, it's still yours."

"Yeah, but to what extent? Who are these people or what are they?"

"I don't know; we don't really know anything. But whoever, what ever they are they're so dangerous that's why as much as I wanted to tell you I just couldn't. I was trying to protect you, in a weird sadistic way."

"This is all so stupid. I'm sorry I just can't, what if they don't do it?" He looked as her inquisitively, "what if it doesn't work, what if the people don't do what you say?" she said giggling still unconvinced.

"Well they usually do and when problems arise, we have," he looked away, "enforcers, liquidators."

Her demeanor changed, "liquidators, as in you..."

"No I don't kill anyone, but they do. You know those people that mysteriously die in their sleep?" she looked at him with disgust. "That's not the worst that could happen Darcy, that's probably the easy way out. See, you don't really feel physical pain, in your dreams, or actually feel anything, that part of your brain doesn't function on a subconscious level."

"That's why I could never feel you?" he nodded as she came to that realization out loud.

"But they found a loop hole. Perception kind of bypasses that, like they have a way I don't know how it works, but I've been told that they can make you believe you're feeling, so you think you are. Torture."

"Why?"

"It's what we're trained for. I've never killed anyone," he thought about his honesty and guilt filled his heart, "but I've done some horrible things. Probably worse."

"There is no worse, besides I know you, you're not a killer." Her words choked him.

"I've done things, I can put pictures in your mind, I've driven sane men mad, I've tortured them with regret and guilt, I've even driven people to …" he stopped short and looked up at her horrified that he had gotten carried away.

"To what? To what?! Say it, say what…"

His eyes fell and his lips trembled, "Darcy I swear it, that wasn't how…"

"How do you know? You said there were others," she was hysterical.

"Darcy, people still have free will, sometimes they just…"

"Just what? Maybe she was tortured. Someone like you, no something like you," Darcy's words flooded out with contempt.

"It's not always like that Darcy people…"

"You want me to believe you? I don't trust anything you say. Was this my torture Jackson? Why didn't you just take me?" She was crying and yelling inconsolably, "I guess you're right there are worst things."

"I would never hurt you; you know that."

"Ha, way too late Jack. Get out Jackson, get out, please, leave me alone. I never want to see you; please I don't want to have anything to do with you."

"Darcy, please…" he was crying, "I just wanted you to know the truth about everything about me. I love you, I would never…I'm different"

"You're not different, get out Jackson."

"Darcy, I've waited so… to be with you, to be able to be here with you, let me be with you." His voice trembled, as he got louder. She wouldn't look at him. "I'll wait, I'll wait forever if I have to." He punched the wall beside him in frustration and stormed out.

Darcy sobbed, but she couldn't tell whom her tears were directed at more. She tried to think about everything Jackson had told her. She thought of her mother and wondered if she'd been plagued by nightmares. Was Jackson telling her the truth about her mother's own devices? Something inside her knew that her mother had been unhappy. She thought of all the arguments she'd seen carefully orchestrated to make sure Daniel felt responsible for her misery, the self-loathing, the pity. She often felt responsible for having derailed her mother's life so abruptly. She remembered the last conversation her mother had had on the phone, how desperate she sounded. Darcy wondered who was on the other end of the line and wished she had paid more attention during her French classes. A horrible guilt enveloped her entire being. She loved Jackson still, but if someone like him could have been responsible for her mother's death, could she ever be with him? On the other hand, if they weren't responsible, then that meant Darcy might have unknowingly been the culprit. Just then she felt awful. Jackson had driven people to kill themselves, people he didn't know, people he had no connection to, by force and she had done the same, to her own mother. Perhaps he wasn't the monster, she was.

She sat at her bay window looking out into her yard and felt drained, defeated. Even after everything Jackson had confessed, she felt indifferent. If life was controlled and cataclysmic by all intentions, why should she expect anything better? Why was it so hard for her? She longed for the days where she was living life in the clueless monotony, days before the move, before Harley, before her mother, before Jackson. Her life seemed to be in a downward spiral. People had always made reference to ups and downs, but to Darcy it seemed not so much hills and valleys, but a pitfall. But as bleak as everything seemed, she couldn't imagine taking herself out completely. Her faith was dissipating.

As she heard the door, she felt a sour burn in her throat. She was sure Jackson wouldn't be on the other end of the door, and she was in no mood for any kind of company. When she finally opened the door and saw Max, she didn't give him a chance to speak. "Max, do me a favor?"

"Hi Darcy," he reiterated in a sarcastic tone. She looked at him pleading. "What, yes of course, anything," he said sarcastically and she smiled.

"Just a ride please."

When they pulled up to the cathedral he sighed.

"Darcy, what is it with you and this place?" They walked in and sat down. She studied the walls and windows with morose. Max stared at her as he often did and remembered watching her look at the same biblical art with wonder and enthusiastic hope; he wondered what had changed her demeanor. After a little while she finally came and sat next to him.

"You were right Max." He looked at her with his brow furrowed but she never looked up. "The world is too ugly for all this. God wouldn't allow all this, he wouldn't create all this."

"Darcy, most of the time, I'm talking out of my ass. Besides I told you about, you know..."

"Colors, yeah but Jack's right colors fade its all...bullshit."

"Jack?" Max was surprised.

"Oh I mean Mack, his first name is actually J..."

"No, I know Jackson Darcy, I just, when did he tell you all this?" He felt a mix of anger and jealousy. He wanted to press her about Jackson and he also wondered why all of a sudden she was referring to him as Jack.

"A while back, look what does it matter? The point is you're both right. It's all for nothing."

"Darcy..."

"Max," her eyes welted up. "Could you, do you think if there was a god, he could forgive" her breaths became labored and as Max stared into her eyes, he could see her soul darken over, "a killer?"

Darcy saw his green eyes glaze over a bit "could you?" he redirected the question with a hopeful inquisition.

She shook her head and as his eyes met the cross at the end of the pulpit his proverbial heart iced over. Then she dropped her head into her hands and wept. "Max, I killed her." He looked back at her but her face was buried. "I killed my mother."

"Darcy, you, what are you talking about? Your mother..." he didn't want to finish his statement.

"She never wanted me. I, I ruined everything and I had no right. I shouldn't be here. If I wasn't she would still be. I took everything from her. You don't know what its like to know you took someone's life. To take something no one has a right to." She was so wrong. He knew exactly what it was like, but he could still not relate to her feelings. He'd never felt that way and he knew he never would. But she was wrong, again.

"Darcy, you didn't kill anyone." He took her shoulders and looked right into her eyes, into her soul. "Don't ever say you shouldn't be here, if anyone deserves any of this, it's you. The world, it's yours Darcy. Don't let your faith die because some assholes that probably don't deserve absolution tell you different or because your mother wasn't strong enough to deal with life." He knew it was a little harsh, but he was unfamiliar with sympathy, especially for someone he considered weak minded. He could see in her face he wasn't getting through to her. He stood up and put his hand over his mouth nervously, "You know how I know there's a god somewhere in all this shit Darcy?" He stared at her with an intensity she did not recognize, "because of you." Darcy did not have a chance to respond, as they both turned when another visitor pulled the doors open. Max turned and walked out.

The conversation on the drive home was absent. Instead they listened to music and Darcy stared out at the monotony of the road. She thought about what Max had said in the church and felt guilty. She reached over and took his hand without looking at him. Initially his reaction was to pull it back as any physical affection with Darcy still made him uncomfortable, but he didn't want to. Instead, he closed his hand around hers as well.

When they reached Darcy's house Jackson was out on his front stoop, smoking. He spotted Max walking Darcy to her door and started in their direction.

"Hey Max, hey Darcy." Max nodded and Darcy brushed passed him and after saying goodbye to Max closed the door behind her.

"Well, Jackson…" Max said sarcastically and raised an eyebrow.

"Yeah well, my parents call me Jackson, so…" He could see the suspicion in Max's eyes.

"So I guess, you're back in the dog house with Darcy." He joked with a hint of satisfaction. Jackson shrugged his shoulders. "You sure have a way with the ladies Jackson. I also heard from a reliable source that Scarlett isn't too pleased with you either."

"I guess its like you said, guys like you and me should probably be alone." Max was relieved that Jackson and Darcy had had a falling out, but he was still concerned. He handed Jackson back his cigarette and that's when he noticed his hand was torn up.

"Rough night?"

"Ah trees and branches."

"Working for your old man?"

"Yup they're gone for two weeks, so…"

There was a thick tension radiating between them and it was obvious.

Something had changed and they both knew they're friendship had taken a turn. Max felt guilty and damaged. Jackson had been the only person who he could ever relate to and for a long time he had been not only his best friend, but his only connection to humanity. Then he thought of Darcy and he knew he'd out grown it. "Jackson there's something I've been…" As he spoke he noticed Jackson attention avert to the silhouette in window and he knew he needed more time.

"what?"

"Nah its nothing, we'll talk about it some other time." Jackson stared at Max with indifference and wondered what would happen if he ever really had to go up against him.

Jackson and Darcy

Saturday morning Jackson sat up almost breathless; he ran to his window and looked up. Nothing. This time, there was no excuse, no obstacle, nothing in his way. He ran across the lawn and rang the bell over and over again.

Darcy was pulled out of her sleep by the sound at the door. She figured she must have been in a deep sleep, because her heart was racing when she sat up. Worried that something terrible must have happened and half traumatized, she ran down to answer the door, nearly killing herself on the way down. "Jackson what the hell…"

"You're okay? Of course you're okay." He ran his hand nervously over his face and that's when she noticed he was in his pajamas. She looked at him bewildered. "How did you do that? Why are you…" She finally realized what he was talking about.

"Go home Jackson, I'm fine." She turned to slam the door and he stuck his hand out instead.

"Darcy, just tell me, did you do something?"

"Yes, okay. I found a way to keep myself from dreaming."

"You what; how?"

"Remember, that night you thought I'd died or something. It was a trick I learned from my grandmother, to help me sleep." She thought about it for a moment. "Is it weird, like abnormal?"

"I, I don't know." He really didn't. He always knew there was something different about Darcy's dreams, but he wondered to what extent.

It hurt to look at him; he was still beautiful in her eyes. He was still everything he'd always been to her. He was still hers. She finally had the courage to meet his eyes and he smiled at her. "Darcy, I"

She wanted so badly to listen whole-heartedly instead she said, "Jackson, you're standing out here half naked, go home. There's really nothing to say." He could sense she was contrite in her words, but he didn't want to exasperate things any further. So he nodded and turned to leave.

"Darcy, jut one thing, I know I have no right to ask, but I need you to do something for me." She looked at him in indifference. "Don't shut out your dreams, because if there was ever anything I had to become involved in, it's the only way I could reach you. I promise, I won't look in on you anymore, I just, if I had to…"

"Fine, but I'll hold you to that promise. We have nothing to say to each other here or anywhere else." When she closed the door behind him, she couldn't help but feel a dark abysmal longing.

She spent the rest of the weekend holed up in her room. She thought about everything and wished for silence. Her thoughts were evolving into visions she could no longer compose.

On Sunday night she could no longer stand the ache that originated in her stomach and now had occupied so much space in her throat she could no longer swallow without feeling pain. She ran down to her parents' room and opened up her mother's closet. There surrounded by the various shades and textures of fabrics eerily hanging lifelessly she broke down. It finally hit her that she would never again see her Jeanette animated through the house or hear her voice radiating off the walls melodically as it often did. And as she took one of the garments separated for dry cleaning, and put it to her cheek, she inhaled the all the scents that infused to make up her mother and realized that faint scent would eventually fade away and there would be no trace left of her mother in any tactile form. She was so angry at her for leaving, and guilt ridden for what she'd done, but mostly she missed her, as she always would. It was a solace she'd never find. She grabbed a sweater and wrapped the flattened arms around her body and clung to it in grief. She knew Max was trying to be helpful but the remark he had made about her mother being weak still irked her.

On Monday morning she felt relieved that when she got back to school, everything was as it was before the accident. No pity, no gossip, no snickers, just the occasional stare. That morning when Clem arrived to take her to school, she had thought about coming clean about the kiss, but then she figured there was no point since she really had no romantic feelings toward Max. After school, they had made plans to go out and get some food, with some friends. As they made their way to Clem's car, they passed Jackson.

"Clem, Darcy, how's everything?" Jackson asked dryly.

"Oh hey Mack," Clem responded as Darcy bit down on her lip and walked passed him. Clem noticed the look of absolute despondency in his face and mouth out an "I'm sorry." He shrugged his shoulders and took a deep ineffective breath.

"Darcy," she whined, "not again, I thought we were passed all that. Are we really back to where we started?"

"Clem, look I promise I have my reasons. Please just let it go."

"Darce, I know I come off a bit intense and a wee heartless at times, but as your best friend I have to say you are being a bit of an arse." Darcy looked at her with widened eyes. "He saved your life Darce, and I probably shouldn't say this, but for some reason I get the impression he really cares for you."

"Saved my life? A bit dramatic."

"Darcy?"

"Clem?" she reiterated sarcastically.

"Fine then, I'll just keep out of your business."

"Thank you." Darcy felt so bad for being crass, but she was having a hard enough time staying away from Jackson, she couldn't take someone making it worse.

The next couple of days went on in the same prosaic mood. Clem was starting to notice how distant Darcy seemed and was tempted to ask her. She also took notice to how visibly rejected Mack looked every time they walked by him and her sympathies animated. Under normal circumstances she'd of obliged her and not pushed the matter, but she knew how sensitive Darcy could be and she didn't want her to fall victim to her own gloomy disposition. Thursday was the last day she could stand to keep her usually emotive opinions to herself.

"Okay Darcy, forgive me please, but I refuse to do this with you."

"What?"

"Really, I'm not going down this depressing rollercoaster with you, so how can I put this gently, get over all your shite please. I know you know that I love you, and I know lord you've had a bad year, but don't make it worse Darcy."

"Worse, is that even possible?"

"Apparently so. There are ways to deal, but pushing everybody out just gets you back to where you're afraid to be," she stared at her blankly, "alone Darcy."

When she got home that afternoon, she made her way to the garden in the back and she walked through inhaling the aromas of the rain that had yet to fall. She came across a tiny wrought iron table with two flimsy chairs whose bits of rust gave them character and sat down pensively.

Again

Jackson walked through the grounds with a heavy stride. His eyes felt dry and worn and his face felt stiff as if he had aged. He wished for the days before everything, before he cared, before his world had collapsed. Sleep had escaped him and even after being called out the past several nights the sleep deprivation he often felt was gone. He searched his soul for a solution, an escape. When he saw Darcy sitting at the table through the corner of his eyes, he felt his heart race. His stuck his hands in his pockets for assurance. The thunder was making its way across the hills. He watched as Darcy stood up startled and gazed out into the direction of the rolling, sonorous boom. She hugged her arms around her body and as he watched her from behind he got an overwhelming nostalgia. As he walked his steps were lighter than they had ever been, almost as if he were walking on air. He had lost all control of his own actions; his body took over.

For a moment Darcy forgot about the world and she was captivated by the abilities of nature as she stood listening to the thunder. She didn't hear the footsteps swiftly making their way to her, but for a second she got the feeling someone was standing behind her. Before she could turn around, she felt his arms embrace her. Her initial reaction was to pull fee, but her body wouldn't allow it. Her heart raced and her breathing became swift and shallow, but she could not move.

Jackson held Darcy like he had held her a hundred times before, but for the first time. As he noticed that she did not protest or push him away he squeezed her tighter as if at any moment they might disappear, he wanted to hold on to her as long as he could. He pushed his face into her neck and took in her essence. As the tip of his nose and the brush of his lips grazed the side of her neck he heard her sigh. It was the soft release of an ecstasy that had been repressed to the point of rupture.

It was just like in her dreams. Darcy could see Jackson's arms around her but over her jacket she could only feel the pressure. When she felt his breath on her neck, her body reacted and she felt a grunt escape her mouth like a teakettle releasing a built up pressure. She felt her body go weak and every nerve in her animated. Warmth passed through her veins. With her teeth clenched she closed her eyes and let go of any and every emotion. She finally broke free and turned to face him. With his forearms clutched in her hands she looked up at him and felt the first drop of rain hit the corner of her mouth.

Jackson's chest burned as every conviction was reborn. He stood staring at her and swallowed hard. When the raindrops hit her face it was poetic almost as if they belonged there. His hand was shaking as he lifted it up to wipe the water gathering on her check.

When his fingers first grazed her cheek, her eyes fell shut and he felt his knees almost giving out on him. It was the first time he had felt her skin under his and it was more than he could bear. His breathing became labored as he ran his hand over her cheek, down the nape of her neck and rested it on her collarbone. Watching her face contort with every slide of his fingers over her immensely silky skin, the moment was culminating. He slid his other hand through her hair over the back of her head and gently pushed her towards him as he bent down he felt a mixture of elation, anticipation, and fear and he slightly brushed his bottom lip over hers. He could feel the pants of her sweet breath against his lips as he felt the water from the rain fall from her lips onto his tongue. His heart was palpitating and he pulled back to study her face and make sure she was okay.

The kiss was slight and soft, but it was the most intense feeling Darcy had ever felt. The rain was coming down harder and they both just stood there in silence. As the water beaded off his lower lip it glistened and reminded her of fruit juicing. She finally had enough fortitude; she looked into his eyes and saw desire, but not the lascivious determined desire she had seen in Harley, it was a longing. She waited as they stood drenched from the crisp waters descending from the smoky sky for him to take her or kiss her with more determination. Instead he took her hand and walked her back towards her house. When they got to her back door, he hesitated, kissed her check, crossed his arms over his chest and started back towards his house. Darcy's mind was reeling with confusion, her insides were flaring and as she closed the door behind her a strange panic set in. She wanted him, more than ever, at that moment, it was resolute.

Closing the door behind him he ran his hands over his head. It was the hardest thing he'd ever had to do, but it was crucial. Every sensation in his body had been triggered and he was sure there would be no containing the lecherous need he had for her if he went any further. His face was burning and his body was aching from detriment. He started up towards his room, when he heard a faint knock at the door. Shivering from the cold rain that still lay soaked in his sweater, he made his way sullenly towards the door. There she stood still drenched, still beautiful. She walked in and he stepped back as she closed the door and leaned against it. He looked at her with his brow furrowed.

"D…"

"Shhh," she walked towards him and he balled his fist for composure. She swallowed the tightness he could hear in her throat and she place one hand on his hip, the other on his chest and went up on the balls of her feet. When she leaned in towards his face, he had no choice, but then again, when it came to Darcy, he had never had one. He wrapped his arms around her and kissed her more intently. The need for air dissipated and with every sweep of her tongue, he could taste her dulcitude. He slid his hands gently beneath the back of her blouse and caressed the small of her back. As he felt her shudder beneath his touch, pants of elation escaped his body without warning. Her body was cold from the rain. He grabbed the bottom of her sweater and blouse collectively and rolled the fabrics in his hands, but could not bring himself to pull away from her lips. After a couple of minutes Darcy pulled back and he noticed her lips trembling. Looking only at her prismatic eyes, he finally pulled her blouse over her head. Her body was trembling; he pulled off his sweater and pressed her body to his. Felling her bare breasts pressed against his skin gave him a euphoric rise. He quickly grabbed a coat and wrapped it around her and when he looked down to see if she was alright, he proceeded to kiss her gently. She pulled back and looked up at him suggestively. Jackson looked at her intensely almost pained, then obligingly took her hand and led her up to his room.

When they reached his bed, he did not lay her down or force her up on it rather she slowly lowered herself onto it and proceeded to remove her shoes and her jeans. He stood over almost paralyzed by attraction. She lay on her back with one hand over her head and the other resting at her side. Jackson lay next to her on his side and positioned his head on his hand; he stared at her with gratitude, gratitude to her for sharing herself with him, as he didn't feel worthy of bearing witness to something so magnificent. Darcy grabbed Jackson's hand and ran it over her body, it felt just as Darcy had described, criminal, like feeling and seeing something forbidden. She released his hand and placed hers on his cheek. The look on her face was pure bliss, she had never loved so incessantly before and she knew she would never again. Jackson bent down and kissed Darcy from head to toe taking in as much of her as he could. He had no objective; he was simply lost in everything she was.

Darcy had never been so sure of anything in her indecisive life. When he finally made his way back to her mouth, she ran her hand over his chest, stomach, and finally brought her hands to rest on his hipbone. She knew he was being careful not to push her, so took the initiative and tugged at his belt loop. "Are you sure Darcy, we really …"

"Jackson, I …"

"I love you Darcy." He leaned in and kissed her edaciously. The copulation was equally indulgent. Darcy did not dream that night. It was the first night where sleep just felt alleviating, without her having to think about it.

Jackson could not bring himself to sleep, he was too afraid of losing the moment. Instead he watched her sleep, the melodic rhythm of her breaths, the way her hair fell over her bare, back. Every so often he would close his eyes and drift away. But when morning broke, he watched as the sun rose in the sky and when the light broke through the window, he watched as it caressed every part of her body until, she was fully illuminated. She opened her eyes and smiled when she saw him and lay over him in a thick embrace. With her body pressed against his, he became aroused, not by the feeling of her skin against his, but this time by the beating of her heart that he could feel against his chest. "You should really get home, your dad is probably going to kill me and we have class."

"Not my dad, but Anne's probably going crazy by now."

"Vere is dat Darcy, I kill her," Jackson mocked as Darcy chuckled.

Darcy bit down on her lower lip and stared at him with an innocence he held sacred. She knew everything changed in that one moment and she couldn't help but wonder how many moments would change her life.

That morning when Clem arrived to pick her up she did not reveal anything. She wasn't sure why; it wasn't a dream anymore, but it still felt like a secret.

The day seemed to drag on longer than it usually did. She had this yearning all day to see him, and thought how ironic it was that when she was avoiding him, he always seemed to pop up and now that she wanted just a glimpse of him, he was nowhere in sight.

The Summon

When Jackson received his summon he was nervous. He knew it wasn't a routine assignment, because he had never been called in during school. He walked through the doors of Dominion with a feeling of apprehension. He took a seat and waited to be called in and thoughts of disturbing possibilities plagued him. He looked down at his hands, and was reminded of where they had spent the night. The sweep of his fingers over the soft convexity of her body gave him solace. The recollection gave him chills and he felt comforted by the thought that no matter what awaited him on the other end of the double doors he had experienced the best thing life could ever offer.

When he saw Dominic on the other end of the table the usual inferiority and aversion he felt towards him had almost given way to indifference. He stood at the foot of the panel and felt the eyes of the thirteen studying his every motion. Dominic's stone colored eyes showing not the slightest of life, almost as if he were staring back at a corpse.

"Jackson," the name escaped his lips like a hiss, "well I see you are still quite efficient at your staple. It should not escape you that you were summoned with substance. Dominion had concerns about your discretion, clearly your capabilities were satisfactory but perhaps the problems lay with your obedience." Jackson did his best not to flinch, but he could feel his heart begin to speed up, so he concentrated on his pulse. There was a couple of seconds of silence, cruel, torturous silence, for Dominic's sadistic benefits.

"However, it seems redemption has your favor, the Watchers were under direction to be more thorough than usual and have reported no unsanctioned movements on your part, as well I see no basis by which to keep this from you, so I can also report that the emissary we had on you has also reported nothing out of regulation." Jackson felt his body immediately relieve itself of the massive tension it had been building. "We weren't too sure if we had the right plebe however, it has been decided that you will be given a more daunting task. As you know we are in a current shift in world leadership, as we would like to get along with the expansion of certain territories, demolition by coercion is in order, just some smaller territories of a less evolved people, nothing too trying. Your next few assignments will all be with the same intention, as it may take a couple of persuasions to get things progressing." Dominic's hand remained up, but he shifted his focus from Jackson to the rest of the panel and as they sat in discussion, their coordinated whispers moved in and out, the sonic waves reminded him of a snake pit.

Jackson lost himself in thought for a while and let a word fall loose from his lips "genocide."

The hissing ceased instantaneously. "Pesticide," Dominic stated with a tone that would almost denote a smile, Jackson panicked and smiled at him for accolade, as far as he could tell it worked and Dominic made it a point to physically reiterate that his hand was still up. "As always our expectations are irrevocable. You will be tasked on your way out. That is of course unless you have any inquiry." He finally let his hand fall, but Jackson knew that his every word, tone, vocal gesture was being looked upon too closely, so instead he offered a nod.

When Jackson walked out he felt a rush of paranoia and made his way into his car and drove towards his house. As Dominic's words played over in his head, he swallowed hard and thought of Darcy, genocide, this would most definitely constitute murder. The other part of the discussion that still had not escaped was the reference to an emissary. A physical spy, how had this escaped him? It seemed almost impossible, but he knew that in the concern of Dominion anything was possible. It wasn't then so much a question of how, rather than who.

DARCY AND MAX: EXPECATIONS

Max hadn't spoken to Darcy in almost a week. After leaving her that afternoon with not much of a valediction, he had spent the whole week, thinking about the kiss, about Darcy, about his life. Max knew he could never have her in the traditional sense, but something inside him stirred when he thought about her, and when she wasn't around, he missed her. He had never been affected by a girl that way before, there was only one solution her could see he had to have her. Perhaps the physical satisfaction would tame the emotional. It was a week of evaluation and resolution. When he was set to submit his report on Jackson, he did it with reprieve. It was seldom when Max felt the justness in his life, but for once in a long time he felt human.

When he pulled up Darcy's drive, he wondered how he should approach her. After a few seconds he heard a car pulling up and it was Jackson. Seeing his friend in the newly lifted haze gave him solace and as he looked over to wave at him he saw something strange in his eye, a look that almost resembled revelation.

When Darcy heard the door she ran down with expectation. Seeing Max at the other end of the door was both surprising and unnerving. They had not spoken since that afternoon in the church and she wondered if had been avoiding her. "Hi." When he smiled at her she couldn't help but return the smile with genuine affection. Max had been her friend unconditionally and she was grateful.

" Max, hey," she hugged him as she had many times before, but for the first time she felt something strange and intimidating radiating between them. "For a minute, I swore, I might never see you again."

She noticed his teeth clench and she knew nothing could be the same between them. "Darcy, you should know me better than that. I just thought you might need some space. So, feeling better about things?"

"Oh you mean after my embarrassing fit?" she blushed slightly. "More or less," she lied. Still she couldn't help thinking about what had occurred the last time they had seen each other.

He looked at her and wanted so desperately to touch her. "Darcy I, I have to tell you, I kinda missed you."

She smiled, "I missed you too Max." It wasn't until she looked up and saw the vehemence in his seemingly apple green hued eyes that she realized the change in connotation. She immediately looked away and bit down on her lower lip. "Max ," she tilted her head to one side, "I think..."

"Darcy, please, don't think anymore." He leaned in and kissed her gently with closed lips. When he pulled back he could see her lips trembling and the realization that he was wrong came over him.

"What was that for?"

"It was just a kiss Darcy. Hey, I have to go, I have a school thing, but," he hesitated as he tried to contain his desire to push further "well, I'll call you later on?" She nodded and smiled in trepidation as she could see Jackson from the corner of her eyes.

Driving off Max felt and that was enough to get him in a place of almost complacency. He decided to take one more glance at his new paragon and when he shifted his mirror, a sway of jealously as he noticed Jackson make his way over to Darcy. He didn't want to arouse suspicion by double backing or lingering, instead he tried his best to maintain his composure and reminded himself that Jackson was no longer a threat as far as he could make out from Darcy.

As Jackson walked over to Darcy, his heart was racing, not from the jealousy that should have erupted when he saw Max kiss Darcy, or from the duplicity of Max's actions towards his best friend, but from the fear of the realization that not only had Max known about Darcy, but how close he was to her now. He needed to do something, anything to get her as far away from Max as possible. "Darcy," he said with his voice shaking.

"Jack, it's not what..."

"Darcy," he reiterated as he gestured her to stop talking and took her by the hand. "Lets go, we have to go now." He pulled her towards his house.

"What; where are we going?"

"It doesn't matter; you're not safe we have to..."

She pulled free and stopped and began walking towards her front door. "Jackson," he was frantically trying to get the door open for her. "Jack," finally she cupped his face in her hands, "stop. Please let's just talk, please."

"Darcy, we can't. Remember I told you how there were others like me?" she nodded. "Well, I think they might know about us and I have to hide you at least for now."

"Wait, what?" She looked horrified. "Jack, I can't just leave, my dad will, well I just can't. Besides with everything you've told me, where could we even go?" Jackson knew she was right there was really nowhere he could ever take her. "Jackson, stop it's okay." He pulled her against him and closed the door.

"I just, Darcy I..."

"I know," she smiled and kissed him.

As she lay strewn across him on her bed, she stared at the window over her bed. "What are you thinking about?" Jackson voice was melodic as he ran his fingers through her hair.

She fiddled with the zipper on his jacket. "When you were gone, I remember laying here staring at her, wishing I could be there, dream of you."

Jackson couldn't help but smile at the notion, that he was responsible for the Sleeping Girl, and somehow it made sense to him. He remembered choosing it during the first years he had met Darcy, and he couldn't help but wonder if even through the orchestrated chaos of their existence, destiny still had a hand in. He had placed it there for her. "So what is going on with Max?" He hadn't led on that Max might be the leak, mostly for her own safety. He knew Darcy's good nature could lead to her own undoing if she tried to talk to Max about what was going on.

"Oh, um, I really don't know. Mixed signals I think." She actually had been preoccupied with the same thought. She knew she would miss Max as her friend and had no idea how she was going to let him down. "Jackson, do you think my mother was weak minded?"

He felt uncomfortable and feared the wrong words might ignite another disagreement, but all he could do was speak honestly. "Um I never really knew your mother, but I don't really think there are weak minded people. People are generally easily affected by situation and emotions. I think, maybe she was just unhappy." He saw a tear build up in her eye and his heart broke. "It wasn't you Darcy; you were probably the best thing that ever happened to her. It really wasn't anyone. There are some people that just don't know how to be happy or even content. It's not any specific thing, most of the times it always something. You understand, there was always going to be a reason for her to be unhappy, and she just couldn't cope. There was nothing you could have said or done, most of the time when people have their mind set on something, I mean really set, the most you can expect to do, is stall. I can't imagine how you feel, angry, sad, um abandoned? I can't offer any real consolation, except to say, that maybe she just needed to find peace."

"You know Jack," she said as she ran her fingers into his, "its just I feel so guilty because as beautiful as she was, and as much as I really loved her, I used to hope that I'd never be like her." The pitch in her voice changed as she was on the verge of tears. "And now there are times that I'm so afraid of ..."

"Darcy, you are not like her. Not like you've described her to me anyway and you are so much stronger than you'll ever know. She knew you loved her Darcy." Jackson wished her could relive her compunction, but that would only come in time.

"Jackson, do you believe in heaven or I mean does it exist, like even if what you say is true; especially if what you say is true?"

"I don't..." he caught himself mid nod and assessed his life, "yes. As bad as things can get, there are still too many beautiful moments. We still die and I have no doubt we go to a better place, well you do anyways and I'm quite sure there's a place for the rest of us. Although," he playfully ran his hand down her back, "I can't imagine how much better anything could possibly feel."

"Jack, this is way off, but what's with the accent?" She chuckled and he smiled. "I mean you never had it before."

"What, you mean you don't find it charming and sexy?" He laughed. "Well. I grew up here so naturally I have the accent. Erm, I guess in your dreams you hear me they way you would hear anyone else. It's all planned out to ensure our discretion I guess. Like from what I have made out, I suppose we get assigned people across the globe, so we don't have any outside connections. I suppose, that's how this happened too, I mean you were my practice, I'm sure they never expected me to go back and see you again and that's why when you moved over I had no way of knowing."

"Don't you kinda of miss it though? Not knowing, being away from everything. Like all those nights, and the mystery of what we would feel like?"

He brushed her hair behind her ear and kissed her gently, "no." They spent the rest of the night in still silence, shut out from the rest of the world as they had been before. With her head on his chest she felt so safe and with the rhythm of his pulse, she fell asleep.

Jackson walked through the empty streets without direction and confused because as far as he could remember, he hadn't crossed over. He came upon the pillars and was surprised that he had still yet to see Darcy. He walked in and the emptiness made him feel uneasy. He walked out into the courtyard still oblivious to why or how he was there. He looked around and felt a nostalgic knot forming his throat. The ground was barren and almost unrecognizable. He sat on the stone bench and tried to picture the days when he and Darcy sat and just talked. He didn't hear the footsteps, but he felt a shift.

"Dd..." when he turned around he was startled to see a woman looking back at him. She was tall and lean, older with olive skin and brown eyes. She looked familiar somehow.

"Not who you were expecting I gather?" All he could manage was a nod. "You know this is what it looked like to her when you didn't come back. Strange really, how a place you knew so well can seem so unfamiliar when someone's missing."

"I'm sorry," strangely enough, he still had his accent, "who are you, where's Darcy?"

She smiled, "sleeping I presume, but we're not in Darcy's dream Jackson?" she questioned his name and he reassured her, "we're in yours."

He smiled to hide a fear that was rising up in him. "No, that's not possible. I don't dream, I can't."

"No, you can, you've just been trained not to."

"Who are you, how do you know about me, about..."

"Not important."

"What...'

"Darcy is the girl. She is very special, but I know you know that. Haven't you figured it out yet or wondered how she is different?" He started at her still bemused. "I know all about you Jackson, what you do, how you do it, why it is that way." Her accent was thick, but her voice was melodic. "I also know, you love Darcy, and she loves you very much, but you're both in a lot of danger."

"Wait, I just, I think I need a minute." He rubbed his forehead "How do you know all this."

"Not important."

"Please, please even just the basics."

"The Dominion has been around longer than you can imagine; they are older, older than beliefs, older than religion, older than time itself. See we believe that we are living, but they figured it out before us. They know that life, this life here is all just a phase of existence; like a dream. And if we can control the events in our lives, our comings and goings, we must be able to do the same in our dreams. See there is a difference between life and existence. Picture a stack of boxes and as you open one, there is another and another. That is existence and life each one box within another and within it our dreams. The core of all existence, the heart and if you can control the heart…"

"You can control life?" A realization came to Jackson a small but relevant moment of truth. "But why…"

"He made the ultimate curse on humanity, on the Gods and formed an unholy bond with damnation. His soul is eternal and as time has gone by he has become more and more ruthless. It's all part of a balance, a secular equilibrium; your dreams represent both perdition and paradise."

"Dominic, but I just…"

"You're not the first to desire what is denied to you, but she'll change you and he knows it. He can't get to her, but he will find a way."

"Who are you and what do you care," she looked at him emotionless.

"There is another like you in her life. He wants her too, but not like you and not by choice. He's unaware that he is being manipulated to lure her in. He won't give her up; it has become an obsession. He's with her now."

"No she's with me now," he blushed and she smiled and placed her hand on his cheek.

"Yes, but she is dreaming and he watches from within. He's good like you, much better than I was."

Jackson sat up from his sleep and took in a deep breath. The sweat that had gathered on his face made its way down and soaked his shirt. Darcy felt the jolt and opened her eyes. "Jack, what's wrong?"

"Darcy," he grabbed her head and put it against his chest. She could hear how fast his heart was racing. "I ,I…" he kissed the top of her head. Was it just a nightmare, his guilt plaguing at him? She smiled and ran her hand down his face.

The next morning he was forced to sneak out as sounds of Daniel's car made their way up the drive. When he got to the cottage his dad was waiting inside. "Nice evening boy?"

He rolled his eyes "she just, I didn't want her to be alone?"

"You mean," his eyes widened, "you were with the Whitten girl?"

"Darcy dad, her name is Darcy."

"Do you know, have you any idea, what you can do to this family? You're going to ruin that girl's life boy! You know, is that what you want or don't you care?"

Jackson double backed "she's the only thing I care about."

He went up to his room and tried to re-sequence his dream any way he could. There was no way to know if she was made up or sent or what she was. He went over every possibility. Was she adversary or emissary, why would she look for him? He closed his eyes, thought of Darcy and tried to think of what he could possibly do to keep her safe.

Darcy and Daniel

Darcy spent Saturday afternoon with Daniel. It was the first time he had slowed down since the overhaul on his life and he was genuinely grateful to Darcy for handling everything in the style and grace she had. They went out for dinner and Darcy had a guilt that had been tearing at her heart. Daniel hadn't spent enough time with Darcy to be able to see beyond her typical emotional visage, but that afternoon, there was something in her eyes. "Darcy, I know we've gone through, that you have had a tough…" she could tell he was struggling.

"We've both had it tough."

He was fiddling with the gold ring round his left and as he tried to keep from trembling. He smiled forcefully and continued "is there something, anything you need to," he hesitated for a moment, "you know I didn't even know her. I mean, no I didn't know her at all. It was like she had a life and I really wasn't in it. Sometimes I look at you and I wonder if I know…"

The mere fact that he was trying with every inclination to reach out made her want to confess. "You know me," she reassured him as much as she could and her smiled through tearful eyes. "It's just, Dad, is it possible to be completely heart broken and still be able to feel happy. I mean, is it wrong with everything, losing mom," she swallowed hard, but her voice still broke when she spoke and a tear build up in the corner of her eye.

"It's okay to be happy Darcy, you're life can't end here. She took her own and that was tragic enough, you shouldn't let her take yours as well." He reached across the table and took her hand as tears streamed down her face. "She made her own choices. You need to have all the wonderful moments life has to offer, joy, success, fulfillment, love." She put her head in her hand and wept. "You're in love?" she nodded. "I didn't even think we'd been here that lo…that's great sweetheart." She looked up with an unsure look on her face. "It really is, he's probably very special to have won someone like you, and I hope he knows how extraordinary you are." His eyes were glassy and she knew he was conclusively sincere.

"Dad," he looked at her as he sipped his water and the music in the room slowed down, "will you dance with me, like we used to?"

He smiled through a heavy heart. "I would want nothing more in the world." They got up and walked to the small wooden dance floor, where a few couples clumsily waddled around. As she put her hand in his, her chest felt tight and she put her head to his heart and they glided. Daniel found a strange peace in every pace. He knew that he could never again feel guilty for what had happened to Jeanette, because Darcy encompassed everything that was right in the world.

When they reached the driveway, she noticed Jackson and Mr. Mackinnon laying mortar in the walkway. Jackson stood up and started towards the door, much to the dismay of his father. As Darcy and Daniel exited the car, her eyes lit up at the sight of Jackson and Daniel furrowed his brow in suspicion.

"Mackinnon?" he whispered into her ear and she shrugged her shoulders.

"Erm hello Mr. Whitten, Darcy," he stood there and felt a little uneasy. As Daniel excused himself for the evening she walked over to Jackson, but before she was able to speak her father turned and took a couple of steps forward.

"Um Mr. Mackinnon," Jackson face lost all its color, "I don't have to tell you my daughter is exceptionally capable, but I'm counting on you to look after her. Even though she is your," he winked at Darcy and she blushed "girlfriend, she's is still my little girl." He smiled and walked in before Jackson could respond. Darcy was still blushing but couldn't help but feel sentimental towards her father's remark.

"Girlfriend? I don't recall ever having ..." Darcy gave him an annoyed glare. "I'm only joking," he playfully took her waist. "I think you have surpassed the term girlfriend Darcy, you're beyond description. You told your dad about me?" A strange sense of normality made him smile.

"No, not everything, just the basics, he sort of figured it out on his own. I should go in, we're having quality time."

"Ah I see, well then I guess I could settle for a good night kiss."

"Well, maybe I could see you later?"

"I thought," then he realized what she meant. "Oh erm, I actually, I have to work," he bit down on his lower lip nervously.

"Oh right." She leaned up to kiss him and as she wrapped her arms around him she secretly prayed for his soul and for those that would perish as a result of whatever he was doing. It made her feel a sense of reprieve on his behalf.

Darcy walked along a curved walkway. The air was infused the thin rows of pine that seemed to climb up beyond the skyline. As she kept walking, the trees seemed to be closing in on each other until there was no light visible between them. Before she realized it she appeared to be in a maze.

He watched as her expression changed when she hit the first dead end. There was always something he found seductive and enticing about mazes. The idea that someone might be lurking around any turn or that someone walked blindly into every corner. He wondered how she'd maneuver through it. The first thing that had attracted him to her was her ability to be cunning and self-assured. He noticed a smile that would crack every time she felt she'd made progress. He chuckled sadistically to himself at the knowledge that there was no way out. He stared at her with appetence.

After a while Darcy began to get nervous. Even though she knew she was dreaming, a strange anxiety built up that she might be stuck. She stopped and took in a deep breath, closed her eyes and tried to calm herself down. She was startled when she felt someone caress her arms from behind. It was Jackson it had to be, but she had never been able to feel him in her dreams before. She thought it maybe had something to do with the fact that they had already been intimate and maybe she'd memorized how her body reacted to his touch. But as he put his lips to her neck, something felt wrong. She tried to turn back to see who it was, but as she began to turn, he placed one hand on her collarbone and the other beneath her chin.

He couldn't understand why she needed the reassurance and then he got a strange arousal from her resistance. As he kissed her neck she squirmed and although he had all the material to mentally make out in his head what he should be feeling it was still not filling.

Darcy tried to wiggle free and the more she tried, the harder he kissed her. She tried to scream, but she had been robbed of her voice. She closed her eyes and with everything she could muster up she was finally able to let escape in a raspy voice a single word. "Jack"

The kissing immediately stopped. But the hands did not lift up instead the one that had resting on her collar snaked its way up her neck and forced close around her throat. As the other followed behind, she panicked and frantically began trying to squirm free.

It took him a while to figure out what had happened. One minute he was riding a wave of ecstasy and the next a rage had overwhelmed him to the point asphyxiation. He couldn't believe what he was doing, but as he held her delicate frame in place, he realized he was as equally aroused by the thought of the life seeping out of her body beneath his fingertips as he had been by kissing her. He squeezed tighter and put his face to her cheek to kiss her one last time. He had never loved, but he knew if he ever had the capability it would have been her.

Remembering what Jackson had told her Darcy reminded herself it was a matter of perception. She relaxed and tried to imagine the breath escaping and reentering her lungs, but when it brought no relief, she realized it was very real. As she was about to loose consciousness, she let her hand fall from the one's clenched around her throat back and reached back to the hip of her assailant.

When he felt her hand grace his body, flashes of all the time they'd spent together ran through his mind. He pictured her face, her body, her laughter, her tears and it was almost as if a transformation occurred in the manner of Jeckyl and Hyde. He quickly realized what was going on and he felt a disdain towards himself. He didn't immediately release her from his grasp, but he let loose his grip slowly.

When Darcy felt the vise lessen, she reached back to one of his hands with both of hers pulled down on his arm and bit down as hard as she could. Then she closed her eyes and with everything she could, willed herself out of the dream.

She awoke gasping for air. She sat up scared and desperate. She wanted to run to Jackson, but she was paralyzed by apprehension. Jackson had been right someone was trying to kill her. She had never fully surrendered the fact that it was a real possibility and she had most certainly not been prepared for what it would be like. The idea that death could sneak up on you in your own dreams, a place that should only be yours, it was a transgression against nature, against human right. Then she realized that she had been right as well, there would be no escape. When she checked her clock it was 5:30 in the morning and there was no way she would be sleeping. Instead she slipped into her coat and slipped out of her house. She stood in front of the cottage and with her cell phone in hand dialed Jackson's number and as she was about to press send she remembered what Jackson had said about working and instead sat on a bench outside her house.

"He's still sleeping I gather." She was startled to see Mr. Mackinnon. "I've personally never seen him awake before noon when he doesn't have school or some other place he feels he needs to be."

She blushed in embarrassment at the fact that she appeared to be stalking him. "Oh, um I just I had a bad dream and ..."

"Ah, may I?" She smiled as he took the seat next to hers. "Sunday, the misses expects me to drive her into town for the 7:00 sermon" he rolled his eyes and looked in the direction of the cottage, "Darcy correct?" She nodded. "I fear your life here hasn't exactly been ideal? Sometimes, I wonder about the world, why things happen the way they do. I have to say though you are one very strong young lady, but now I wonder, what would someone like you want with my son?" Darcy looked to the ground visibly taken back. "Don't get me wrong, I love my son very much, and you most certainly exceed anything I would want for him, but you just seem like such a bright determined person and he's so lax it irks me. I see no direction in him, no pride, I fear for him, perhaps because I just don't understand him." He looked away and Darcy noticed his concern was genuine.

They sat in silence and finally she spoke. "He's funny and smart and..." beautiful, lovely, compassionate, strong, she wanted to use so many different words, but she could never say that to his father, "amazing." He nodded and smiled.

"He makes you feel special then does he?" She nodded and added

"and safe."

"Well, then I guess there's not much more I could hope for." He stood up as Mrs. Mackinnon appeared from inside, "well, young lady, if he ever crosses you, you come and see me; I'll get him straightened out." She chuckled and looked up, as the sun appeared to be rising. "Go on in; see if you can't get him up with the rest of the world. Might do him a bit of good?"

Darcy waited until Mrs. Mackinnon was in the car and walked into the cottage. As she stood in the living room she got a strange nostalgia. As she walked through the house, up to his room, she could vividly picture every moment as it had been that first night. She got to his door and smiled as she could feel the fluttering in her stomach. When she walked in he was sleeping face down and she could see the definition in his arms as they were set above his head. She walked over to him and ran her hand down his arm. Then she bent down and put her lips to his shoulder and proceeded to his kiss down his back gently.

Jackson opened his eyes startled and although he flinched, he took in a deep breath and let out a moan of rapture. He turned over and as Darcy stood over his bed he gave her a wicked smile. He moved over, she slid into his bed, into his arms and as he enveloped her in his embrace she closed her eyes and felt safe again. She thought about telling him about what had happened, but she didn't want him to do something rash. They just lay there in beautifully relieving stillness. She loved being in his arms and could not imagine a better place.

As he stroked the back of her hair, he noticed his hand and the memory of the night swept over him. He quickly put it back over his head and underneath his pillow and reminded himself to bandage it over.

By Monday, things seemed to have reached stability. Afraid and newly aware of the consequences from sleep deprivation, Darcy used her white wall to fall asleep Sunday night. She figured if Jackson needed to reach her for one reason or another he could simply go to her. Jackson drove Darcy to school and Clem was glad that Darcy was finally able to surrender herself to her own emotions.

PENITENCE

Jackson thought it was strange that during one of his classes he received a message to meet Max. When the scholastic day was over, he found Clem and Darcy out in the parking lot and asked Clem to please take Darcy home for him. He whispered to Darcy that he'd explain it to her later and kissed her goodbye. When he reached Max's door, he felt strange as if he should be on his guard. He was well aware that he did not want to be there, by now he knew better; he braced himself when he heard the door handle turn. Max appeared in the door way unlike Jackson had seen him before. His usually well styled hair sat messily atop his head, his eyes were glazed over with the small veins within them exponentially highlighted, and he was shrouded in an old t shirt, jeans and tennis shoes. "Hey Jackson," his voice was raspy.

"How's it going; I got your message." He stood straight faced, but never let on that he was aware of the shift in perception.

"Yeah, I just figured we could hang out, don't see you too much these days. Been keeping busy?" Max winked playfully.

They walked out into the busy streets and set off with no direction. After a while the hollowed conversation had dissipated and as they continued on in silence, Jackson wondered where they were headed. When they stood at the front steps of the cathedral, Jack furrowed his brow in confusion. "You ever been in here Jack?" he asked in a somewhat maniacal undertone.

"Can't say that I have really."

"Well I have; a couple of times actually."

"Fan of the confessional?" Jackson smiled.

"Repent and all shall be forgiven," he preached mockingly. "Let's go in." Max continued on in the same playful banter.

His behavior was so erratic, but Jackson obliged and followed him in. It had been a while since Jackson had been before an altar. He felt like he was trespassing, he wasn't worthy of the privilege of salvation. It was empty, but still gave him a sense of warmth. As he looked around he felt strangely empowered.

"Look around you Jackson my boy, behold the eternal peace, for hidden within these scriptures lies our salvation," his voice stronger and preachy, he laughed at the sound of his own pretense and jumped down from behind the pulpit. Back in his own voice he added slowly "that you and I will never know.

Coming here used to give me, oh I don't know hope, now it just reminds me how fucked we really are huh?" he laughed.

"What happened to repent and all shall be forgiven?" Jackson walked towards him with his hands tucked in his pockets.

"It's a ruse. Like the truth will set you free, bullshit. The truth will screw you over in the end. A lame approach at an inquisition, you spill your guts and then get fucked over." They stood there staring at each other in silence, "the truth sets you free, and omission keeps you alive. Not a very tough choice huh? Just guilt them into reparations right?"

"So then why come here, if none of this is for us eh?"

"For a while I guess I really thought maybe, just maybe, there was something that could change it. A balance, we get fucked over but here's your consolation prize. Something beautiful to hang off the arm of the monster," he sighed, "didn't that ever bother you? In all those old movies the beautiful woman always fell in love with the monster, but then in the end, the monster was still destroyed and the woman stays behind crying and shit. She was the only one who knew the real him, the soul within the abyss. It was usually, uh no, always her fault he got killed anyway. If she'd of just left him alone; or if he had killed her like he wanted to initially, he'd be fine. Instead she gets him killed, they all learn compassion and life goes on," he winked at Jackson "but not for the monster, he got screwed and not literally either for that matter, ah he's probably better off."

"And it's not his fault, the unscrupulous depravities, he was made that way right, the real victim, Frankenstein like."

"Exactly," he winked and clapped his hands up to his mouth. "See Jackson my man, you get it. You always did and that's why we were friends."

"Were?"

"Were, are, same shit right? Nah, let's go with are, sit better with you?"

Jackson stood up from the bench. "Well, this has been really enlightening, but I think I'm gonna head off. You?"

He stared at him with contempt and then smiled. "I'm gonna stick around, who knows, maybe God will stop by." Jackson nodded at his blasphemy and walked out.

He reached Gidding's Hill and noticed that Clem's car was not in the drive. He walked over to the main house where Anne proceeded to tell him that Darcy hadn't gotten home yet. He picked up his cell phone to dial then he saw a car driving down the road. It was Max; suddenly he was grateful for the fact that Darcy had not made it home yet. Jackson walked down the stone steps as Max was getting out of his car.

"Looking for someone Jackson? How'd you do it?" Max's tone was no longer playfull, but sarcastic and angry. "Fuck her, cause you did right? I mean besides metaphorically speaking. Let's just ask her then." Max walked up towards the house.

"She's not here Max." As Jackson spoke, Max studied him for a while.

"Hmmmm no, I don't believe you," he said and pushed past him and made his way into the house. "Darcy! Darcy!" He shouted through the foyer.

"I told you man she's not here!" As Max continued on his quest, Anne came out from the kitchen at the sign of the commotion.

"Max, Yackson, vat, vat is happen?"

Jackson's eyes widened, "Anne its okay, stay there, everything's fine, just stay, there."

She didn't heed and kept grumbling as she walked towards the staircase where Max was still shouting up at and now climbing. Jackson turned to check the door and by the time he had turned back, he saw Max moving determined towards Anne grumbling t her to shut up. "Max, Max," it was too late he had his arms on her head and with one quick swift he'd snapped her neck and her lifeless corpse hit the floor. Max looked up at Jackson surprised at his own action. "Bloody fuck Max, what did you do?"

"I, I, I don't know, she was screaming and it was just, I just…" He stared down at Anne then shifted his attention back to Jackson who was standing there horrified. "This is all your fault."

"What, how?" Jackson said defensively.

"You broke the rules man, you went against everything we were told, you put her in danger and I still fucking absolved you asshole. I knew, I fucking knew but I thought it was done. But you, you kept on, you couldn't just let it go. Let her go and now…"

"What you're gonna kill her too is that it?"

"No you're wrong Jackson, that's all on you. You killed her, because you were too fucking selfish to leave her alone. You knew exactly what would happen and you let it. You think you love her, if you loved her you wouldn't have condemned her like this asshole."

"She doesn't know anything Max," Jackson pleaded.

"That's bullshit Jackson, we both know its bullshit."

"She doesn't I swear it. She had some doubts but I swear she has no idea."

"Let Dominion decide." When those words escaped Max's lips, anger, a hate, raged up from within Jackson's soul.

"You can't, you know they'll kill her, you know it."

"No, they won't, I won't tell them who it was, I'll act like I have no idea; they can take care of you."

"You think they won't find out eh? They will eventually. You know they know, they always know. After they deal with me, they'll… and what, you gonna be the one to take me out then?"

"That's what I'm counting on," Max was shouting.

"So come on then, do it now if your so set then. What do ya think is in it for you, think she'll submit when I'm gone then? She's not blind Max; she's not a fucking idiot." Max had reached his end, he knew he couldn't kill Jackson without being commissioned first, but he could still make him hurt. He threw the first punch, but Jackson was surprisingly quick to retaliate.

He had always been aware of Max's brute strength, but it wasn't until he felt it against his face that he truly saw his potential. The first blow was the worst, perhaps because it had been unanticipated. It was as if the side of his face had been run into a brick wall. With the black still lifting from his vision, he was up and swinging with all his strength. Every punch seemed to braze over his face with a burn. Tired, crushed, beaten, he stood against everything Max offered up. About five eternal minutes into the brawl he noticed Max stall and as he was about to take advantage of the opportunity Max spoke, "shh, hold on…" Max climbed to his feet and turned to face the door in horror. It pushed open and there she stood.

"That won't work, stay the fuck away from her" exclaimed Jackson as he threw one last blow in Max's direction. Max face turned with the impact, but his recovery was impressive. That's when Jackson saw her too.

"Oi, what the fuck's going on, you guys fightin' to see who's got bigger bollocks? I just left Darcy to pick up her car and she should be…" with the scuffle they had forgotten about Anne. When she noticed the lifeless housekeeper on the ground with her head unnaturally turned out she lifted her hand to her mouth in horror. "Wha, what…"

"Oh yeah," Max made his way towards her, "we think she fell down the stairs, Mack heard a scream and found her that way?" He stared at Jackson intensely.

She turned to Jackson and he looked away. "Shouldn't we do something, call someone?" She was close to hysterics.

"Ambulance is on their way," added Max.

Clem's pallor gave way to a look of fear and confusion. "Is she…" she looked to Jackson and noticed the look of pain in his face as his jaw clenched. "Oh my god," she put her hand over her mouth as Max walked over and took her in his embrace.

"You really shouldn't have to stay here like this, you don't look too good. You want me to get you home or if you're too upset to be alone we could go my place for a while until you feel better. Mack you can handle this right?"

Jackson was impressed at how easy Max was able to manipulate someone. As he walked Clem out the front door, he looked back at Jackson with a sinister smirk and winked.

He was still panting from the fight and the metallic taste from the blood in his mouth added to a sudden rush of nausea he felt when he looked a back at Anne. He looked around and wondered if he should call for help. Then when he saw his reflection in the hallway mirror, he realized it might not look too good to the police. There was no way around it; he had to get rid of the body. He looked back down at her one last time and whispered, "I'm so sorry." Then he headed out to the garden shed to see if he could find anything useful. When he turned the corner he noticed the shed was open. He walked in and was surprised to find his father inside. He wondered if his dad had not heard the scuffle between he and Max.

"Dad?"

"Boy," he turned to face Jackson, "what happened to you?"

"Oh umm got in fight, at school."

"You causing trouble again boy?"

"No sir, it was just a scuffle, no trouble sir."

"What brings ya out here then eh?"

He thought for a minute then spoke. "I was looking for you actually."

"Is that so?"

"Yes sir, it's just, I thought I heard someone scream from the main house. You didn't happen to hear anything did you?"

"I was out in the garden boy, I heard nothing. But I suppose I should check it out eh? Your girl..."

"Oh um she's out getting her car from the mechanic."

He followed close behind his father and waited when his father pushed open the door with a guilt that held his feet back. "Ello? Anyone there, Ms. Anne...Oi bloody hell. Boy, boy, come in quick." Jackson walked in to find his father examining the lifeless corpse on the ground. "Call the ambulance!" Jackson pulled out his phone and began dialing as his father examined the scene more closely. "No need to be too quick, I gather they should probably send a hearse really. Poor girl, supposing she fell down the stairs." As his father assessed the scene, Jackson became nervous at the thought that perhaps if someone were really to look in on the scene more methodically, they might find the body misplaced.

They waited for the medics to arrive. As his father gave a statement to the police that had arrived at the house first, he noticed a small patch of blood on the wood floor, which he quickly covered with his shoe. Jack then noticed a bit of dry blood on his knuckles and he frantically washed his hands over the kitchen sink. His over shirt was also splattered on and he immediately pulled it off and tucked it into a kitchen cabinet. With so much blood the police might begin asking questions he might not be able to answer; he wondered if most of it was his or Max's, then another vastly more important realization ensued, there was no blood of Anne's at the foot of the stairs. He wondered if the officers, both of whom already appeared dense, would question that fact. They never did.

As they loaded the black bag into the back of the ambulance, Darcy pulled up into the drive. "Boy, boy! Go see to your girl." His father's voice brought him back. He was lost in a daze.

"Jack, what happened to your face?" As she spoke Darcy lifted her hands to his face. By this point his eye was almost swollen shut, the bruises around his busted lip and cheeks were seeping through.

"I'm fine, it's nothing. There's more important, it's Anne, she had...an accident." He turned to Darcy and let his face fall "she took a tumble down the stairs they presume."

"Oh my god, are you serious? Is she gonna be okay?" His look all but told the truth about the state she was really in. "How did they, I mean who found the...her?

"Oh erm, I, my dad and I came over to check on, I heard a scream and we just..." he gave her a look as if to say he could say no more. He had promised her he'd never lie to her again.

His nervousness was apparent to her; she knew almost each and every one of his expressions by heart. She felt paranoid, but she couldn't help but wonder what he was keeping. "Now I feel bad I never really got to know her." She sat against the hood of her car. "Makes you wonder, who's next," she whispered as she bit the corner of her mouth.

"What makes you think anyone would be next?"

She held up three fingers to him. "You know what they say?"

"That's just superstition." Jackson's words caused the corner of his mouth to rip a little further causing him to flinch in pain.

"If anyone of us should be devoid of skepticism it should be you. You, more than anyone else, should understand the possibilities of the impossible or improbable." As Darcy spoke, Jackson couldn't help but role his eyes.

He wasn't too sure why but he couldn't help but think of Clem. He wondered if she was really in any danger from Max. The last thing she said before she walked out of the house earlier was for Jackson to make sure Darcy would be all right without her. The words seemed almost prophetic. He shuddered at the thought that they probably were to some extent. He grabbed Darcy and pushed her into his embrace in an attempt to express how much she really meant to him. She wrapped her arms warmly around his waist. Mr. Mackinnon uncomfortably walked over to pat Jackson on the shoulder. Darcy blushed at the sight of him.

"Bb, Son, we've got to get down to the hospital and straighten all this out; should only take a couple of hours." He turned his attention to Darcy, "if you feel ill about staying here on your own, the missus is doing some laundry..."

"It's okay I'm okay." Darcy felt nervous about looking Mr. Mackinnon in the eyes as she spoke to him and she didn't know why.

"No Darcy, I think maybe you should go in and stay with my mum."

"Well, I sort of wanted to shower and stuff, but I guess I could just walk over if I feel bad or something. Jack, I'm okay really and anyways Clem is supposed to be by so I'll be fine."

He didn't have the heart to tell her. "Darcy if you need anything I swear I'll run over if I have to." She smiled and kissed him gently on the cheek. "I love you, I'll get over here as soon as I can." She grabbed his hands and felt the bandage beneath her fingers.

"What happened to your hand?" He studied it and became aware that it had completely slipped his mind.

"Oh, erm, it's nothing."

"Just like nothing happened to your face?" Darcy asked sarcastically.

"Fair enough, look I'll explain it to you later okay?" She nodded apprehensively. Jackson felt strange about leaving her alone with death seemingly trailing so close behind, but he figured the most he had to fear was from Max and he was off with Clem anyhow.

As she walked into her house she felt a cold within her bones. She looked at the stairway expecting to see blood, or at the very least scuff marks, but there was nothing. She walked toward the stairs and tried to picture how it may have happened, perhaps she just slipped and landed at the foot end, or maybe she just took a misstep. But no blood? She couldn't bring herself to walk up so instead she walked into the kitchen for a glass of water. She leaned against the window and looked out at the cottage. The idea that Mrs. Mackinnon was a stones throw away gave her solace, but something was still eating at her. She closed her eyes and tried to remember if she had seen the bandage on his hand earlier or even the morning before. Why hadn't she paid enough attention?

There was just no way her fears could be justified. She couldn't help but wonder as she stood in the kitchen, she closed her eyes and tried to picture it. She lifted her hands to her throat and turned her head in the direction she had the night before. She bit down tenderly just enough to mark, and when she brought then back down her heart stopped still. Impossible, unlikely, there was no way. As quickly as it has been conceived, the thought dissipated. She sat on a stool at the island in the middle of the kitchen and lay her head down on her arms; that's when she saw the piece of familiar black plaid fabric peeking out, provoking from the corner of the cabinet beneath the sink. She was frozen, a stone version of herself that could not be animated. After a couple of eternally torturous seconds she stood and walked towards it. She stared at it for a couple minutes more then tugged at it until it materialized before her. She knew it well, but just to be sure she lifted it to her face. The delicious scent that still lingered was unmistakable, but entangled within another unmistakable scent one she had smelled only once before.

When she reopened her eyes to examine it, the red splatters that were drying over were validating, convicting, condemning. She let it fall to the floor and stared at it with contempt she had never felt towards any inanimate object before. She ran for the door and looked back at the stairway picturing Anne, Jackson, the blood riddled shirt, the bandaged hand, she didn't know what to make of any of it. She needed to think. She ran out to her car and turned the ignition.

When she parked the car, the only thoughts running through her mind were involving Jackson. She'd gone over it a dozen times. She knew him, more than anyone else did, he had divulged every detail of his existence to her, there was no way he was a murderer. There had to be something more, something she was missing. Focusing her attention on his recondite recollection of the events in which Anne was found, the shirt, his face, she refused to mind the suspicion that he might have been the mysterious hands that had earlier tried to strangle her. She only knew of one other person she could trust enough to help her.

DISPLACEMENT

She walked into Max's building as she had done so many times before.

As he washed his hands, he knew things had been set in motion. He was quite amused with himself; at how well he had thought things through, at how well they would play out. He was surprised at the fact that the sound of someone at the door had actually startled him. When he saw her face through the peephole his insides crawled. Magnificent. The convenience of an inconvenient visit seemed almost orchestrated. He opened the door and she looked at him a bit confused.

"Hey Darcy, how's it going?" he asked a bit under enthused.

"Max, your" she put her hand up to his cheek that was slit and purple. His eyes mechanically fell shut at the touch of her hand.

"Yeah well, I guess I underestimated Jackson's right hook." He stated surprised that she seemed unaware.

"Jackson? "

"He didn't tell you?" He raised his eyebrow in a petty attempt to reiterate the omissions. She shook her head. "Have you seen him?"

"Yeah, but I guess with the whole circus of Anne and everything... oh I didn't, you remember my housekeeper Anne..."

"The guardian?" he joked much to her disapproval. "Sorry..."

"Yeah well, she had an accident and..."

"Oh yeah I know, I'm really sorry."

"Wait, what, how would you know..."

He was taken back at the fact that Jackson had neglected to mention Max in any of this and wondered what he had told her. "Well, because I saw her, I was there."

"Where?" She was visibly upset.

"At your house, where do you think Jackson and I, Darcy, did he tell you anything?"

"Just that he and his dad had found her..."

"His dad? As far as I remember it was just Jack and I until Clem walked in." She felt sick and completely confused. "Hey, you look a little...do you want some water?"

"No I just need to sit." He led her over to the sofa and she sat down and rubbed her face. "Just, what happened?" Darcy asked reluctantly.

"I don't really know. I went over to your house to see you only when I walked up, the door was kinda open, so I walked in and called your name." He paused for effect and to get his fictitious details as sorted as possible. "When Jack came up to me I was a little surprised at first and when I asked for you he seemed to get kinda weird about it almost like he was mad or jealous. He was like "No she's not here and even if she was I really don't think you should be coming around." Or something like that, I don't remember, anyway he seemed nervous and I swear like for a second I thought something was going on, like you were in trouble or something, plus I thought he was lying, so I pushed my way in to make sure you really weren't there, and that's when I saw the, your housekeeper. Jack told me he had just found her like that and I told him to call for help and he said he had it all under control. That's when he got all weird and defensive again and we were arguing and things got heated and he just lost it and came at me. It wasn't too long before your friend Clem walked in and saw everything. It was pretty nasty." He studied her reaction and was pleased at his abilities.

"I have to go." She got up to walk out and he followed close behind.

"Look Darcy, I know maybe things between us got complicated and I don't really know what you and Mackinnon have going on, but be careful. Also, I just," she stared at him with a heavy heart, "you know I'd kill him. Maybe it's not the right way or the romantic way, but it's my way. I can't tell you I love you, or even show you all that well, but..." she sighed and nodded, she knew.

The drive home was pensive. Every time Max spoke it was almost as if she were hearing about a stranger. That was not Jackson, not like she knew him, not like he ever could be. On one hand she was relieved to discover the blood splatters were probably from Max, but why would he lie about Anne, and why hadn't Clem called to tell her any of this? Her head was throbbing; she had never felt so beaten down.

When she got to her drive she saw her dad's car, she should have figured upon hearing about what had happened he'd be there. She walked into her house to face confusion and wait for Jack to get home.

Max and Jackson: Vindication

He walked up to the gates determined yet still apprehensive. He lit a cigarette and paced the ground. Every time he took a drag the corner of his raw lip burned fierce and simply justified what he was doing there. He wanted her, anyway he could have her or maybe he didn't. He couldn't be sure, but he knew so long as the other was still around she'd never be vulnerable. Could he do it though; up until a couple of hours before, he had never killed anyone within his own intent. As doubt crept in, the door opened up and surprised him. "Max?" The face was new and unrecognizable, her red dress stood out against the blandness of her pale skin and platinum hair. "Dominic will see you now."

"What? How did he even know I was here?" She smiled and shrugged her shoulders as he followed her in. She smiled; she was normal. He had no idea why but as she walked away from him he got an odd feeling. He couldn't place it, but it was almost as if he should remember her for some reason. He walked into a room he had never been in before. It made him a bit nervous that he wasn't just going before the panel. The room was odd, the walls were a slate grey and barren, no windows or decorations of any kind, the floor was a black tile and there was a black desk that was equally vacant. Had it not been for the fact that not a speck of dust could be seen anywhere he would have thought it abandoned.

"Please sit." He recognized the voice, but it still managed to send chills down his spine. He hadn't even heard the door. "So there was something plaguing you I presume. You've been pacing out there irritatingly." Max was a little unnerved to be alone with Dominic and it would be a lot harder to communicate with him as his hands were crossed over his chest rather than in a position to signal a response. His stone eyes lit up as he took to the chair behind the desk. "I have to say I was rather appeased to find you had come to countermand your previous testimony."

"You say that like you already knew."

"Is that not why you are here?" Max took a deep breath and nodded. "Right well, I have to say for a minute I thought you had capitulated from your humanity; that or perhaps that I had two insubordinates to have to deal with."

"You knew about Jackson? Then why…"

"My boy, I make it a point to know all. It's just a matter of finding out how far the contamination has spread. It's also a good test to your loyalty. You know, I rarely make it a point to speak to anyone on a basis such as this, but it befalls me to tell you I am pleased with your callousness. I find sometimes it is more difficult to separate those that tend to be tied to the aphoristic soul. So, I presume to be right in assuming that our advisor has not yet seen the error of his way. Yes, well, I had already been informed earlier from a more palpable source. Usually this is a matter I take up with my lesser endowed associates, but he has proved time and time again to be one of the more gifted..." he trailed away in thought. Max looked down at his feet nervously. "Right, then I suppose..." Before he was able to finish his sentence, the woman in red walked through the door and handed him something, Max squinted his eyes to get a better view; it was a task. The very thought that he knew all too well what name lay chiseled on that task gave him a feeling of bereavement. Max was aware that if he carried out this assignment he would officially and completely have lost himself.

"Is that mine?" Max asked uncomfortably.

Dominic gazed at him for a moment. "You were made aware that you'd be the one to effectuate the situation." He handed Max the paper and Max made his way to his feet to walk out. "Open it." Max stopped and looked at him puzzled. "In case there is any perplexity." He couldn't help but wonder if it was another test to see how he would react. He knew every twitch and blink would be scrutinized so as he unfolded the paper in his hand he mentally prepared himself to see Jackson's name on the other end. He looked down and he felt his heart stop beating all together. His insides were shaking and it took everything to maintain his composure.

"Darcy Whitten?" he whispered, trying to keep his eyes from glazing over.

"It was a difficult decision but upon weighing the two, I have decided to spare Jackson for the immediate time being seeing as how he is working on a very important development of mine. I presume you were aware that this was the obstacle; are you familiar with the girl?"

He searched for his voice and struggled to keep it from trembling. "Yes." He could feel Dominic burning through him with his eyes. "I've seen them together."

"Of course you have and apart, from my understanding." Max looked up at him through furrowed brow. "I do make it a point to know all." Max made his way towards the door. "Shouldn't prove too trying, if she's as…what would be the best term, ah weak minded as her mother. Very clever, you handled that with charisma. From what I gathered you rather enjoyed it." Max nodded and walked out militantly.

As soon as he was out of the gates he finally released the breath that had been caught in his chest. He knew Dominic had made him look at her name for his own sick delectation. He hated himself more than he ever had. Jackson was right; Darcy had no chance. As he drove home he could feel his lips tremble, his hands were mechanical in making their way back, as he was miles away in thought. He felt a strong emotion, an emotion he had not felt in a long time, an emotion he usually provoked, he was afraid. The epitaph in his pocket burned through into his chest.

Darcy sat on her bed thinking about everything that had happened. She had waited for Daniel to get home before having the courage to go up to her room. With what had happened to Anne earlier, they were both on edge, and as he awaited Mr. Mackinnon to return, she just as eagerly awaited Jackson's. She couldn't help but wonder why Clem had not called her to tell her what she had seen. She had already called several times and left a couple of messages, but the calls went without response. She threw herself on her bed in a haze of emotional exhaustion. As she stared up at the mural over her bed, she couldn't help but feel, feel elated, feel nostalgic, feel for her Jackson. It didn't make sense everything that Max had said added up, but just didn't make sense; something had to be missing. She buried her face in her hands.

"You're so beautiful." He startled her; she hadn't even heard him enter the room. "Your dad is outside getting the gist from my dad, so I came up to see how you're doing." As she stared up at him she couldn't help but notice the bruises on his face had taken full form and his busted lip had turned to a deep hue of red, but he was still painfully beautiful.

"I went to see Max, Jack." She looked to his face for a reaction of any kind.

"What?! Why?! Why would you do that?" He was visibly upset and it made her wonder why.

"What, what do you mean? He's still my friend Jackson."

"Your fri…Darcy, he's not your friend. How come you don't get that? Why don't you see that he doesn't want to be your friend," he snapped sarcastically. She thought about what Max had said and the bruises were a reiteration of it.

"What is going on with you? You're yelling at me, you're fighting with Max, and now you're acting insane. Max is right, maybe I don't really know you."

"Know me?! You know everything about me. I always tell you the truth."

"The truth? Which version? What really happened downstairs Jackson, you said you and your dad found Anne, but Max told me he was with you, and the bloody shirt, and the fight, and your hand?"

He felt a fire building up inside him. "My hand what's my hand…" He unraveled the bandage on and revealed a gash where she had half expected to see a bite mark. "I didn't want you to worry, it was from the other night, when I had to cross over, no big deal; same reason I hid the shirt after the fight with Max. If anyone has their own versions of the truth…" he wondered how much more he should say. "He's maniacal Darcy; you don't know him at all. He's evil and repulsive and a liar."

"A liar, that's a little hypocritical, because as I recall you don't exactly have the best track record for coming clean, and besides he said Clem could…"

"Clem," he interrupted excitedly, "what did he say about her? Have you spoken to her Darce, is she answering your phone calls? No I bet not, eh? You should have asked him what he did with her."

"What the hell are you talking about? Why would he have done anything with her?" Darcy was becoming more irritated and it was apparent in her voice.

"That's what I'm trying to tell you, he's a…he probably killed her. There, there was just no other way to tell you," Jackson said.

"Jackson, you're starting to freak me out now."

"What you don't…" as if fate were taunting him perversely, Darcy's phone went off. It was Clem; as Darcy mentioned her name he was taken back. He went over the events of the day in head and couldn't figure out what had happened. He was sure Max would try to get rid of her and he wondered what he was playing at. As Darcy pressed Clem about what had happened her eyes widened and he felt more and more confused.

"…so when you came in they were already fighting…" he looked up at her and as she stared into his eyes her heart ached. "…he said what…yeah, no, no I'm fine really. Weird like how…yeah Max told me the same. Yeah, I'll call you tomorrow, bye." When she hung up the phone she stared at him in silence.

"What?" Jackson asked somewhat confused.

"Nothing, I just, I don't get it," she responded.

"What, what don't you get now Darcy?"

"It's just, her story sounds more like Max's than yours."

"So we're back there again eh, you still don't trust me."

"How can I when you're still not telling me everything. Look, it's been a long afternoon, I just, I need to think." Darcy couldn't help but feel bad as she spoke.

"Darcy," he put his hand on her shoulder and she subconsciously pulled away. He nodded as instead he placed his hands atop his head.

"Just," she bit down on her lip for stability, "what happened to Anne, Jackson really? I checked the floor no blood, no scuff marks…"

He looked up at her for a moment, and saw something in her eyes he hadn't yet seen, doubt and a bit of fear. "Do you, you don't think I could have…"

"Darcy, Jackson," Daniel's timing was conveniently inconvenient, "sorry, I just wanted to see if you were alright."

"I'm fine dad, we were just talking," Darcy said.

"Actually, I was heading off." Jackson sounded upset.

"Oh, I hope your not leaving on my behalf," Daniel was still a bit uncomfortable at the idea of Darcy as an adult.

"Er, no I just think we've pretty much said all there is to say so I'll get out of your way. Darcy, Mr. Whitten." As he walked away Darcy felt gross. She wanted to call out to him, to go after him; she hated herself for letting him walk away thinking she thought he could ever do anything less than chaste.

As she lay in her bed that night she tried to put things into perspective. She knew all her doubts had been cleared up when she saw his hand, but why was he still holding out on her? Did it matter? She knew that no matter what he was or did, she could never stop loving him; she would live in the beatific existence with him or follow him through the depths of hell. She picked up the phone and dialed his number, to no avail. He was upset with her, rightfully so. She threw her phone down, picked up her sweatshirt and began putting on her shoes, when her phone beeped. It was a text from Jackson. "Sorry, there's something I have to do, I'll explain later. Sleep well; I love you." She lay back down. Feeling relief that he wasn't just avoiding her altogether, she slipped into bed, pulled on her earphones and concentrated as she slipped away.

Max sat at the edge of his bed with a blank stare. After hours of musing, his mental exhaustion had given way to lethargy. He put his head in his hands. How could he do it; would his body let him go through the motions. He tried to comfort himself with the notion that at the very least he could make it quick and virtually painless. Max lay back on his bed and rested his head on crossed arms. He closed his eyes and tried to slip away. When he found he couldn't, he squeezed them tighter, and instead of attainment, tears slithered down his face. He sat up reached into his nightstand drawer, pulled out her t-shirt, and dug his face into it.

He knew he loved her, as vexatious and inexorable as it was. He let the delusions of solution fill his head. He thought about kidnapping her or taking her away, away from London, away from Jackson, but he knew Jackson was right; Dominion would never be far behind. Even if he lied about killing her, the watcher would find her eventually. If he killed himself instead, they'd just replace him with another assassin. Then the pictures of the tortures that they could afflict, the tortures he had committed onto others, began to take form in his head. There was no way around it, at every turn, a brick wall.

He stood up, got his coat and walked out. His feet carried him to where his heart could not find its way. He sat in his car with the knowledge that he was about to betray everything that made the world worth living in it, to cauterize the last vein pumping life into his proverbial heart. He drove, hoping and praying for intervention. As much as he loathed Jackson, a part of him secretly hoped he would be there to stop him, to protect her, but when he arrived at the house, just silence.

Daniel was home, but Max had snuck past Anne at least a dozen times, and he knew it would not prove too trying. He stood at the doorway of her bedroom and he knew that walking into the room would change everything.

When Darcy found herself standing in the white cube, she was confused. As far as she could remember she had fallen asleep, determined not to dream. She looked around but could only see white, a hue so bright she almost felt she should be shielding her eyes as one does from the sun. Then she swore she could hear a faint whisper, but the noise was so muffled she could not make out the exact phrase. The four syllables bounced off the walls as they were repeated over and over again.

She turned in every direction and leaned her ear against every side of the cube. After a while it was hard for her to distinguish side from floor or ceiling as she moved through it. "What! What, I can't hear you, what are you saying?" The noises stopped finally. She looked around very confused and now somewhat unbalanced. Suddenly something caught her eye; small print appeared on the wall opposite her. Letter by letter as if someone were typing it out, she made her way closer to it.

W- a- k- e U- p D- a- r- c- y When she was finally able to make it out, it began to appear on all sides of the cube over and over in bigger, bolder scripts. She tried her very best to pull herself out of her dream and finally…

DIFFIDENCE

She sat up in a cold sweat, gasping for air as if she had been suffocated. "Bad dreams," the voice startled her. She quickly reached over and switched on her lamp. He was standing by her window, as if he had been looking out.

"Max," she whispered, "what are you doing here? My dad…"

"He's sleeping," he rolled his eyes at her. "Hmph I remember the days when you would practically beg me to stay with you and now…"

"That's not what I meant, you just scared me." He chuckled at the notion as it reminded him of the conversation he had had with Jackson in the church. "So what happened with Mackinnon then? Did you work it out?" She looked away nervously as the question made her feel uncomfortable. "Ah come on Darcy don't treat me like a little kid. I'm not stupid really."

"I know, it's just, I never even thought you liked me in that way, until…"

"Until you kissed me?" She blushed and under the glow of the light she looked even brighter than usual. "Yeah well, I guess I never knew myself," he walked over and sat at the edge of her bed. "I mean I always knew I might, erm, care for you, more than I ever had for anyone before, but then I guess something just changed. Sometimes I really wish it hadn't. I wish we could just hang out like we used to, watch crappy movies together, eat crappy pizza, just talk…"

She made her way over to where he sat facing the wall and wrapped her arms around him from behind. She pushed her face into his neck "I'm so sorry Max."

He giggled only slightly amused, "sorry you kissed me?"

"No, sorry things aren't the same … or different." She knew if her heart had not belonged to Jackson, she could have easily taken to Max. He closed his eyes and as she buried her face in his neck, he felt her tears on his skin. He reached up with his hands shaking and caressed her hair. "Max?" He turned to face her and she noticed a change that had built up in his eyes.

"Darcy, I," as he looked into her eyes, he saw a pleading. He couldn't do it. He cupped her face in his hands and kissed her. It wasn't a forceful, determined kiss; it was lingering and emotional. She closed her eyes and knew it would be the last time she would feel Max. When he pulled back she rubbed her cheek against his hand and as she sniffled from her tears, something made its way to her nose. A scent, a familiar scent; one she had smelt before. At first she hadn't made it out, but then flashes of the maze, the hands, the lingering on Jackson's shirt. Her stomach fluttered, she took his hand and ran it under the lamp. At first he was confused by her actions, but then as it shone there confessing beneath the light of the lamp, it came to him. The bite mark had almost all but disappeared, only a light trace of her teeth lay telling on his hand.

"Max," she let out his name like a gasp. "You, you, you're..."

"What Darcy, what am I? Evil, mean, a monster?" He stood up from the bed and walked back towards the window.

Her voice trembled when she spoke, "I was going to say like Jackson." She couldn't move.

He laughed a little as he opened a window and lit a cigarette. "Like Jackson, really Darcy? I mean, seriously how can that be, if you just can't help but love him and can't help to not love me? Couldn't help your mother, can't help yourself. Come to think of it, is there anything that you can help ever?"

"Max stop, that's not fair."

"Oh sorry Darcy but didn't anyone tell you life's not fair. Just tell me this please cause I'm really curious. Why not me huh, I mean if I'm like Jackson?"

"I meant that you could do what he does." He nodded, as he now understood what she meant.

"I see and what is it that Jackson can do exactly?" She was afraid, so afraid that every individual nerve in her body shook independently. "Right, no, I'm nothing like Jackson, what I do takes a lot more balls. Excuse my language, but don't kid yourself, he's just as fucked up as I am."

"But you're wrong Max, I loved you, maybe not like Jack, you were my best friend but Jackson, he, he loved me."

"Loved you? Don't you know yet or haven't you figured it out?" His voice became course and more forceful. "He's killed you, set you up to die. Like I said, don't fool yourself Darcy he's done things just like I have, but I did everything, everything to keep you from getting hurt. I loved you and it took everything not to tell you, not to want to touch you, I cared enough to let you have a chance. He didn't don't you see." His eyes began to welt up and her heart ached for him. He fell to his knees and buried his face I her lap. "I, I just wanted something, something good, and something beautiful and when I saw you I just knew...

She hadn't heard him enter the room but at the sound of the clapping they were both surprised. "That's great Max, phenomenal performance, but why don't you tell her what you're really doing here mate. Tell her the truth; you've come to show her how much you love her then? He's here to carry out his task Darcy." Max climbed to his feet. "He's here to kill you." Darcy's expression fell and she felt her throat closing. "Couldn't get to her through her dreams, surprised?"

"I didn't even try. I'm not a fucking coward like you Jackson, I came to tell her like a man, who I really was. Not hiding and running like a little boy." Max spoke through his teeth.

"Oh yeah okay then who are you, a fucking murderer?" Jackson was able to keep his voice from trembling as he spoke.

"I don't have a choice asshole, you did. You could have saved her, or did you leave that bit out," Max said pleased at himself.

"A choice, a fucking choice, everyone has a choice Max. Who sent you Dominic? You all set to carry it out, for what for accolades? You were probably so taut at the idea that..." Jackson was not allowed to finish.

"What the hell do you know; you think I didn't way my options here. There aren't any. If I don't do it someone else will and worse."

"That's the difference between us friend, I'd rather it me be than her."

"Then we're pretty much in agreement, because I'd rather it be you as well." Max smiled as he spoke now.

"You're going to have to kill me first."

"I can't;" Max said, as his expression changed.

"Can't or won't." Jackson taunted Max with his words.

"No Jack, I would, but you know I can't."

"Why Max scared of Dominion, scared Dominic will come after you then eh? You scared to die Max? I'm not, I know where I'm headed and that's the most I can fear, not knowing. But you know, you laid it out all for me in the church the other day, we know our place, it's not there or here so what of it mate eh, you kill me, they kill you and she's left, free."

"You think it's that simple Jackson?"

"Well, isn't it?" Jackson replied.

"I'm game. Came in together, go out together, why not?"

Neither one could call the other's bluff as they stared at each other straight-faced. Darcy couldn't believe what she was hearing. Her head was spinning; her heart was stone cold. "Or," she whispered as they both stopped and turned to face her, "if it was just me then…"

"Darcy don't!" Jackson scorned as he moved in and took her by the hand.

"Jack…"

"I mean it Darce, just…don't"

"Max if it was me, then would it be just me?" Jackson stared at him with a look of contempt as Darcy asked.

"Yes. It's just you." Max's eyes fell as he answered her.

Her skin crawled and it was an emotional itch she could not relieve. She forced free from Jack and reached for a box cutter from her desk. "Darcy, what the hell are you doing? Put that down, stop it!" Jackson spoke with love, through fear as he made his way towards her. His lips quivered and he reached out to her with shaky hands.

Max could not speak, partly because he was secretly hoping that at any moment she would bring an end to everything and partly because he was afraid, of the titillation that seemed to makes it appearance around death and decay. She looked to Jackson, "please you know I don't want to do this, please just stay there or I will and then…"

"Okay, okay, I'll stand over here, but please…"

"Jackson, remember when we talked about the stars about seeing something prolific?" her voice shook as tears made their way down his face. She looked over to Max and he wasn't sure why but he obligingly stepped out of the room. She walked towards Jackson and put her hands on his cheeks. "You gave me the stars Jackson, you're my heaven."

"Darcy," the tears burned down his face. "Let's go Darcy I'll take you away I can keep you safe, I can save you."

She looked at him and smiled, "no, Max can save me." He looked at her with a furrowed brow.

"What, I don't…" The tremble made it's way back to Jackson's voice.

"If I do it," she bit her lip.

"No Darcy, I'm not going to let him."

"There's no other way," Darcy said.

"It wont save me, I'll just have to..." As Jackson spoke, he founded more difficult to complete a thought.

"You can't, promise me. You said there was something after, something better, you have to meet me there. I'm going to wait for you and you promised you would always be there."

Jackson could no longer breathe through the wails that were logged in his throat. "Darcy, what if I can't go there, what if I can't meet you. Exoneration is not..."

"Jackson, go to our place," she winked. He broke down; he grabbed her and held her with every muscle in his body. He squeezed her as hard as he could without compressing the life out of her. He kissed her hard.

"Just," he whispered, "give me tonight." He was well aware that Max was listening.

"Sure why not." They both turned when Max walked in. "It will give me a chance to get things going. I mean what's one more day right." He disappeared through the doorway.

Jackson was confused and suspicious as to why Max has been so obliging, he wondered if it was going to be harder than Max had thought. Could he commit such a sin, crucifying a cherub? Whatever his motives, Jackson was just grateful for the time.

They didn't speak. There was nothing more to say. As they lay there together lost among the glowing art and in awe of each other's majesty, each were preoccupied. Darcy had begun their last night together trying to take in as much of Jackson as she could. She memorized his face, his voice, his smell. After a while her thoughts drifted to her father, her family, her life, and she became afraid. Afraid she might lose her nerve. What would Daniel do without her?

With undaunted fingers, Jackson traced every curve of her body, just in case. He kissed her almost to the point of suffocation. When he noticed she'd closed her eyes and drifted off in his arms, he began to think of every possible scenario. An unending array of escapes flooded his mind. There had to be something, something he was missing. He held her hand and knew he couldn't ever let it go. He leaned over and whispered in her ear. "We have the night right Darcy? You'll still be here in the morning?"

"Mmm hmmm," she grumbled in her sleep.

"I love you more than everything Darcy," he kissed her cheek.

"I love you too Jackson," she held back her unsteady voice.

Even after his breathing became more steady and profound, it wasn't until she felt his hand relax, that she knew he was truly out. She studied him one last time and kissed him tenderly.

Reckoning

When he heard the door he knew, it was culminating. When he opened it and saw her on the other end of it, he pictured her as he had seen her the first day they met, the last day of his life the way he had known it. "You got here faster than I thought."

"You knew I would come?" Darcy asked Max.

"I know you better than you know yourself, and I know you know Jackson better than he knows himself." Max spoke in a different colder tone than usual.

"Well, you are my best friend." She caught herself and she immediately looked up at his face. A pained almost remorseful look shot across it. "Were you really going to kill me tonight?"

"Yes." He didn't so much as flinch when he said it and was sure he was being honest.

"Still are?" Darcy smiled playfully though her tears as she asked. He nodded and she wiped the tears away as she swallowed hard. "Did you always know, who I was? Is that why you wanted to be my friend?"

He thought for a moment. "No, I had no idea." He paused for a moment. "But then, that night when you asked me to stay with you, in your sleep, you called out his name and I guess I figured it out. For what its worth, I tried to keep you away. I wanted you to want to stay away, so..."

"The nightmares..." she said and he nodded. She sniffled, as she knew she could not stop the tears, "Well, thanks, it is worth a lot. To me anyways." Darcy sniffled again and looked away. "Will it hurt Max?"

"I won't let it," he nodded. An anger began to rise within her heart.

"No, I mean will it hurt you?" She cried and put her head into his chest. "I want to hate you, but I can't. I don't get it. I really thought you cared for me. That's the worst part. If you'd just been anyone else, if I didn't know you. Why the whole show? If you knew who I was why didn't you just stay away and it would have made this easier."

"I didn't want to," Max whispered. "I tried but I just couldn't. I guess, I'm just as bad as Jackson huh." He pressed his forehead to hers and the familiar scent of cherry escaped from her panting breaths.

He looked up for abatement and as he kissed the top of her head his tears deluged.

Jackson found himself standing in front of the pillars confused. He walked in and saw her standing there expectantly. "Oh bloody hell , thank god, you have to help me. I only have tonight to save her. What can I do?"

"You already did." She smiled.

"What, no Max, he's going to ..."

"Jackson," she took his hand "you don't get. It's all just part of the plan."

"What, what plan..." he pulled his hand out of the cold grip of hers.

"Yours," she spoke in a playful connotation. "See, he chose you and now he won't try to get to her..."

"What, but that's ..."

"Couldn't through me, and now he won't through you..."

Finally revelation, "shit, shit.." At first he was confused, so he ran through it all in his mind. "No, not, no, it can't be, but she's still with me, just now she's sleeping in my arms, she's safe!" As she smiled in contentment, the iris of her eyes turned to pale slate. "Ah Darcy, fuck."

Jackson shot up in the dark and when he turned over she was gone. He ran down the stairs and out the front door without vigilance. He patted his legs and found his keys were in his house. As he made it to the front door, he noticed it was open. Jackson walked in with an odd feeling in his chest. He got his keys and as he walked out, he passed his father reexamining the new walkway.

"Going out at this hour boy?" His father spoke in a somewhat "matter of fact" tone, and this made Jackson feel eerily uncomfortable.

"Yes erm, it's an emergency, so I really have to go and your blocking..."

"I'll be done in a minute; nothing urgent enough that you wouldn't call for police for eh boy?"

"Actually I really, it's quite urgent, plea..." Jackson spoke as he climbed into his car.

"Your girl?" He interrupted Jackson and spoke in the same cold undertone as usual. Before Jack could answer, he continued on "didn't that get all taken care of?"

"What?" As Jackson spoke, he felt his pulse begin to race a little. "I'm not really sure exactly what you, I mean I don't..."

"It's for the best. I'm only disappointed that your convictions weren't stronger." As Mr. Mackinnon spoke, Jackson began to feel sick. He had no idea who the stranger before him was and a rage began to build up, peppered with disgust. "I have to say," he continued on, "I told Dominic it'd never work, that you were stronger than that, but he saw something in you and he knew." Jackson felt ill as if at any moment he might simply pass out.

"Get the hell out of my way before I run you the fuck over." Jackson's voice trembled as he spoke. He turned the ignition with pure detriment running through his veins. The first blow was excruciating as if something was trying to claw its way out of his head, but after the second, waves of black fell over his eyes and he was gone.

"Ah Jackson, you never fail to disappointment me, at least you're consistent. You could have been the best. Throw it all away and for what?" As he yelled the tendons on his neck flickered. "I knew that little bitch was trouble, the moment I saw her. Played you both for fools she did."

He was still strewn out on the gravel when he came too, the bloody shovel at his side. The adrenaline still thick in his veins brought him to his feet surprisingly steady. Jackson could not contain his fury and with a balled fist, he raised his hand at his father for the first time. He couldn't be too sure and although his father didn't so much as flinch, he saw a flash on fear in his eyes. "Shut your mouth old man, you don't know shit. Look at you now, I could kill you where you stand and no one would find whatever was left of you." As Jackson spoke the blood from his head tricked down and the metallic taste caused him to spit out.

Jackson's father let out a sardonic chuckle before he spoke. "That's it, there's the boy I raised. I always thought you'd of made a better assassin. Look at that recovery. You belonged with Max and me out there not with those lot of fucking intellectuals." When he saw the look in Jackson's face, he felt appeased. "What, surprised boy?"

"No, it makes sense you're just as big an asshole as Max. Now get the fuck out of my way or I'll tear you apart." Jackson spoke those words with a pure determination even his father could not deny.

When he saw his father lift up the sheers in his hand he was quick to let out a massive swing. He knew when he struck his father's arm that although it would not bring him down, it would be enough to disarm him. It worked well enough for Jackson to get in a few good strikes.

Jackson had always known his father was strong, but he was a better fighter than Jackson was. It was clear how good he must have been at his lot, and considering his age, in his prime Jackson was sure he must have even been better than Max. Jackson was stronger than he thought he was and the fact that he could think on his feet gave him an advantage. His ignition was still running, and all he had to do was get close enough to slip into his car. He knew time was not on his side or Darcy's for that matter. As they continued to wrestle around on the ground, Jackson was growing more and more tired and less apt to come out from under his father. Just as he was about to take what would have been a final blow, through the corner of his eye he spotted his escape.

Salvation came in the form of a rusty, blood riddled shovel. Mr. Mackinnon had no idea what had hit him and as he keeled over all he mustered up was a raspy "well, played."

Jackson's guilt was short-lived as he sped off to Max's.

And to this…

Darcy closed her eyes and prayed for a quick release. Max stood behind her and ran his hands down her arms. She thought hard about Jackson, about Max. She didn't want to die. She knew she wasn't born to be a martyr, but she was sure there was no way she could escape Max.

Max took in one last deep breath. Until the whole situation with Anne earlier that day he had never killed anyone outside the breech, he wasn't sure he could do it again. When he slipped his hands over her throat, they trembled wickedly.

Jackson wasn't careless enough to barge in guns blazing. He knew very well the only advantage that he had over Max was that he was presumed to be dead; or at least held back. When he slipped through the bedroom window, he saw Darcy's shirt folded up on the night-stand. It was enough to reignite a furry that had begun to dissipate and give way to desperation. He wasn't foolish or gallant enough to attempt a naïve move like trying to rush Max. He needed a weapon. Jackson looked around the room as quietly as he could, until he eyed an old duffle bag under the bed. It couldn't have been more perfect than if it had been a gun.

It was much worse than Darcy had imagined it'd be. As Max's hands closed tighter around her throat, not only had she lost her breath, but flailing around had simply made it happen a lot sooner than she expected. As she gasped once more, she began to feel a pressure rise up in her face, and her eyes felt like they might simply explode. As she began to fall limply into Max's arms, he raised one of his hands off her throat and placed the trembling hand over her mouth and nose, all the while shushing her as one would a small child.

Just as she was about to slip off completely she swore she saw something in the reflection of Max's window. And as she saw Jackson raise the bat over Max's head, she was out.

EPILOGUE

Darcy quickly made her way out the back door. Somehow, everything was green again. She made her way to the stone bench and sat desperately searching her memory for relevance. She couldn't remember how she'd gotten there. The fine line that had once scarcely separated reverie from reality dissipated. Their place had come back to life and somehow she'd gotten back.

"Hi."

When she heard his voice she nearly jumped up.

"Darcy," he took her in his arms and kissed her deeply.

"Oh my god Jackson; I thought you were gone." Her heart began beat frantically in her chest and a mix of emotions ensued.

"No, not just yet." He smiled at her and kissed the top of her hand.

"What is this why are we here?" Darcy asked still trying to remember past her night at Max's. "How?" She bit down on her lip. "Are we dead?" She finally had the nerve to ask as her eyes began to welt up.

"I'm so sorry Darcy, I'm so sorry." Jackson's reply was morose and genuine.

"There's nothing to be sorry about Jack," she cupped his face in her hands. "I'm fine, I'm here with you." She starred at him with the same affection she always did. "But will you be there when I open my eyes, I mean if I…?"

"I hope so, but don't open them just yet," Jackson pleaded.

She wrapped her arms around his waist and began to sway. "I always wondered why this place was always in my dreams, I was a little afraid of it at first. I guess it was always meant to be ours. I also always thought you were sent to me, but I was wrong Jack, maybe I was sent to you. You can stop it Jack, all of it, Dominion."

"Darcy I don't care about Dominion, I just want you; I should have just left you alone."

"Why would I have ever wanted to be alone, when I could have been with you?"

"I'm so scared to open my eyes Darcy."

"So am I."

"What if you're not there?" Jackson asked knowing she would not have that answer either.

"Then I'll be here, waiting for you every night just like you were here for me." She ran her fingers down the side of his neck and as she pressed her lips to his he could taste her still; the moisture of her lips stirred him.

When the light came through the window, it was almost painfully luminous. Recollection of the night was hazy, almost completely severed, and as gratitude consumed the soul, "I'm, I am still alive," the words were just an affirmation.